PRAISE FOR THE VEIN

excavating rich horror and glimmers of humanity across a century of greed, lies, and even love. *The Vein* is a treasure for fans of mature dark fiction."

—Gordon B. White, Shirley Jackson and Bram Stoker Awards finalist

"*The Vein* is a horror thriller that is pacy, atmospheric, and heart-wrenching. Nelson weaves local lore and intricate plotting in a literary voice similar to C. J. Cooke's, but entirely her own. Certainly an author to watch."

—Eliane Boey, author of *Other Minds*

"Steph Nelson weaves past and present nightmares together to create a tale as rich and layered as any vein of silver. Below the civilized exterior of Pate, Idaho, generations of greed and grief fester. Readers will yearn to venture deeper still, where malevolent riches sleep."

—Drew Huff, author of *Free Burn*

"Nelson's small-town terror tale drills deep for a cross-generational look at characters who can't let go of loved ones, and secrets that refuse to stay hidden. An engrossing read."

—Patrick Barb, author of *Pre-Approved for Haunting*

"A chilling, masterful, and deeply moving story about a strange small town haunted by its past. This astonishing debut is one you won't forget."

—Faith Gardner, author of *Violet Is Nowhere*

"Steph Nelson's ability to draw in the reader with a perfect mix of horror, noir, and Americana is only surpassed by her knack for wrapping up a tale with a truly satisfying ending."

—Brian Rosten, Editor of *The Maul Magazine*

THE VEIN

CONTENT WARNING

This novel contains brief, non-explicit scenes of the sexual abuse of a child. It also includes suicide. Please read with care.

Edited by Rob Carroll
Book Design and Layout by Rob Carroll
Cover Design by Rob Carroll

ISBN 978-1-958598-15-3 (paperback)
ISBN 978-1-958598-41-2 (eBook)
ISBN 978-1-958598-42-9 (audiobook)

darkmatter-ink.com

THE VEIN

STEPH NELSON

DARK
MATTER
INK

THE VEIN

STEPH NELSON

DARK
MATTER
INK

For my mom, Denette Dresback
and
For my dad, Jim Dresback

Thank you for giving me life.

PATE, IDAHO

August 1979

ONE

DAWN WINTON WAS too young to be carrying dynamite in her hiking pack, but you didn't argue with Dad. You obeyed. *Slow obey is no obey.*

"My pack's full. You carry these."

Dawn nodded fast before she could cry or refuse and stomp her foot and run into the house like she wanted. You didn't do that around Dad, and definitely not when he was obeying the Lord. It was the Lord telling him to bring the dynamite along on their hike into the woods for Apocalypse Survival Week, and Dad was thinking about that, not about his daughter's safety.

Dad knelt down beside her and stuffed two faded red sticks in with the rest of her gear, wicks facing up and nearly poking out the top, as if to be lit on a moment's notice.

Squinting hard against the morning sunlight as it broke through the landscape of pine trees, Dawn tried not to think about Dad or the dynamite. She kicked the dirt in front of her, but it was no use. She couldn't stop imagining dynamite exploding on her back, how she wouldn't live beyond eight years old because she'd die by dynamite today. Or maybe tomorrow. But certainly, she'd die by dynamite.

Dad had never brought explosives along before, but nobody could stop him. Mom, Dad, and Dawn all lived way out in the woods, in a tiny old cabin that no one ever visited, and the nearest town was a few miles away, down the mountain and into the valley some.

Dawn had wanted to run away to town ever since she was old enough to make sense of the idea, but she could never leave Mom, and Mom would never leave Dad, so Dawn was stuck, probably forever.

"You hear me, girl?" Dad said. "The kingdom of God suffers violence…" He paused before completing the verse and nodded at Dawn, signaling for her to finish.

"…And the violent take it by force," she answered.

"That's right." He pulled the strap of her bag so tight, she nearly fell backwards onto the seat of her pants. The dynamite was now sealed inside.

"But Daddy, why do we need the dynamite?"

She felt him suddenly tense up behind her. It was a bratty, stubborn question, and Dad hated those. *Stupid, stupid, stupid.* She turned to see him rise to his full height, more than twice hers, and he looked down at her.

"To be ready for the End of Days," he answered. "You know that. When the apocalypse comes, we ain't got but an hour, maybe two, 'fore the whole system falls apart and people start going crazy lootin' and killin' each other over food and simple supplies. That verse is proof the Lord knows it'll get ugly, and He's all for us defending ourselves against those with the mark of the beast." He dipped his chin, got closer to her face, and narrowed his eyes. His hair was so dark and greasy. "Feels like I gotta tell you this over and over again. You forgettin'? Or bein' willfully disobedient?"

Dawn hadn't forgotten. The End of Days was more real than breakfast, lunch, and dinner. More inevitable than the sun tucking itself into bed each night. Dawn only had two jobs in this world: to be ready for the End of Days, and to make sure she was right with the Lord. The first job was easy—Dad had taught her how to hunt, fish, trap, skin, sew, chop wood, start a fire, find fresh water, tend a wound, siphon gas, wire explosives, even make a battery from scratch. Dawn had all the skills needed to survive. It was the second job, being right with the Lord, that worried her. What if she accidentally sinned right before dying—before she had time to repent?

Did the Lord take that into account? The End of Days and the apocalypse were temporary because eventually she would die. But not being right with the Lord? That was for all eternity.

The best way to avoid such a mistake was by keeping Jesus inside your heart at all times. So, she pictured the door to her heart closed tight, with Jesus stuck in there. The dark cavern of her ribcage would no doubt be windowless, and the door would be thick like a bank vault and heavy, secured by a million locks, all of which would be so complicated that even Jesus couldn't figure them out.

Sometimes when she thought on it too long, she felt bad for Jesus, being trapped in there all alone. But the truth was simple. If it came down to Jesus being stuck inside the cold darkness of her heart, or Dawn spending all of eternity in Hell, where the worm doesn't die and the fire is not quenched, the choice was easy. Jesus would just have to make do.

"Look me in the eyes," Dad demanded, his rank breath now too close to her face.

Dawn hadn't even realized she was looking away. She met his gaze and lied, "I'm sorry, Daddy. I'm just forgetful, I guess." In that moment of sin, she imagined the door to her heart cracking open just enough for Jesus to peek out. But she quickly repented, promised never to lie again. Thankfully, the door shut and locked quick enough to keep Jesus inside.

Dad grunted his disappointment with Dawn's answer and marched off into the woods without her.

Dawn wiped the tears from her eyes and chased after him.

PATE, IDAHO

July 1989

FATE, IDAHO

July 1985

TWO

SYL DIXON HAD only been back in Pate for a few weeks. A month at most, but it felt much longer. Time ticked by more slowly now that she wasn't a detective and didn't have a family to think about.

Pate had certainly grown over the past twenty seven years. The silver mines were mostly closed, abandoned. And then there were the portraits, or pictures maybe? She didn't know what the hell to call them, but they littered the fronts of homes. Framed images of people—always people, never landscapes or animals—hung next to mailboxes and house numbers. They could be black and white, or sepia from age, it didn't seem to matter. Syl had even seen a few framed Polaroids. Nobody would tell her why the pictures were outside, and it wasn't for lack of asking.

Gran's house was the same as she remembered it though. And that's why she was back. To clean up the property and list it for sale. The old house was paid off, and there was time. Syl was probably going to be in Pate awhile. After all, Carl had moved Lucas to Florida after the divorce; they weren't in Spokane anymore, either. Not that it mattered. Lucas could live down the street, and she probably wouldn't take a step toward visiting him anyway. She'd considered calling him many times since she moved here, but the closest she came was staring at the phone on the wall, unable to lift the receiver off the hook.

Syl drove her unmarked 1987 Crown Victoria with windows down—fast, always too fast—along the empty two-lane road.

Just follow the river, Pate sheriff, Roger Mock, had said.

So that's what she was doing. Following the river at the base of these steep mountains, driving toward what would soon be sunset. Syl glanced periodically at the empty passenger's seat, where her chicken-scratched note fluttered in the wind underneath the latest Michael Crichton novel.

Directions to one abandoned Lucky Dog Mine, where the body was found.

Pate County had so many abandoned silver mines. Some bigger than others, but there was no way she'd find this particular one without detailed instructions to get there. Roger had given them to her over the phone earlier today.

Syl had been turning down Roger's attempts to convince her to join their small police force ever since she got here. She never had any trouble shooting him down. The most recent rejection of his offer happened in the cereal aisle of the only grocery store in town.

"You become a cop right out of high school?" Roger had asked as an opener. A jab at her height, of course. So predictable. She was more than used to those comments. It was too big an idea for small minds that a woman who didn't break five-feet tall could join the police, become a detective.

"Just after sixth grade, actually. A child prodigy," she'd said, reaching for a box of Cinnamon Toast Crunch.

He had chuckled. "I like a woman you can razz without upsetting her. Most women are so goddamn touchy about everything."

She had rolled her eyes before turning around to face him.

Roger immediately asked her again if she'd be interested in joining the *small but mighty* Pate Sheriff's Department.

"No," she'd said. "I gave up police work."

He handed her his card, which he'd already done three or four times, and said she could call him if she changed her mind.

She gave up police work, and yet, here she was, on her way to meet Roger at a crime scene. To offer her initial opinions on the body they discovered inside Lucky Dog Mine.

It would have been wiser to say no, but something about being back in Pate worked on her as the weeks dragged on. The first six years of her life—the years she spent here—had always been a blank space in her memory, but now she was recalling things. Nothing concrete, more like feelings that came and went. Even though the house had been a rental for over twenty years, it was the same burlap weave wallpaper upstairs. The same smell of cigarette smoke, seeping from the drapes—Gran's smell. The same yellow-splashed kitchen. These sensory details surfaced a question she'd previously spent little to no time on.

What had happened to Gran all those years ago?

Syl's parents were already dead by the time she was six, and Gran was her guardian. But then Gran vanished.

It wasn't like this dead body in the mine was connected to Gran's 1962 disappearance, but after weeks of boredom in this tiny town, and zero motivation to organize Gran's shit, Syl's mind had naturally gravitated toward the mystery, and the pressure to find answers had built up exponentially since that day in the cereal aisle. So when Roger called today, she found herself saying yes. And now here she was, telling herself that helping him out may lead to opportunities to poke around about Gran without anyone realizing it.

Syl arrived at the spot where the piece of paper said to go. Two regular vehicles and a police cruiser were parked by the river. Across the water, Roger stood, messing around with that ball cap he always seemed to be wearing. It had an old Seattle Mariners logo, an upside-down trident in the shape of an M.

She slammed the door of the Vicky and walked across the little footbridge toward him.

"Any trouble finding this place?" Roger asked.

"No, not at all. It's not like there's another mine around here anywhere."

Roger chuckled at her sarcasm and quickly turned to lead the way like they were running a relay race and she was passing him the baton. It made her feel like some newbie. Someone he had to make sure knew their place.

Syl jogged to catch up with him. "Look, I'll tell you what I think, but that's all. I don't want to be involved with any sort of investigation."

"You'll change your mind once you get eyes on the body," Roger said.

How the hell do you know what I'll do?

Syl held the irritation in, and stayed close to him the whole hike up to the mine's entrance. They walked in single-file silence until Roger finally spoke.

"It's Alex Conder."

"I don't know who that is."

He stopped walking. The man was seriously out of breath, and no wonder. He was at least twice her age and his rotund belly sat above a formidable ass and thin legs that didn't look capable of supporting the weight. Roger unwrapped a piece of gum and balled up the foil wrapper, shoved it into his pocket. "You're a Dixon."

"Yeah, so?"

"Dixons and Conders go way back."

"I moved to Spokane as a kid. Haven't been back since."

"Right," Roger said. He returned to walking. "Male, forty-six years old. Works construction, family man. We know it's him, and he wasn't brought here against his will."

"Why do you say that?"

Roger turned and pointed to a beat-up truck parked right next to Syl's. "That's his rig. Hen verified it, although he didn't need to. We all know it's Alex's."

"Who's Hen?"

God, if he made her ask every time he name-dropped, she was going to lose her mind.

"Ed Hendon. He's new to the force. He and Dan MacCarel both. My last two guys were up for retirement at the same time over a year ago. I was too. We all joined upon returning from the war. Department's too small to have a full-time detective, so we take turns on rotation. But my rookies aren't ready yet."

The only thing in that statement Roger hadn't already told her was that the rookie's name was Hendon. The fact that they didn't hire detectives was the main reason she turned him down in the past. Investigating was actually interesting to her even though she was pretty shitty at it. But going back to patrol? Never would she ever. Especially in this boring small town.

"Cause of death?" Syl asked.

"That's a problem." Roger removed the ball cap and wiped his bald head with a quick hand. His face was red, his breath ragged.

"Why?"

"Because it doesn't make sense. Hendon said it looks like Alex died of starvation."

"Okay, and that doesn't make sense because…?"

"Because you can't starve inside of twenty-four hours. Alex was home with his kid last night. Kyle was in bed when his dad turned on the TV to watch a program."

Syl's mind stalled a bit. It felt like trying to fit a square peg into a round hole. Then she stepped in front of Roger. He was going way too goddamn slow.

"By all means, lead the way," Roger said, annoyance plain in his voice. But when he didn't try to keep up, she knew she'd done him a favor. Now the man could go at his own pace.

THREE

SYL REACHED FLAT ground outside the mine's entrance well before Roger. Two other cops hung around, smoking. They tossed their cigarettes and stamped them out as soon as Roger came into view. One of them had a thick, black mustache.

"Body's pretty far in, sheriff," Mustache Cop said once Roger made it to the top. Then he pulled the arms of the locked gate out, and the slack created a space below. Mustache Cop crawled under the fence.

Roger grunted something unintelligible and spit out his gum before unclasping a key ring attached to his belt. He gave the other two cops a look Syl had been on the receiving side of one too many times. *You idiot, why didn't you think to do this?* The padlock came loose, and the gate swung open. The other cop handed them orange hardhats.

"Be careful," Roger said, giving Syl a flashlight. "These abandoned mines aren't exactly safe to run around in. Most been sitting for at least a decade. Some of them, like Lucky Dog here, much longer."

Inside the mine, every splash of July sunshine was gone. Lucky Dog seemed like a big, rocky tunnel. *Drip, drip, drip,* was all she heard, along with four sets of feet shuffling around. Roger led, Syl came next, and the two cops followed behind her. Nobody said a single word. No jokes, no macho banter. She shivered, then tripped over something, but caught herself before a tumble. She pointed her flashlight at it. Railroad tracks?

Roger heard the commotion and turned around. "Ore cart tracks. Watch out for those too."

"Thanks for the heads up."

Roger chuckled again.

Every step took them deeper into blackness. How far were they going?

"Should have put up shop lights, Hen," Roger said.

"With what electrical outlet?" Mustache Cop—apparently Hen—said.

Roger shimmied out a shrug that Syl doubted the cops behind her could see. "Use a generator or something. Figure it out. Job's all about problem solving."

The air coming from deeper inside the mine was frigid.

"You cold?" Not-Hen said directly behind her.

"I'm good."

"I can run back to the cruiser and grab you my jacket."

"No, I'll manage."

A mumble came from the end of the line. It was Hen. He said the other cop's name, Mac. Something about Mac looking for a reason to bail. Mac said shut up, and then quiet returned.

"Sheriff," Syl said, "Who in the world came in here far enough to find the body?"

"Some EPA guy. There's a few of them around town, starting that mine cleanup project. One's a glutton for punishment, apparently. Was asking around about which mine was creepiest, and someone told him Lucky Dog. Locals know *all* mines are creepy this far in, so I'm not sure why Lucky Dog came up, specifically. Anyways, that guy happened upon Alex. Scared him shitless, but I guess he got his cheap, small-town thrill."

Hen and Mac laughed, and it echoed throughout the mine.

"The timing's odd though. What are the chances he'd come so close after Alex? Did you question him?"

"Course." Roger was defensive, but she ignored it.

"And?"

"Poor guy didn't have any clue who Alex was, or really even what month it was. He was in such bad shock, the hospital didn't want him traveling home to Boise yet."

Seemed like a big reaction over just a dead body. Sure, it was a harrowing experience, especially your first time seeing one, but not enough to make you lose your mind like that.

"Here we are," Roger finally said, his blade of light swinging inside a cavern. "Be extra careful with your steps now. There's a steep drop-off." He shined his light where the rock floor stopped. Then he went up to the edge, and bending down with some effort, because his gut made him front-heavy, Roger picked up a rock about the size of a golf-ball. He tossed it into the hole, then turned to Syl, waited.

"Is something supposed to—" Syl began.

"Shh." Roger said.

Syl stuffed down more irritation.

Hen and Mac were motionless, arms hanging at their sides like scared kids.

Roger shined the flashlight on his silver wristwatch.

Syl started again. "Sheriff—"

He put a finger up to silence her, and she gave a loose sigh.

Plink.

The tiny sound of a rock hitting water.

Roger brushed his hands together. "That's how far the drop is."

Holy shit. Syl chewed the inside of one cheek. That was indeed one hell of a drop.

Hen pushed through Mac and Syl to reach Roger at the front. "This way," he said. They all followed him along the wall to the left of the cavern.

Yellow evidence tape came into view, and Syl ducked under it when she got there. Roger stayed outside the perimeter.

Inside the small, cordoned area, there was a corpse laid out on its back. She inched closer, shining light directly on the face. It was shriveled up, severely decomposed, but not like typical body decomposition. The eye sockets were empty, and the skin was pulled taut around protruding teeth. It looked like rawhide. The corpse's Wranglers were still belted loosely around the waist, and a white crew neck tee too big for the body's remains exposed an emaciated shoulder. But the worst part was the mouth, which was wide open as if caught in a scream.

"Looks like he's been dead for years," she whispered. "Forget starvation, this is a fucking mummy."

Nobody commented. Syl tried to reconcile what she saw with the information she'd gathered so far.

"Alex Conder was seen yesterday, okay, but are you sure this is him?"

Roger squatted next to her, staying outside the tape. "Alex was accident prone. Cut that one off with a band saw in his high school shop class—" Roger flashed the light on the spot where the corpse's left pinky should be. "Cut that one off with a table saw just a few years ago." He pointed to the space where a right index finger was missing. "So sure, maybe it's not Alex. But then it's some guy nobody knows, who happens to have two fingers missing in the same spots as Alex. And drives his rig."

"And you're positive he was seen yesterday?"

"That's what his wife said on the phone. I'll take you over there tomorrow, and you can ask the kid yourself."

"Hen, did you take any photographs of the scene before tromping all over?" Syl asked.

"No."

She snapped pictures, and the flash filled up the whole space. Since she gave no warning, they all groaned for their eyes.

"Did you call the coroner?" she asked.

Hen shook his head.

"Make that happen. You're responsible for the scene until he comes."

He looked at Roger for interpretation.

What was she doing? She wasn't in charge here. Didn't *want* to be in charge. But now here she was, doling out orders.

"Oh, God," Roger mumbled and shook his head.

She knew why. Since Hendon was a rookie, making him responsible for the scene was the same as making Roger himself responsible for it without having to ask him to do it.

"Tough break, sheriff," Syl said, smiling to herself. Then she began setting up evidence markers. The least she could do was get them started by gathering evidence and preparing the site for the coroner. Then she'd be done with it.

"There's some blood here. I want to know what blood type," Syl said. "Hard to tell if Alex has any cuts. Could be the attacker's." She placed a yellow marker labeled "3" next to the drops of blood on the ground.

"Hen, your bag," Syl said, reaching for it. She rummaged around and found a pair of tweezers, used them to retrieve something from the corpse's chest. Holding it up, she said, "Let's test fibers. See where this came from."

"Lab's in Boise, eight hours away," Roger said. "It'll be days—weeks—before you hear back from them on blood type, let alone fibers."

"That's fine."

Roger smacked his gum so loud that she had to grit her teeth to keep from saying something. His nervous energy was over the top.

"What's wrong?" she finally asked.

"Hate these damned mines."

"Yeah, my grandma hated them too."

Syl had never been inside one, and that had been Gran's doing. Even when it was Grandpa offering to take her on a tour of his workplace.

"I'm sure she did," Roger muttered. Syl wanted to ask more. Why would he say that? What does he know about Gran? But it wasn't the time.

"By the way, you didn't set up an outer perimeter either, Hen," Syl said. "The mine entrance should be taped off. Why isn't it?"

"Was locked, so I figured it didn't matter. Nobody would come this far in anyway."

"Right," she said. "Nobody like Alex Conder would ever venture inside. Or the press. Hell, when they find out—"

"I got it," Roger interrupted. He reached down for the roll of yellow police tape. She would have sent one of the rookies, but he was gone before she could protest.

FOUR

ROGER WASN'T A pussy or anything, but he hated the mines and hadn't come back to this one in particular since his senior year in high school. Back when he and some buddies from the football team thought it'd be *swell* to explore an abandoned mine. God, were they stupid.

Lucky Dog Mine went deep, but it was also one of the first to close in the 1930s, when the silver dried up and the price of ore dipped. In the spring of 1942, before Roger had any sense, Lucky Dog seemed to him and his friends to be the perfect place to get up to some last hurrahs before they graduated high school and shipped off to war.

They'd brought their girls and a case of beer along. But one of the guys went missing that night and was never found.

Roger groaned. This was the last thing he should be thinking about right now. A flash of fear rose up in his chest, and he picked up his pace like when you turn off lights in a basement and run up the stairs as fast as you can because you're sure something is pressing against your back, nipping at your heels.

People disappeared all the time around Pate. There were ghost stories and theories about why. Of course, these were all made up by bullies and babysitters, but everything felt true in the dark.

Breaking into the warm light outside, Roger took a deep breath. He'd feel much better when he was completely out of these woods though. He set to work affixing yellow tape across the opening of the mine in an X-shape, then folded a piece of Big Red into his mouth. Roger waited, watching the sun melt behind treed mountains. They probably had about thirty minutes of daylight left.

The corpse came to mind, and Roger had to remind himself this was Alex. Not some nameless fool. But then again, none of them were nameless to Roger. Protecting the town was his job, and he failed. He'd failed so many times over the years. This felt like his opportunity to make up for it. If he could solve this case, maybe his tenure as sheriff wouldn't be a total waste.

But the Pate County Sheriff's department wasn't equipped to handle shit like this. Especially with Hendon and Mac. They were Tweedle Dee and Tweedle Dum, just without the striped pajamas and spinning propeller beanies. Although sometimes, Roger imagined them wearing that shit, and it made him laugh.

He had to keep Syl interested in the case.

After about twenty minutes, Syl emerged from the mine, followed by Hen and Mac. Roger was just about to ask what she thought about the body when he noticed Mac whispering to Hendon like the *psh-psh-psh* of little girls.

"By all means, Mac, share with the class," Roger said.

"It's nothing."

Roger stared, waiting for one of them to speak actual words that meant something.

"Mac thinks it's the same thing that got John Winton," Hendon spurted. Mac shoved him.

Yep, Tweedle Dee and Tweedle Dum.

Roger was too old for this. What had he done in a past life to deserve it? He didn't want to talk about John Winton or Pate's own unique brand of crazy. He was already unlikely to convince Syl to stay on the case, and that would not help.

God, this town is cracked.

"Well, shit," he said. He rubbed his stubbly cheek like he could loosen a genie from a lamp, take his three wishes, and get the hell out of there.

Maybe Syl wouldn't require him to get too far into the weeds about it. Maybe she'd accept a vague explanation, and then all the John Winton talk would fizzle away like a bad dream. But the look on her face said otherwise. Big blue eyes wide, eyebrows raised.

He was screwed.

Roger nodded toward the cars, indicating he wanted to talk in private, so they half-walked, half-slid down the gravelly hill.

"Who's John Winton?" Syl asked, not even waiting until they got to the cars.

"A guy who disappeared about ten years ago. Summer of 1979."

"Do you have his case file?"

"Won't need it."

"I won't need the case file from an incident other cops think relates to this?"

And there it was, underneath the question: classic female ridicule. Women were experts at making you feel an inch tall without outright insulting you.

"Not related. Not even close. John Winton's case is nothing like Alex's."

"Tell her about the Markwells too," Mac shouted from the mine entrance.

Roger groaned.

Syl folded her arms across her tiny chest. "More related incidents that you don't think relate?"

Well shit. He'd have to tell her. About John Winton, about why Winton's case wasn't special or unique. God, about the Markwells! He knew how it'd sound because he'd been up to his eyeballs in alligators working with the Pate mayor to cast this town as a good place to raise kids—low crime, old-fashioned morals, etcetera. But the more the words *Markwell* and *Winton* floated through the air, the more paranoia would grow. And now he was being summoned as that lunacy's spokesperson, for Christ's sake! Sure, the town was cracked, but he didn't want to pull down its pants for this woman to examine.

"Not related incidents," Roger said. "I've never seen anything like what's in that mine."

PATE, IDAHO

January 1962

FIVE

LOU DIXON GENTLY **LOU DIXON GENTLY** closed the bedroom door behind her, careful not to wake her six-year-old granddaughter, Syl, who was finally asleep. She leaned against the hallway wall, fished a Pall Mall from the pocket of her housecoat and lit it.

She took long, slow drags from the cigarette so as to savor it, really enjoy it, like she used to when she was young, back when she still had healthy lungs and a lifetime left to waste.

The humming, like dull electricity inside her, had quieted even though it'd been steady, relentless all week. If only it'd stay that way, let her have some peace. But she knew better. She'd spent decades pushing it aside, ignoring it, trying to box it up like Harold's things out in the barn. It used to give her breaks, trick her into believing it was gone. But it always came back, ringing through her bones like shots fired in a canyon.

Stranger padded up the stairs, nails clicking wood with each step. The old dog's hips bothered him, so he plopped down sideways, and stared up at Lou with tired eyes. Her heart sank. She hadn't made a plan for him, which meant he'd likely spend his twilight years homeless. Lou couldn't think about that right now.

"I know, old boy," she said. "I got plenty to do besides frittering time away like this." Lou scratched Stranger behind his ears. "Maybe because the time's short, that's why I'm movin' so damn slow. Cut me a break, will ya?"

Stranger followed Lou downstairs, where she poured a cup of coffee from the percolator, drummed up a few pens from an untidy drawer, and laid out a stack of stationery. She sat down at the kitchen table to write.

The other preparations had all been made days ago. This letter was the last thing on her list, just as Lou had planned it. It was her only chance to explain things to Syl, like the girl deserved. She'd take her time with it.

January 8, 1962

Dear Syl,

If you got this, it means I'm dead, and on one hand, good riddance. Not to you, of course, my sweet pup, but to this life. Been full of pain. On the other hand, I don't want to go. Feels like I just started living here with you. You make everything brighter and happier, so I'm tempted to believe our days can go on this way until my natural end. But it's "time" for reasons I'll explain here.

I'm no writer, so excuse my wandering. I'm not going to fuss over it. The story is the story. I want you to know more about us, your family, but I also want you to know about the biggest mistake of my life and the reason I have to go. You should hear it right from the horse's mouth. Knowing you, you won't be satisfied until you do.

Your father, Mason, died last week.

I never been a good mother, you'll see by this letter's end. But I tried to be a good grandmother. I love you very much. You're asleep, warm in your bed right now, probably sucking that damn thumb. It gives me a gut punch to think you don't have a clue what's happening. You're just a baby, and you deserve so much more. But this is all I can give you.

I was a baby myself when my family moved to Pate from the Boise area. My father mined silver down in Idaho City and wanted to come up north where it seemed the galena was never-ending. (Galena is lead and silver ore, pup. It's what's in these mountains.) By the time my family got here, it wasn't the same as in those first days of mining where anyone could strike rich. Most claims were staked, but it didn't stop men and their lust of silver. Lots of them still panned, prospected, hoped to find riches. My pa was one of them. Spent his Sundays panning along the river, remote as possible. Mostly, though, he was a regular miner, working six days a week for the mine boss, pulling out that galena. Round that time miners were starting to organize. My pa was paid well by the mine boss to help patrol against the union, and I ain't proud of this, specially since my Harold, your grandpa, was so active in the union later on.

One of the men in charge of organizing died while working down on a level he knew well. My pa was this man's boss, and he tried to say the man slipped and fell down the chute, but he wouldn't have. He'd have known better. They never did find that man's body, and his death was written off as a mining accident. Thing was, my pa had warned him off organizing a week before it happened, but we didn't tell anyone that. Man's family thought it was murder, but it was never investigated.

Pate's full of dark secrets like this.

Your grandpa came from miners too. He saw how the lust of silver poisoned his own father and brothers and because of it, he never cared to strike it rich. He worked the mines, sure, but only for the salary and benefits, which weren't bad by the time we were married and on our way. I'm not like Grandpa though, pup. I always been someone who's got to feel out trouble for herself. Can't ever just watch and learn.

You don't know this, but we had a little girl after your father was born. Never could talk about her. I guess it hurt too much. She was only three years old when she vanished. Your father, Mason, was at school that day. Third grade at the time. Grandpa had asked me to walk to town instead of driving because it was smack during the Depression, and we were pinching pennies. The price of ore had dropped again, and the mines were laying men off. Grandpa kept his post because he was one of the best, but he could only get work four days a week. I needed flour to make Shit on a Shingle for supper. Least, that's what I told myself since it was Grandpa's favorite meal. Truth was, I'd polished off my last bottle of whiskey and I was in a big hurry to get more.

This was just months before Prohibition ended and it was easy to get the stuff by then. I always had a whiskey problem. Inherited it from my mother. She drank herself dead and couldn't stop even when she knew she was dyin', when her liver was making her skin yellow. Practically died with a bottle in her hand. Hell, pup, you never know what's lying around in your family history, inside your own bones. To me, that might be the scariest thing about this life. Thinking I may have sent some of these bad ways down the line to you. Well, I managed to kick my drinking to the curb by the time you came along, thank God. Anyways, I always was a good liar, so I hid my habit from Grandpa real easy. Took money from the jar and made up stories about why.

So, there I was, driving our old Model T into town. There Rose was next to me, singing Twinkle, Twinkle, Little Star. *She had this squeaky laugh, and she was trying to stand up in the front seat. I was grabbing her by the skirt of her dress and pulling her down, telling her to plant her batootie. Only made her laugh harder. When I looked back at the road, there was all these crows smack dab in the middle. I never seen that many crows all at once. I tried to dodge them, but I jerked the rig too hard, and it went off into the ditch.*

When I woke up, my head was bleeding. Were no crows in sight. I couldn't find Rose. Looked until I was sober too. Then I high-tailed it home and called the old sheriff. Told him Rose was gone. Sheriff went with me out to the accident site, and he looked around a bit, mostly to oblige me. He gave up. Said he had his doubts she survived the accident. If she did, she probably wandered off. But why would a three-year-old wander into the woods? It made no sense. I asked him to help me look further in, but he refused. Said I ought to know the woods were too deep to comb and the department too small for the task.

But Rose was my girl, so I set my mind to find her myself…

PATE, IDAHO

July 1989

SIX

ESMA WINTON STARED at the blank sketchbook laid open on the kitchen table. She'd just finished reading *Conjuring Your Inner Child*, and the book said this exercise would help her move forward, help her heal from all the troubles in her past, and she desperately wanted that. Needed it.

Thanks to the book, Esma could finally see that a lot of her irrational fears, her constant negativity—even the headaches—were due to past traumas. The headaches had disappeared almost right after John did, but the pain of her childhood was more stubborn. She used to have special gifts, like the ability to lucid dream, to control what went on in her mind during sleep, but this ability, like all of them, had faded with time. According to the book, her wounded inner child was to blame.

Esma held a blue ballpoint pen in her right hand and a red one in her left, just like chapter three instructed.

According to the book, a person's dominant hand writes the thoughts of their adult self, and a person's non-dominant hand writes the thoughts of their subconscious inner child. The non-dominant hand has easier access to the parts of the brain that govern intuition, spirituality, and emotion, so it was the perfect conduit for bringing subconscious thoughts to light. Once in the light, the person's consciousness could address them, even make peace with them. You weren't supposed to think too hard about it though. You just had to let the conversation flow.

She started with the blue pen.

Dear Little Esma, my darling inner child, I hope we can talk a bit. Would that be okay with you?

Her left hand awkwardly gripped the red pen, like a wall-flower at a school dance, waiting to be asked. Was something supposed to magically happen? Then her left hand wrote:

GEUSS SO. WHAT SHUOLD WE TALK BOUT

Look at that! The book even said sometimes the inner child couldn't spell as well as the adult. This was amazing; the words formed without any forethought on her part. The blue pen went to paper again.

How are you feeling today?

Red pen touched paper eagerly now.

OK I GEUSS. NOT SLEEPING VERY GOOD CUZ OF BAD DREEMS

Do you want to tell me about them?

CAN SHOW YOU

Esma's left hand didn't respond in letters, but drew instead.

A circle at the top of the page, lines all around it—a sun maybe? Then some more lines came up from the bottom and stopped almost where the circle was. The lines intersected diagonally. Trees? Or really bad stick people, Esma wasn't sure. The hand began to draw another shape, but stalled, then scribbled:

SHES COMING. HAFTA GO

Mom. Surely that was the "she" Little Esma was referring to. Esma put the pens down. She had a familiar feeling. Unsettled, but excited. Like peeking out from behind Mom's open bedroom doorway as a kid, watching her apply red lipstick, perfume, craving closeness, but willing herself to be invisible, praying Mom wouldn't catch her, yet still unable to stop looking.

Dawn's car door slammed at the base of the hill leading up to their cabin, startling Esma. Was Dawn's shift already over? She lifted a loose wood slat from the floor underneath the kitchen table and shoved the sketchbook into the cabin's foundation, hiding the evidence. Well, not *hiding*. Not exactly. She didn't need to hide from her eighteen-year-old daughter.

Then again, what would happen if Dawn saw what Esma was reading? The girl would scream about witchcraft. About how Esma was opening the door to the devil. John used to talk like that. Esma had always thought it was a little extreme, but she never could talk John out of his ideas.

Esma looked out the window. Dawn juggled her cleaning caddy, trying to unload it from the car, so Esma ran water at the old drainboard sink. Dawn would walk in to see her doing dishes. She'd like that. Dawn always said the place looked like—what did she call it? A FEMA disaster area? But Esma liked her things out and around. Nothing was worse than bare surfaces, that feeling of open space. Whenever she set out to clean, it was like throwing away memories. If she forced herself to keep cleaning, she'd erase their future too. Esma was most decidedly not ready for that. But inevitably, whenever she cleaned, she thought of death. The end of things for her, just like the end of this Velveeta carton, or the destruction of that grocery sack.

Dawn walked to the hand pump on the side of the cabin to clean out her mop bucket. The girl was so tidy. Esma looked all around to be sure nothing was out that might anger her. Dawn had John's temper.

Esma had put Dawn into public school after John disappeared, and she graduated with straight As. But her social life was— Esma reached for the small frying pan and ran the grease down the sink—Dawn's social life was hell. There was no nice way to put it. All those days watching her run around with druggies from school. They'd park their junkers where Dawn couldn't quite see them because the cabin was so far up the steep hill. They never bothered with a phone call to say they were coming, so Dawn was always by the window, sticking her head out the door or standing on the porch straining to see, like some sad Rapunzel.

"Why don't they call first?" Esma had asked once. "Why won't they come up and meet me?"

Dawn had rolled her eyes and ran out in a halter top and a super short jean skirt, jumping into the arms of whoever was her current love interest. The clothes were way too revealing for a fifteen-year-old, but Esma would have allowed them if she could make a clean trade for no more druggies.

Esma supposed every teenager went through a rebellious phase, but by the time Dawn was seventeen, she was scary. If Esma told her no about anything, Dawn got up in her face and screamed so hard, Esma could feel the hot spray of spit. And then one day Dawn just changed, became religious. Like turning a dial to change the station on the radio. Of course, Dawn had gone along with John's faith when he was around. She was just a child. But without John, Esma was not motivated to crack that whip and so all the religion stuff sort of sloughed off. And then there was teenager Dawn, putting it all back on again like wet jeans. Where did she even get the idea? What was the appeal?

The whole thing had spun Esma out a little because the change from Scary Dawn to Jesus Dawn had been so quick, so thorough. She was happy that Dawn wanted to be good. Yet, could she trust it? Scary Dawn had to be in there somewhere, dormant, waiting to show up and pounce when Esma least expected it. Her solution was to leave Dawn be, let her figure life out, try not to get in the way.

Esma sniffed the Brillo pad she was using to scrub the pan. So *that* was where the nasty smell came from! She threw it at the garbage can and missed, then opened drawers in search of another pad. Out of luck, she settled for a clean washrag. Or at least, it didn't smell like mildew.

Dawn was finally in a good place now, that was what mattered. She was holding a job, going to church. So what if it came in a strange, plastic package? Sure, Esma had to hide her projects from Dawn in order to keep her on this good path. Had to pretend she still believed in the Bible and church and all that, but she'd do that and more if necessary.

Dawn's old druggie friends were all over Pate. People like that never left the spot they were born. Esma couldn't risk Dawn running back to them if the anger won her over again. But then again, that was what Scary Dawn would do. What would Jesus Dawn do?

Dawn walked through the back door, and it slammed behind her. Esma hated the harsh slap of that door. She cringed.

"Gosh, it's so hot out!" Dawn wiped her forehead with the front of her T-shirt.

"Sure is," Esma said, making a show of turning a Corelle bowl upside down to dry on the dish rack.

Hey, Dawn, look, I'm doing the dishes!

Esma accidentally flung a drop of water onto her long crepe skirt in the process. She was back to wearing her "hippie clothes," as John called them. It's what she wore when she actually *was* a hippie. She'd always meant to travel the world. But the only time it happened was when she hitchhiked across the country to attend Woodstock. She got saved on that trip, in a VW van with a bunch of Jesus People. They'd pulled off the freeway and baptized her in a pond just outside the festival. Those were the days when people were only interested in loving God and loving each other. Faith was simple.

"We should go to the lake tonight, Mom. Wouldn't that be fun? What do you have going on?"

Esma didn't turn around, but she felt the dimples in Dawn's smile anyway. Esma hated the water, but for all her nerves about the change in Dawn, she owed her. Dawn supported them financially. She got the job as a housekeeper at Great Pine Hotel right out of high school. Sure, it wasn't very much money, but it bought food, along with gas for Dawn's car. It was plenty for Esma, and a lot more than they had before.

"Nothing really. Thought I might work on my projects a little."

Dawn smacked her forehead with her palm. "I forgot I told Pastor I'd pick up his kids from Bible study after work. His wife isn't feeling good and he doesn't want to leave her alone. Sorry, I guess I can't go to the lake."

"What's wrong with her?" Esma asked, not caring a whit for the lake.

"I think it's just a bug. But it seems like she's sick a lot." And then, like it just occurred to her, she announced, "We should pray for her! It's probably just an attack. Nothing the Lord can't handle!"

It was that singsong Pollyanna voice that refused to acknowledge anything bad. The woman couldn't simply be sick, she was being *attacked*. If you forced Esma to pinpoint it, this was the thing that bothered her most about Dawn's recovered faith. Esma believed very much in putting out good energy and receiving it back, but this felt more like being afraid to see reality.

"Yes, of course," Esma said.

Dawn must have walked over, because Esma felt the heat of July coming off her skin from behind.

"Oh, right now?" Esma turned and wiped her hands on her long skirt.

"If we don't do it when the Holy Spirit reminds us, we'll just forget." Dawn flopped her shoulders in a shrug that made her long, blonde ponytail swing.

"True," Esma said. No use arguing with Dawn.

SEVEN

DAWN CAME OUT of the cabin and the back door slammed. Mom hated that, but Dawn forgot. She checked to make sure she had her car keys in hand and walked down the rickety steps. The woodshed caught her eye.

The old shed was rotten in spots, and it sat behind the cabin, at the base of a little hill that climbed up until it flattened out into a meadow. Beyond that, trees lined the mountain all the way to downtown Pate. It was quite a drive to get downtown because you had to go all the way around the mountains. But you could take this hill behind the house on foot at an angle and be downtown in thirty minutes or less. You had to walk fast to make that kind of time though.

Along the side of the shed was a huge gas tank Dad installed, who knew why. He was always bringing home vehicles that were lemons, so sure he could restore them. He brought home all kinds of strange things, actually. Like those sticks of dynamite on their last Apocalypse Survival Week. They never did light those, but of course, they didn't have time. Dad disappeared so soon after they arrived at camp. Dad wanted cars parked all over so that when the end times came, he'd be ready, a car within walking distance no matter where they happened to be when everything fell apart. They'd drive up the remainder of the Idaho panhandle and deep into Canada. Dawn never understood how Canada would save them from an apocalypse, but it didn't matter now. He didn't get those old cars running, or off their property for that matter, and they littered the weeds like rusty ghosts.

Dawn avoided the shed. It was her reminder that religion could be violent. Her dad showed her this, but Dawn's very first experience with the violence of religion didn't come from him. It came from a large painting displayed above the fireplace in the cabin.

A picture of an almost naked man. His body hung, baking in the desert. He was stuck between two other men, one's head hung like he was already dead. The man in the middle's head glowed like a red orb. Glints of metal visible in sunlight, his eyes strained upward, asking for something. Help maybe? Dawn didn't know. There was the charcoal sky about to cover up the sun, his skin sagging off rib bones, more metal around his hands and feet. Women sprawled at those feet, crying. Later, she learned it was the crucifixion of Christ. Mom pulled the painting down after Dad disappeared. Dawn didn't even ask her to.

When she was about three years old, Dawn sat on a circle rug in front of the fireplace, staring at the painting while she was supposed to be memorizing scripture. Sometimes she'd get stuck there. Hours passed and she'd come to, realizing she'd been there a long time. Mom never noticed her sitting there, but then again, Mom never really noticed her at all. Dad was all Mom lived for and cared about. Nothing had changed there.

Once, back before Dad disappeared, Dawn had been staring at the crucifixion while Mom slept in the back bedroom. Dad found Dawn like that. He clomped in with those boots he wore and sat down on the couch.

"This is what God's love looks like." He pulled her up on his lap and pointed at the painting. "Never forget what our Lord did for us. The Bible says 'the eyes of the Lord are in every place, beholding the evil and the good.' Nothing you do passes without Him seeing it, girl."

But all Dawn saw was blood and pain. God's love must be pain. Pain was love, and blood was devotion. Hopelessness, sunburn, hunger, and lots of crying was God's love.

His eye is beholding the evil, Dawn. He's watching you all the time.

Dawn tried every day to get Mom out of bed, but the headaches always won. Tried to show her the new puppet show she made up, the costumes she'd designed for her stuffed animals. Mom never stirred.

Dad watched the puppet shows. He had a great laugh and when he'd tip his head back, it boomed and she knew she really hit his funny bone. Otherwise, Dawn hated Dad's watching. It was like he could see through the walls of the house, and if she forgot to say prayers in bed, he knew. He noticed if she didn't scratch her scalp very well in the bathtub. He knew if she didn't change her socks. Then the practice in holiness started.

"When I call, you come, girl," he'd say. "Slow obey is no obey."

He'd whisper her name from another room. She swore it was inaudible at times. It got to where she could tell when he was gearing up to do this little exercise, and she'd pay extra attention. The way he'd clear his throat, that he hadn't picked up his Bible, yet he was sitting at the kitchen table. Sometimes he didn't call her name at all and then she'd hear hard boots falling on worn wood. She'd explain that she was listening and he hadn't called her. But that wasn't a possibility in her dad's mind. If Dawn didn't come running, it was that she heard, but refused to obey.

He pulled her by the hair, the ear, the arm, bruising, ripping, tearing her from her play and into the shed. He closed the door, putting them in darkness. The shed had no windows. He had to light a lantern to see.

Dad reached for a switch or an old newspaper he rolled up, or he'd remove his belt.

Dawn prayed to God for the switch over the belt. She'd take a crowbar over the belt because of what came after.

"It's your job to listen," he'd say. "Like the good sheep that hears the Shepherd and responds to the still, small voice."

He'd pull down her pants and lay her on top of his knees, spanking until she was bruised and bleeding. He kept it up until she had a good attitude. Until she wasn't crying and she could smile while receiving discipline.

"Spare the rod, spoil the child," he'd say, almost apologetically.

Sometimes it was easy to stop crying, to show Dad she could *rule her spirit*. That was Dad's term for not allowing your emotions to dominate you. Usually, it'd take a solid two, maybe three minutes of spankings.

It wasn't just the spankings either. Dad's version of toilet training was shutting her outside in the dead of winter when she had an accident. Rewards for making it to the toilet on time were ice cream for dinner and skipping naps. She'd cry outside and still, Mom never stirred.

"Get a good attitude and learn to love discipline!" Her dad would shout inside the woodshed and spank her again.

The only way to calm herself down during spankings was to make herself disappear. One day she noticed an old photograph of a man and a woman, lit by the lantern's glow. It was a black-and-white framed image, leaning up against the wall. She'd focus on them, even make up stories about them. Were they in love? They didn't seem very happy, but nobody smiled in those old pictures. This couple had a child, but he wasn't in the picture. He was underneath the shed. She met him the first time she imagined disappearing under there. It was her trick for making everything hurt a little less. She'd close her eyes and feel the darkness, like sludge, sucking her down, pulling her just below the surface of dirt where she'd stay hidden until it was all over. That's where the little boy lived. He was six years old and he was her friend. He helped her during the spankings. Dawn got so good at disappearing that she could stay gone all the way through the cleansing, which followed every spanking session when the belt came off. It was why she hated the belt so much.

"This hurts me more than it hurts you, Dawny," Dad would say, catching his breath from the exertion. "You know I love you. Do you love me?"

He set her on her feet and she scrambled to pull up her pants and run, like a mouse when the cat's paw released.

"Whoa, whoa. Where you going? You can't leave me here like this. All full of sin! It's *your* sin that's got me so I'm not right with God. You know I can't make myself clean." He'd slip off his suspenders and unbutton the front of his pants.

"You need to help me get all the sin out. We can't have it in this home."

He'd place her hand on it and help at first. She'd rub and rub until she saw the sin heaving out of him in white, wet strings. He always smiled.

"God loves you, Dawn." He'd kiss her forehead afterward. As Dawn grew, her dad always chose the belt. And then the cleansing.

EIGHT

SYL'S EYES BLINKED open. The clock by her bed read 3:03 a.m. The three o'clock hour was her own personal witching hour. Ray Bradbury was right to call it the "soulless" hour. Nothing more evil than waking up when it's too early to get up and too late to fall back to sleep. Goddamn insomnia.

The moonlight turned her bedroom ceiling a light shade of blue. Syl stared at it, thinking about that creepy-ass mine. The practically mummified body, the *drip, drip, drip*. About the portraits all over town.

She pushed the comforter off. No sense trying to sleep, it never worked. She'd lie in bed for hours and hours, only getting more frustrated that sleep wasn't coming. Syl used to be a good sleeper. It drove Carl crazy because she'd be deep in slumber, kicking all night long and keeping him awake until he retreated to the couch. She never remembered doing it.

God, her back hurt. Buying a new bed had been on her list of things to do since moving back to Pate, but she sucked at to-do lists.

In the kitchen, Syl could see the dilapidated white barn out back, just a shadow backlit by the moon and stars. She spooned Folgers into the paper filter and started the miracle machine. Stray grounds stared up from the yellow tile countertop and she swiped her hand across, dumping a handful into the trash. She pushed her index finger into a deep nick in one of the tiles. The renters, bless their hearts, hadn't kept the house up, but they hadn't completely trashed it either.

Wrestling her hair into a ponytail and listening to the coffee maker gurgle, she found no hair band in her robe's pocket. She went into the bathroom to find one, and there she was in the mirror. Bangs a mess, split down the middle, one side levitating. Typical for a first look after sleep, but even so, she smashed them down, brushed them together furiously to cover the split.

Out of nowhere, Lucas came to mind.

I can't think about him.

(Why not?)

Nothing I can do about it.

(You could visit him.)

I can't.

(You going to abandon your boy? That's your play?)

Ah, screw it. She stopped arguing with her hair and walked back into the kitchen to stare at the coffee pot. Make it go faster. Why did everything take so goddamn long? After a minute watching it drip, she poured the half a cup the machine had produced so far and took such a big drink that she burned her tongue.

I could just wait the seven seconds it takes to cool off so I don't burn my mouth.

Too bad God passed her over in the patience department. Yet, despite the patience problem, she'd moved to Pate where everything took twice as long as it did in Spokane. But she had to leave that city. She was suffocating. This wasn't ideal, but at least she could breathe.

Syl did quite a few years on patrol before she made detective in Spokane, and that was after taking the detective's test a couple times and being passed over. But how could you compete with men in a culture that encouraged them to pursue police work when they were boys? Men whose dads and uncles were police officers before them and who happily shared those connections. Syl didn't like to jump to the sexism argument, but there it was.

Her final attempt at detective coincided with the police department's new PR campaign last year. They were working hard to recruit and promote more women and minorities. She was one of only two in either category trying for detective, so of course *then* she was the most *qualified*.

"Don't depend on that smile to get you by, Dixon," Sheriff Cummings had said as a welcome to the homicide department.

Goddamn Cummings. What did that even mean in terms of police work? No criminal had been hip-swayed and winky-eyed into confessing to murder that she knew of. And if it brought a confession, she doubted Cummings would object anyway.

It would have all worked out fine if not for the insomnia. She'd had her share of sleep deprivation when Lucas was a baby, and handled it. Somewhere around his toddler years, she stopped sleeping at night. Started feeling trapped in her life. But what really ruined her were the many times she fell asleep on duty at the station. The first time it happened, she'd just made detective. She passed out full-on, head down, drooling and snoring at 10 a.m. That was the beginning of the end.

Turned out she could handle the pussy jokes and dyke comments—all white noise. But something like falling asleep on the job was chumming the water for sharks. The ones who ate careers.

Around that time, Syl's doctor introduced her to some lovely little friends, the sleeping pills. The pills arrived too late to help her overcome her record though. She was demoted to patrol, and nothing about that was appealing. The only reason she became a police officer was so she could eventually be a detective. If that gig was up, what else was there? Plus, she still had the insomnia to deal with. The sleeping pills worked wonders for getting to sleep, but staying asleep was a different thing, it turned out.

The other thing was her solve-rate problem. Would Cummings have kept her on with the sleeping problem if she didn't also have the solve-rate problem? Maybe. Syl followed her gut more than other detectives. Unlike in the movies, this didn't usually pan out and the county prosecutors were just about done with what they called her "thin reasoning" for warrants and her "feelings-based" facts. The sleeping problem only helped Cummings to edge her out politely.

Growing up, she'd been obsessed with *Nancy Drew* and any other mystery book she found at the library. But reading about solving crimes didn't promise you'd be good at solving them yourself. Plus, the way Cummings wanted her to investigate was a lot more procedural and boring than Nancy Drew. All the hoops she had to jump through to make sure things were nice and tidy for court. Exhausting.

Nothing boring about the way they found Conder in that mine though. What could cause that?

It didn't matter, she'd meet up with Roger to interview Alex's widow later because she said she would, and then she'd bow out. It'd be a favor to Roger to bow out, even if he didn't see it that way. He thinks she quit investigating to move here and she was fine with his delusion that she was a good detective. No reason for him to learn otherwise.

She could use the cash flow though.

Syl yawned and rubbed her eyes. It wasn't logical to solve this identity crisis at 3 a.m. Or before the coffee kicked in.

She poured another mug and sat at the kitchen table, wishing for a cigarette. But she had quit smoking and she would hold that line. Succeed at this one thing in the midst of the graveyard of Syl Dixon failures also known as her life. Fingers fluffing bangs mindlessly, as she stared out back.

Seeing that barn made her think about sorting through Gran's shit. The barn was a doozy and if she could get through all that, boxing up the house would be a cinch. Maybe she was jumping into the deep end though. She had that tendency. Take on the biggest task available, botch it, ignore it, or otherwise put it off, and then feel sorry for yourself about being such a goddamn failure. No, the barn wasn't the place to start. Gran was the biggest pack rat Syl ever knew. She should start inside the house where there was less clutter. Get a little win.

She took a drink of coffee, this time without scorching her tongue.

Gran would be almost eighty-seven now, so Syl had no hope of actually finding her. Not alive, at least. Although, if anyone could stay spry as they rounded the corner to ninety, it was

Gran. The weird thing was Gran left no note, although she did arrange for Syl to live with Aunt Shirley, Gran's sister, in Spokane. Syl's father had died in a trucking accident just prior to when Gran went missing. Her mom died in childbirth.

Would she even be successful finding out what happened to Gran? Success wasn't really her thing. She imagined headstones in the graveyard of her life. RIP decluttering. RIP parenting. RIP investigating.

NINE

ESMA WOKE UP that morning thinking about John.

She'd been trying not to think about him so much lately and even started to wonder if it was time to move past him. He wasn't coming back.

Why was he constantly on her mind now? More than usual. Maybe it was all that focus on healing past trauma. She'd had another dream last night, and it had been almost impossible to change. At the last minute, she'd managed to create something different in the dream, but what if that stopped working? What if she became like everyone else: stuck in whatever dream your subconscious comes up with?

It was her wounded inner child acting up again. She needed to do the work to heal in order to strengthen her gifts. She pulled out the sketchbook and picked up the pens, starting with blue.

Hello there, Little Esma! How are you today?

Red pen marks scratched across the page.

SCARED. MOM HAS A NEW BOYFREIND

Esma's stomach turned over.

Just stay out of their way.

The red pen didn't budge. Didn't respond at all. Dang it! Questions. Only ask questions, the book said. Esma tried a different approach even though she already knew the answer.

What are you scared of, Little Esma?

WHEN THEY LOCK ME UP

Tears pinched at the back of Esma's nose. Like she was the one there with Mom again. Whenever Mom had a new boyfriend, they'd put her in the closet and leave the house. Go dancing at the bar all night. Sometimes Mom didn't come home for days.

You're safe now, Little Esma. We're safe. They can't hurt you anymore. Did you know you have special gifts?

I DO?

Yes! You can change your dreams at night and sense things.

Most of the time, at least. Esma didn't need to go into those details right now though.

MOMS BAD

Esma knew that wasn't true, that her mom had her own trauma, but it was hard to disagree with.

Why do you think that, Little Esma?

I KNOW IT. YOU SAY I KNOW STUF

Mom can't hurt us anymore. We're happy and safe.

Were they happy though? Esma looked around the cabin and saw only the pain and heartbreak the past years had brought. Just then, she remembered the drawing. She'd ask Little Esma to finish, but before she could, her left hand scribbled:

YOUR THINKIN OF JOHN ALOT

The pen rose from the paper and Esma felt a flash of heat from her heart chakra into her face. How would Little Esma know that? But then she relaxed. Of course she knows! Little

Esma was *her*. It was all her own mind. Just to be sure, though, Esma had an idea for a test.

How's your dog?

CARMENS GREAT SHES MY BEST FREIND

Carmen was Esma's only friend for most of her childhood. A mangy dog she found one day. She was shocked when Mom let her keep it. Fact was, nobody else knew about Carmen. Well, nobody except Mom. Esma kept her inside the house until she ran away one day. By then, even Mom had forgotten she had the dog. The little mutt was so quiet, so happy to be warm and loved.

She's such a good girl. You take good care of her for me. And you're right, I am thinking of John. I miss him.

HE MISESS YOU TO

Esma slammed the pens down and pushed the kitchen chair back, metal scraping wood floors. The energy was wonky. She stretched her neck from side to side, feeling very tired. Something was unproductive about this. She'd pick up *Conjuring Your Inner Child* later to see what she was doing wrong. That's probably all it was. But she couldn't help asking and so she picked up the pens again.

How could you know that?

"Mom?" Dawn called as the back door swung open.

Esma closed the sketchbook in one quick motion.

"I forgot my Bible," Dawn yelled, walking into her bedroom without coming into the kitchen. Esma held still, as if she could be invisible.

"Whatcha doing?" Dawn was suddenly behind her.

"Oh, just drawing a little something. Trying out a new approach to prayer."

Esma hated lying to her, but she couldn't tell her the truth. It'd set her off.

"Cool! Can I see?" Dawn came closer.

"I don't ask to see your prayer journal."

It came out so much more forceful than Esma meant it to. She smiled, but what if it was too late? What if Dawn got mad? She slowly placed both hands on the sketch pad.

"Oh. All right. I wasn't trying to snoop, just curious to know about your new approach." Dawn's voice was tight, controlled. She walked past Esma and back toward her room and then turned around, her voice softer, more singsong, "Are you coming to church this Sunday?"

"Yes, sure, sweetie."

Liar, liar pants on fire.

"I'm so glad to hear it!" Dawn's arms were out, reaching for a hug. Esma took it. "There's something special about you, and I believe the Lord will give you the answers we need! Pastor says it's the next generation that'll lead us,"—she pulled away to face Esma—"but I think it's you and your spiritual gifts."

Esma was so surprised that she just stood there, stiff, blinking, until Dawn went out the back door again.

How did Dawn know about her gifts? She felt exposed. She'd never mentioned them. Had the girl gotten into her books and seen what Esma was studying? No. If she had, Dawn would most certainly be mad. Esma watched Dawn's car until she couldn't see it anymore, and then she scrambled to open the sketchbook, picked up the pens.

What did you mean that John misses me?

HES COMING

The blue pen in her right hand hesitated. The correct thing to do was drop the whole business. But what if she could see John again?

John disappeared. It's been ten years. He's not coming back.

Esma held red pen to the paper, feeling like Little Esma wanted to say something else.

CROSS MY HART HES COMING HOME

Esma shut the sketchbook fast. This was crazy! She was talking to her more-enlightened self in order to heal past trauma and all she was getting was proof of her own lunacy. Maybe this exercise worked for everyone else, but it was just making Esma more confused.

Plus, what was Little Esma even talking about? How could she know what John was going to do? And by *she*, she meant herself. Little Esma was *her*, but Esma didn't have the first clue what John was going to do or whether he was even alive anymore. But then, what if John really could return? She either needed to stop trying to rationalize this and go with it, or she needed to put the sketchbook away for good. Esma tucked it under the floorboard, but her hand lingered over the big knot in the wood. She really, really wanted to see John again. How she loved him! They had been so happy together, the three of them, living like little pioneers in the wilderness. Why did it have to end?

What if he was still out there somewhere? What if he could return? She shouldn't set her heart on it, and yet, she couldn't resist the hope in this moment. To have John back... Tears leapt into Esma's eyes at the idea, and she brushed them off her face.

SPOKANE, WASHINGTON

May 1901

TEN

LILY CARDING SAT on a rust-colored boulder. Hugging her knees, she looked down at the Spokane River. Massive rocks lined the edge of a small canyon and white-capped currents rushed fast far below. Her home was set a little way downriver from the Spokane Falls, but she could still hear the distant crashing. Father's mill was at the falls. The sun warmed her face as it crested over faraway blue mountains, tipped with a thin veil of fog. The whole scene, along with the sound of the roaring water, sparked wildness inside her. Lily closed her eyes and listened to the water's power, like it was medicine for a sickness. She came out here to skip chores and to get away from her little sister. This morning, she imagined she was free. Wind pushed against her skin, twisting her long, dark hair into a tangle. It'd make her mother cross, and the thought of that made Lily smile.

The town was growing fast. Father had bought the mill when its original owner went bankrupt, and the Carding family swiftly became part of the elite in this small, western town. He commissioned a home designed by the famous Kirtland Cutter, which meant they were in the company of the most beautiful and unique estates in the northwest. But all that shimmer didn't cover up what was underneath. What went on inside the home.

Last night at supper, Lily had asked her father if she could study painting in Europe once she was done with her schooling. Her governess said she had talent, and she wanted to develop it, plus she was set on getting away from home even though she was only sixteen.

Lily's family was intolerable. The one person she cared to be around was Holver, their stable hand, but there was no way this arrangement would be palatable to her parents. Her father didn't even want her to be married. The few times she'd overheard her mother mention it to him, he'd flown into a rage, like usual. That was fine with Lily. She didn't want to marry either, and Europe would solve it all. Father certainly had the money to send her. But he'd said no. He couldn't stand to see her leave home.

A small marmot approached the rock she occupied and holding as still as possible, she willed it to come closer. The sun grew warmer as it rose, and Lily relished it. She was a creature of light and hated the cold, dark days. Winter was still two seasons away, and it was plenty of time to plan an escape. She'd get out before those awful days when the sun was stingy with its presence, rising late and setting much too soon. But today, the sun tanned her face, which would also make her mother cross.

It was certain Europe wouldn't happen, so she needed to find another way out. Marriage would get her away from this place, but it wouldn't help her reach her goal of being free. It would simply be a different sort of cage.

The marmot came up to her foot and sniffed at it. She wanted to pet the little rodent, but if she did, it'd run away into its hole in the ground.

Why couldn't she have been born a boy? *That* was freedom—to be a man. But here she was, stuck inside this prison of her own body. She had just as many wits about her as men did. More than most men, actually.

Lily's foot slipped from its hold on the boulder, and the scraping noise chased her marmot away.

"Lillly?"

It was Margaret. Lily groaned.

Hadn't she gone far enough from the house to avoid that confounded pest? Margaret was only twelve, but still. She hated, hated, *hated* Margaret. The adorable little girl, with her constant smiles and laughs. Begging Lily to do a picnic in the forest together. "Just like Little Red Riding Hood!" Margaret always said. She didn't seem to realize how the fairy tale ended. The only thing that stuck in Margaret's small mind, no matter how many times the governess read the story to her, was the picnic basket and the woods. Fool.

"Lil?" Closer now.

Lily held still, hoping the scant timber would hide her. Maybe she'd blend in. Out of the corner of her eye, she could see Margaret hopping on her right leg, and then her left. She loped over the long grass and milkweeds leading to the cliff's edge. Trailing behind her was that mangy Saint Bernard dog, Sadie. It followed her everywhere, staying extra close whenever it saw Lily.

That was due to last year when Lily had tied Sadie's furry legs together. The front two and then the back two, and oh how the animal had cried! It wasn't that Lily enjoyed doing it, she didn't. But it was necessary in order to show Margaret that she was serious about being left alone. Especially when she was out here, or when she was reading, or painting. The dog was vexing, but it wasn't the dog she took issue with.

Margaret had intervened on Sadie's behalf that day. Just before Lily finished the task of shoving a wooden stake under the ropes to hang the dog upside down from two trees, like a tied hog.

"Lil! What are you doing? Stop it. Stop!" Margaret had wailed, pushing her out of the way and working fast to untie the knots as Sadie made chirping noises that weren't quite howls but also weren't any form of barking. Lily stood back, arms crossed under her bosom, trying not to laugh at Margaret.

"It isn't funny! She's hurting. Why do you hate Sadie so much?" Margaret demanded, wrapping her arms around the huge dog, now free of its bonds.

Lily bent down and put her face into Margaret's, arms still crossed. "I don't hate Sadie. I hate you," she whispered through clenched teeth.

All expression and color vacated Margaret's face. The girl cried, but Lily wasn't sure if it was due to the dog being tied up or from what she'd said.

Now here was Margaret, coming toward her, as if Lily had never hurt her dog. As if Lily were actually the sister Margaret thought she was. As if Lily would jump up and agree to play a game or read a story together.

Please, God, make her disappear.

"Hi, Lil! I've been looking all over for you." Margaret smiled when she finally reached Lily. Her brown curls bounced once more after she stopped. She was out of breath. "Mr. George is going into town, and I know how much you love town. Want to go?"

"No, Margaret, I want to be *here*. Alone!" she hissed through a clenched jaw.

"Why don't you call me Meg like everyone else does?" Margaret swished her lacy dress. The movement made her curls bob again. Would Lily's teeth crack from the clenching?

"Because that's not your name. Now *go away!*"

"I'm sorry for making you cross, Lil."

"Blast it, Margaret, stop calling me 'Lil!' And get this dog out of here!" She made a sweeping motion toward Sadie, who cowered, then hid behind Margaret.

"I have something for you. You can read it when I leave," Margaret said and skipped away before Lily could refuse. Sadie hopped along like Margaret's shadow, barking at every butterfly along the way.

Margaret was unflappable. She acted as if Lily hadn't just screamed at her. It made her even more angry with the child. Why couldn't Margaret just get mad at Lily and stay away? If she'd be angry, or even afraid, maybe it would help. Maybe then Lily wouldn't feel so driven to torment her. But she knew it was a delusion. In order for her and Margaret to coexist, Margaret would need to pretend like Lily didn't exist. It was supremely unlikely to ever happen.

Lily opened up the card and saw Miss Jackson's handwriting. Margaret was capable of writing her own letters, and yet she'd probably whined until the governess offered to do it for her. It read:

Dear Lil,

Please join me for a picnic lunch in the woods at noonday.

Sincerely yours,

Meg

No.
But then, just as Lily twisted the card to tear it up, an idea came to her. She folded the card in half and put it into her dress apron's pocket.

PATE, IDAHO

July 1989

FAYE, IDAHO

July 1989

ELEVEN

SYL PULLED UP to the address Roger gave her—the Conder house. Trailer, rather. His rig was parked outside the single wide, surrounded by weeds, cheat grass, and the like. She spied buttercups and bluebells, too, but no lawn grass or other typical yard stuff. Not even the landfill-crap trailers notoriously displayed all over their properties. No half-torn couches, no broken toilets. The place was neat and spare, like somebody plopped a trailer down in a field dotted by a few pine trees. The trailer itself was set a ways back from Main Street, at the base of a mountain. This made it so the place wasn't in town, but it wasn't quite in the thick of the forest either.

The choppy trill of bluebirds and some wind rustling pine needles made Syl smile, something she'd done so rarely over the past year. It was beautiful here in Pate. Her smile faded when she remembered she was involved in police work. It had happened in a breath, so naturally, like picking up a piece of litter from the ground. There was still some resistance to the idea, but she felt an inevitability to it.

Syl walked up the tiny dirt path where Roger stood guard. Two goddamn framed pictures stared at her from near the trailer's metal door, mocking her. Holding a secret she was too much of an outsider to know about.

Roger smacked his gum, waiting.

As she got closer, she saw one black and white portrait of a man, and a color photograph that looked newer. Judging by the bell-bottoms the two people wore in the second photo, it was likely taken during the seventies.

"What are all these portraits for? I've seen them on houses all over Pate."

"Town's big into family," Roger said with a shrug.

Typical answer. She narrowed her eyes at him and waited to see if he'd say more, but he didn't.

"Did you just quit smoking?" Syl asked.

"What does that have to do with anything?"

"The obsessive gum chewing."

"Had a heart attack a couple months ago, and the doctor told me it was the smokes or my life."

Roger took the metal steps up to the trailer's clipped porch. She followed.

"Did Hendon pull the John Winton case file for me?"

Roger moved his hand like he was batting away the question. "One thing at a time. First, interview Betty and Kyle, then you can chase rabbit trails that go nowhere." Then he turned and smiled, as if realizing something. "That mean you're helping with the case?"

"I didn't say that."

Betty Conder opened the door after Roger's quick knock. She looked like a version of Alex—a skeleton with some obligatory skin covering bone nakedness, and a loose button-up house dress from the sixties. It had massive orange, green, and yellow flowers, and looked five sizes too big. Betty clearly smoked too much and ate too little. Her round, brown eyes were red-rimmed from crying, no doubt. But they seemed ancient, like the woman had seen everything life had to offer. She couldn't be *that* old though. How old did Roger say Alex was? In his forties? Still, this woman had to have logged extra years. Like her life had been on fast-forward.

Betty held a menthol cigarette tight between her lips. It wagged up and down as she said, "You the big city detective who gonna solve all this?"

"Sort of. I mean—"

"You're *sort of* gonna solve it? Or you're *sort of* a big city detective?"

"Both. Sort of both. I'm Syl Dixon."

"Lou's girl. I remember you, although you were knee-high to a grasshopper last time I saw you."

Syl tried to hide how thrilled she was that somebody remembered her. She wanted to ask Betty more about Gran, but Betty went right on to the next thing.

"You gonna catch the sonabitch who did this to my Alex?"

"That's the plan."

It wasn't exactly her plan; she was still hoping to bow out of the whole thing. But the reality that she would end up helping with this case pinched at her tighter and tighter with every step forward.

Betty waved them inside the trailer and through the kitchen. Fabric, thread, sewing pins, and buttons were scattered across every surface like debris from a wind storm.

"You like to sew." It was a question, but Syl said it like a fact.

Betty stopped walking and leaned against the chipped sink, removed her cigarette and said, "I make Barbie clothes." Her voice dragged like a pitchfork along a bed of rocks. "For the girls around town, but sometimes I go into Spokane and sell 'em at market. Gives me some walkin' around money. Plus, Alex wanted me to quit the smokes. Got to where he wouldn't let me use his money on 'em. So, I started buying those with my Barbie money too."

Syl held up one of the few finished dresses in the pile. It was lavender, with tiny black jewels across the bodice. Long sleeves, puffed slightly. It had minuscule buttons up the back. The work was detailed, and Syl was impressed.

"They're pretty."

Betty tipped her head like she already knew that.

"Can you write down the names of anyone you saw at the grocery store last night?" Syl said, putting the dress down carefully. "Just need to confirm you were there."

It wasn't something you could ask in a larger city, but even just a few weeks in, Syl knew from experience you always saw someone at the store around here.

Betty nodded and looked around for a scrap of paper.

The woman must have spent all of her time sewing Barbie dresses, based on the condition of the home. The red brick-pattered linoleum was coming up in the corners of the kitchen, and it wasn't just the smell of menthol cigarettes Syl picked up. There was a significant whiff of mildew, like maybe the woman forgot a load of clothes in the washer all week. All month? Crumbs were all over the kitchen counter. Three glass ashtrays were full of mountainous butts in ash. That was just in the kitchen.

She couldn't judge. There was something almost beautiful about a woman—a housewife, no less—who invited people into her disgusting house unashamedly. Syl only wished for that sort of confidence.

Betty set the pen down, handed Syl the paper with two names, and wafted her cigarette hand toward an open box of Hostess donuts. The lid was crumpled like maybe it'd been open for a long time.

"You guys want one? Cops and donuts and all."

Hell no.

"Oh, no thank you," Syl said. "If I could talk to Kyle now, that would be best. Does he know about the condition his dad was found in?"

"No. Figured him not knowing was better," she mumbled around the cigarette and nodded toward the other room. "He's in there."

Roger was reaching into the Hostess box when Syl walked out.

Kyle sat on a torn brown couch, the kind you usually found in front of a trailer. He had a brown mullet. Permed, no less. Interesting financial priority: your eleven-year-old's hairdo. He played Super Mario Brothers on the Nintendo.

"He's tired," Betty yelled from the kitchen. "Not sure what kinda luck you're gonna have!"

Syl sat down next to the boy.

"I love video games," she said.

Kyle rolled his eyes like she was just some old lady. They were rimmed bright red like his mom's, purple underneath.

"Kyle, I'm going to ask you a few questions." She didn't wait for his response, and he didn't offer one. "Do you remember what happened last night?"

Kyle shook his head, not taking his eyes off the TV.

"Did you see someone other than your dad?"

Shook his head again.

She sucked at this. Two attempts in, and she'd only fed him yes or no questions.

"Kyle, I need you to try to think hard about it. What do you remember?"

Kyle shrugged.

"What did you see or hear?"

Another shrug. And then the kid spoke. "You don't look like a cop. Where's your uniform?"

"I'm not really on duty. Plus, detectives usually don't wear one."

"You're a detective, like Sherlock Holmes?"

"Kind of. But more boring than Sherlock Holmes. And without the cool hat."

Or the kick-ass solve-rate.

Kyle went back to his video game.

"You look really tired. Why is that?" she asked.

"Can't sleep. Keep having bad dreams."

He was playing tough, but he had just lost his dad. She put this at the front of her mind as she asked another question.

"Dreams about what?"

Kyle acted like she hadn't spoken at all. He played in silence. Syl sat there, feeling like he might say something, with absolutely no evidence in favor of it.

Then he changed, softened. He hesitated, put the controller down and said, "You ever heard of people who glow silver?"

"What do you mean?"

He turned his arm so it was wrist up. Pointed at his veins. "Like here. These blood vessels, glowing silver all over. Glowing silver eyes too."

"No, I'm sorry. Did you see someone like that?"

"Kept showing up in my dream. I woke up and then fell back to sleep and there it was again."

"Anyone you recognize?"

Tears filled Kyle's eyes. "My dad." Then he stiffened and said, "My dad looked like a monster."

"What sort of monster?"

"A mummy."

SPOKANE, WASHINGTON

May 1901

TWELVE

"I CAN'T BELIEVE you're here, coming to my picnic in the woods!" Margaret said, carrying the picnic basket with both hands, swaying to leverage the weight of it.

Lily had agreed to come on one condition: No Sadie.

Margaret instantly shook on it.

"This looks like a good place right here," Margaret said and bent down to set the basket on the pine-needle-covered ground, but Lily wasn't ready to be done walking.

"Here? No. We need to experience the woods. Like Little Red Riding Hood," Lily said, trying to smile, trying on *Nice-to-Margaret* and finding it alien and cold.

Margaret picked up the basket again and put one foot in front of the other. Lily could tell each step was difficult, but her sister was driven by that maddening optimism of hers. What had the fool packed, an entire Christmas turkey?

They had walked almost an hour when Margaret said, "I'm hungry, Lil. Can we have the picnic here?"

Rage rose inside Lily, but she pushed it down—kept pushing it down every time it sprung up into expression. Why should Margaret get her way every time? Get to be a child still, perfectly innocent and untainted, with so many years of freedom ahead. No pressure to marry, no pressure at all. Lily was jealous, she didn't deny it. She knew it wasn't Margaret's fault, but that didn't make it fair. Why should she get to play with a dog and eat sandwiches in the woods? Why should she make all the decisions? And why should she sleep in perfect peace at night, while Lily was forced to spend all of her time trying to find a way out? Surviving.

"No, Meg, let's keep going. I'm sure Red Riding Hood was hungry too."

Margaret straightened up and smiled, revived by Lily's usage of her nickname. "You called me *Meg.*"

The innocence in Margaret's response poked at the rage inside Lily again. It made no sense, but it infuriated her.

Once they'd walked another half hour, their feet plodding along and Lily's stomach growling too, Margaret dropped the basket. She announced like a spoiled child, "I'm not walking anymore. We're having the picnic right here." ·

Lily looked around and supposed here was as good a place as any. "All right."

Margaret bent over to get the cloth out of the basket. "I'm so happy you're here with me, Lil. I've wanted to picnic with you for so long. Why did you decide that today—"

Thunk.

Margaret fell face-down after one hard blow to the back of the head. Lily had used the first downed branch she found.

Lily stood back, waiting, shaking now. Had she meant to hit Margaret that hard? Was her sister dead? No, there, she was moaning and moving her arms a bit. But then instead of helping Margaret, instead of apologizing, she raised the branch up high and brought it down again across her sister's back this time.

Crack.

Margaret screamed, scrambling away from Lily, not looking back. Lily caught up and hit her across the back again. It wasn't like they never had lashes across the back. This was a regular occurrence in their house. For being late to wash up for supper, for mistakes in their needlework, for leaving the window open when it rained, for mumbling prayers instead of *e-nun-ci-at-ing,* as Mother said.

Margaret had fewer lashes than Lily, and it wasn't just that the child was younger. She was good. So dastardly *good.* Rage fully matured inside Lily in this moment, sixteen years of fear and anger she'd shoved deeper and deeper down. She was drunk with it, like how Father got drunk before pushing open her door after Mother was asleep. Stinky, slurry, deliriously numb-drunk, crawling into her small bed, his large hands feeling for the bottom ruffle of her night dress, pulling it up.

Lily tried to push him away, but always failed. She was Sisyphus, condemned to this struggle, and no matter how hard she fought, no matter how much ground she seemed to gain, he'd end up in her bed again anyway. Margaret never, not once, had gone through this.

She squared up to where Margaret's head was slowly moving forward, still trying to escape. Something inside Lily said to stop, but it was too quiet, and Lily wasn't listening. Her legs spread for balance underneath her full skirt. She could see her legs, but they didn't feel connected to her. She was floating above, like watching the whole thing happen and powerless to stop it.

Margaret rolled to her back, tears mixed with dirt anointing her cheeks. Her words came out in strings of red, running down her pointy little chin. Lily only saw one functioning eye. "Lil—Lily, I mean." Margaret tried to speak through a swollen and bloody mouth. "Please don't. I won't bother you again. Please, please."

Lily brought the branch down again, this time slamming it into what used to be Margaret's pretty face. She was lost again, thinking about Father. How she couldn't leave the house, but how she couldn't stay either.

Blood sprayed across Lily's face and dress in one strong burst, startling, rousing her awake like cold water poured over you while you sleep. She was here now, in the woods, and the sun was on the other side. How did it get this late? Margaret was on her back, arms spread as if she were doing a back float down the Spokane River. Her face was caved, a bloody crater.

A single loud sob erupted out of Lily. What had she done? She sat in the pine needles until dark, trying to remember how she got here, to this point where she could hurt her own sister. She did that until it didn't make sense to do it anymore and then a cold numbness took over.

Quick now, hide the body.

It was the voice inside that tried to stop her before. Now she was listening to it.

Lily looked around, past tree upon tree until she saw the biggest one. She dragged Margaret's body by its black-booted feet and shoved it into an animal's den at the base of the tree. The corpse was folded in half, like how Mother taught Lily to fold the linens for the closet. Lily kicked the forest floor to spread out dirt marks from the scuffle even though she didn't need to. Right then, the sky cracked, and a downpour of rain came on.

Lily's stomach roared with hunger. She set up the picnic to look like they simply got caught in the rain and separated, then shoved three tea sandwiches into her mouth before she ran home.

PATE, IDAHO

July 1989

THIRTEEN

DAWN ALWAYS USED bleach because it really did the job. Troy, the manager, wanted her to use products the hotel provided, but they just didn't work as well. Dawn snuck bleach into her little caddy, under a pile of dirty towels. The hotel watered down it's supplies, and so it took her twice as long to do the job. Safer for the surfaces, Troy would say. But Dawn wasn't stupid. The real reason was to save money and Dawn was angry just thinking about it. That they'd make her job harder on purpose to save a few bucks. Plus it wasn't like anyone else cared much for the condition of the rooms.

For example, last week someone had peed all over the bathroom floor. Not even close to the toilet. She didn't understand, since this was supposed to be the town's "nice" hotel. Why would someone paying for a nice hotel do a thing like that? Perhaps it was a child, although it was a lot of urine.

Troy had shrugged and said, "Another day, another dollar."

Dawn was annoyed that time, but she focused on her paycheck and all that she could do for God's kingdom with her money. All the children she could help someday, once she'd saved up a nice nest egg. But it was so demeaning to clean up another person's bodily fluids. With watered-down products, no less!

Another time, before the urine on the floor, she'd opened the door to room 341, and there was vomit all over one of the beds. Like the person didn't bother to try for the toilet and instead sprayed the bed repeatedly with puke. When she walked into the room that day, she covered her nose and gagged.

Troy said, "It is what it is," and then, "I'll leave you to it."

Dawn tried to plug her nose from the inside and breathe out her mouth so she could use her hands to work. She was afraid of adding her own stamp of stomach acid to what was already there, but she kept gagging, tasting the smell of it. The whole time she thought about Troy, about how she was a housekeeper, not a nurse in a hospital. They didn't pay her enough for this!

Today, somebody had defecated in the bathtub. It was smeared all over the countertop too. Again, could have been a child, but she'd changed diapers in the church nursery, and this didn't look like a child-sized job.

She thought about calling Troy, but decided against it. He'd just offer another cliché like "When life gives you lemons, make lemonade," or "C'est la vie." Or even worse, he'd be angry. The last time she complained about the state of the rooms, he'd rolled his eyes.

Dawn disposed of the bulk, flushing it down the toilet, then poured the bleach and watched it expand across one of Troy's beloved bathroom countertops. Anger crawled up inside her again.

It wasn't as much cleaning up the mess that ticked her off, it was thinking about Troy. How he made her feel so small. A generic middle manager who acted like the king.

Rule your spirit, Dawn.

Dad's voice was in her mind. Smile, control yourself. If you ever want to be useful to the Lord, you have to keep your feelings in check.

Why did his voice still pop into her mind? She hated it. Plus, did "rule your spirit" even mean "show no emotion?" Probably not. Hardly anything he taught her was interpreted correctly, if it was actually in the Bible. He made stuff up all the time.

And Mom missed him! How ridiculous. Mom had hung that picture of him outside the house right after Dad disappeared. Dawn never looked at it. Didn't understand why people around town hung pictures up outside. Was it some shrine? It felt pretty pagan to her, so she asked Mom about it once. Mom brushed her off, like usual. There was so much Mom had no clue about even though she fancied herself a spiritual person. How could someone who claimed to be so enlightened also be so blind? She was too busy reading about meditation and other weird stuff to notice things in her own home. Dawn had found Mom's little hiding place under the loose floorboard years ago. One time, she'd reached in to riffle through the stash and see what Mom was hiding. The family Bible, on top of a stack of books, stopped her cold.

He's always watching you, Dawn.

Next to that was a picture of Mom smiling. She was beautiful, and Dawn guessed it was their wedding day, Mom must have torn it in half when she got the hair-brained idea to hang Dad's picture up outside. Mom was wasting her time grieving Dad, wishing he would return. Dawn was glad he was gone, felt like an answer to a prayer she never had the guts to pray. But Mom's memories were nothing like reality. She had those headaches that kept her in bed most days back then and never, not once, saw or knew about what Dad did to Dawn.

Dawn dropped the sponge on the linoleum floor. It was so heavy with liquid that it went *thunk* and splashed up a small, brown-tinted torrent onto her work dress.

She poured a bit of bleach on the skirt. Luckily, it was white. She squeezed the excess from the sponge in order to mop some more from the countertop.

Standing back, she looked around. The mess was really only in the bathroom, easy to clean. Maybe she should tell Troy about it though. Then again, Troy didn't like Dawn, because she was a Christian. She found this out the day she witnessed to him. He'd said Christianity was just a crutch for weak people. In that moment, she'd thought of the Bible verse, "If anyone will not listen to your words, leave and shake the dust off your feet." He could rot in Hell for all Dawn cared. It wasn't her fault Troy wasn't chosen, couldn't accept Christ as his Savior. She tried to show him how to be saved.

So, no, she definitely couldn't tell him about this mess. What if he fired her? Thought she was high maintenance? How would she take care of her mom? How would she save up to help abused children? It'd have to stay a secret.

Thinking of secrets made Monte Shrake jump into her mind, and her stomach flipped over. They'd just become friends, and while she liked him, he wasn't exactly godly. She didn't want Mom to know about him because she'd get all excited and start asking, "When's the wedding? How soon will I have grandchildren?" Dawn was saving herself for someone special. Someone who had saved himself too. She doubted Monte fit this category, knowing what she did about him.

Dawn reviewed a checklist in her mind to make sure she didn't forget anything before she left the room.

Beds made.

Bath linens replaced.

Bathroom sparkling.

Yes, if forced to choose, guests would rather have a super clean bathroom over any damage bleach caused.

Once Dawn was satisfied, and she couldn't see or smell anything left over, she removed her gloves and turned them inside out. She'd need to throw them away and better not to do it at home. Mom was still in the habit of combing through Dawn's trash. It wasn't like throwing gloves away was a big deal, but Mom could get paranoid and read into things.

She looked at herself up close in the mirror to see if she got all that crap off her uniform. A shower would definitely need to happen before meeting up with Monte tonight.

FOURTEEN

"I'M GOING BACK to the scene by myself," Syl said to Roger outside the Conders' place.

What Kyle said about Alex looking like a mummy pushed her off the fence. Especially after Betty confirmed a second time that there was no way Kyle could have heard about the condition of Alex's body. He'd been home the whole time, not spoken to anyone but her, only allowed to play video games. No TV. Just in case something came on the news about it. Nothing had been on the news anyway, but the precaution was smart and Syl told her so.

"Back to Lucky Dog?" Roger asked.

"No. More like the woods around the area."

"Why the hell would you do that?"

"It's my process."

"That's not the right way to come at this thing. I really don't think you should go back out there."

Syl didn't reply.

"I just mean, I don't think you'll find anything." Roger spit his gum out and reached in his shirt pocket for another. The pack was empty and he sighed.

"Don't know unless I go."

Roger grunted in defeat and then said, "Meant to thank you for coming out. Last thing I wanted was to call in someone from outside Pate."

"Why? I'm from outside Pate."

"Yes, but you're a Dixon."

"So?"

Roger took off that ball cap he always wore. Plenty of nasty sweat marks. He ran a palm once over his bald head, replaced the hat. After a pause, he said, "Well, Dixons are so goddamn meddling. I just thought it might come in handy here."

Syl chewed the inside of her cheek.

It was settled then. She was helping.

"Get me those John Winton case files, too, please," she added like an afterthought.

He removed that hat and held it with the same hand he used to rub his head again.

SYL TURNED HER music off as she drove alongside the river.

Gran had taught her about the woods, lessons most little girls never learn. Lessons all little girls *should* learn. There were predators and prey, and you could be either at any given time. *Don't fear the woods. See it as a place that holds food for the winter. A place to find or create shelter from the elements. A place to re-energize. Learn how to be a local instead of a tourist in nature.*

Syl always laughed when she read fairy tales as a child, those pages with sets of eyes peering out through the blackness of the forest. As if the forest itself was lying in wait to hurt you. Gran said the forest was neutral, perhaps even intelligent. She even thought the trees talked to each other, although she didn't have proof, just her "caveman voice" inside telling her it was true.

Anything in Gran's world could be sorted by an afternoon in nature. It was her church. It was her hospital. One time she said it was the closest place she could get to the god she hoped existed.

Gran, you were a goddamn poet.

Syl opened the car door and stepped into the light fog, clearing fast as the sun rose over the mountains. It was probably close to lunch time. The river rushed loud as she crossed the footbridge.

Thing was, although this looked like any old forest in the northwest, it didn't feel like your average forest. Syl couldn't explain why. She was never nervous in the woods and it wasn't like she was nervous now, but that feeling hung. It was just different. Had Gran ever caught that? Probably not, because these were the only woods Gran really knew. But Syl had hunted, hiked, fished in other areas, and she sensed something here. It was like the forest *did* have eyes. Against everything she believed about outdoor spaces, this place didn't feel neutral. It was why she returned this afternoon. To talk herself out of that gut feeling. She would approach the woods how Gran taught her and probably just see that she was psyching herself out.

"Listen to the sounds like you're putting them into a funnel. The big sounds first, the ones everyone hears, down to the ones so small, nobody else notices. Once you know what you're hearing, you can put it away and move on to other sounds," Gran had said.

It was a process of organizing nature, packaging it so the brain had room to recognize a threat. If you knew what all the sounds were, you'd know the instant you heard something out of the ordinary.

"How will I know it's a threat?" Syl had asked back then.

"It won't stay tucked away. It'll keep coming up and running round and round in your mind."

Syl was across the footbridge and just about to approach the steep gravel leading up to the mine. But she didn't want to be in the mine again. Not exactly. She stepped off the trail with high knees, walking over tall weeds, dodging low bushes.

The river wasn't loud, but the water burbled as it moved along rocks. It was the most obvious noise. She noted it and tucked it away.

Birds called out. Crows.

They swirled in the warm air currents above her.

She waited for more sounds.

I hate waiting.

(What would Gran say?)

Shut up and wait.

Dry, fallen pine needles from God-knew-how-many-seasons crunched under her feet. She took more steps away from the trail. Lucky Dog Mine was up the steep cliff behind, off her right shoulder.

The sound of water was quieter now. She was deeper into the trees, which blocked the noise.

A single bird cried against the racket the crows made. Sounded like a hawk. It was too far above for her to be sure what kind, but definitely a bird of prey.

Pine needles underfoot were white noise now, familiar and put away. Ditto bird noises.

What was she smelling? Definitely pine, but almost a hint of wetness even though it hadn't rained last night.

"Get to where it's like your body is floating in a huge tank of water," Gran would say, standing with her arms and legs apart, trying to act it out for five-year-old Syl.

This was the part Syl couldn't grasp until recently. It took years and years of practice until one day she stumbled into what Gran had tried to explain. Anything you could experience in nature was like a ripple or wave in the water. Once you tucked your observations away, the water went still again, and so the quicker you recognized things, the better. Then, it didn't matter whether a deer stepped into the woods, or a squirrel was watching you. It'd sent a nudge through the water. You felt it strike your body, in a sense, and it'd jar you out of what you thought you knew. Show you things.

The sun cut slats through the tall tree trunks like little laser beams. A chipmunk chattered from a high branch, like a last stand. Territorial little buggers.

Then something hit the ground. She stopped walking. Her gut said it was just a pine cone falling, but she waited to be sure, or else it'd nag at her. There it was again, but this time she saw the movement and confirmed it was pine cones, so she tucked it away. Syl kept at this until she wasn't thinking about Gran anymore. Just the woods. Why they felt so different than other nature spots she'd been in. What a threat would feel like here.

Syl pulled up a mental picture of Alex Conder in the mine.

The crows seemed to caw louder just then. She blinked, watched them. It was nothing out of the ordinary.

Then she heard a howl.

A quivering, high-pitched wail. One low note, and then a higher note that held on for a long time.

Not low like a wolf.

Softer than a coyote.

A bird maybe?

It sounded like a common loon, but it couldn't be. They really didn't stray from bodies of water, and she was too far from Great Pine Lake to hear a bird calling out.

The other thing was, loons really only made these noises at night. And it was usually a call and response.

This sounded like a single loon calling out. Not by a lake, not in response to another loon.

Then it stopped. She waited to see if it would start up again, but it didn't.

The sun was hot now. She'd been at it at least an hour, maybe more. The wetness of morning was gone, leaving only the hot-dirt scent of pine needles. She was desperate for clues about what happened to Alex. The only unexplainable thing she'd found out here was the howling. It bugged her that it didn't make sense, because she couldn't tuck it away.

She sat down and crossed her legs. With her hands on her knees, waiting wasn't as hard. If she was to take something away from this, her mind had to be clear. And since she was still talking to herself, she wasn't there yet.

THE LOON CALLED out, loud, louder still. Syl covered her ears, but the sound leaked through. She tried to run, but her feet wouldn't move. The pine needles on the ground stood on end and wrapped around her ankles, her calves. Pine needles twisted up her body, changed into veins, started to glow. She tried to scream but couldn't hear her own voice over the howling of the lonely bird.

When Syl woke up in a burst, ready to fight somebody, it was silent. She'd fallen asleep and had a bad dream, that was all.

The golden hues of daylight shone behind the mountain in the distance. It was dusk.

Dusk and absolute stillness. No crows, no water rushing, no pine cones falling. No loon calling.

Then she felt a nudge, like a ripple against the proverbial water. It was close, but she didn't see anything out of the ordinary. The dead silence was absolutely extraordinary, but how could she know—

There, she felt it again. Moving in slow motion she stood, turned in a circle, eyes scanning, ears perked. What was she missing? The feeling was gone for a beat, but it came again and again, like waves lapping the lake shore.

Something was watching her.

PATE, IDAHO

January 1962

FIFTEEN

LOU STUBBED OUT her cigarette and lit another. Only an hour had passed and she'd already told so much. She could still toss out what she'd scratched up and start over. Maybe she should. Or, she could just forget the whole thing.

She took a pull of her cigarette and sighed, releasing a cloud of smoke.

No. Lou had to do right by the girl, if anything, here at the end. But Jesus, she wasn't even through the first page and already she'd told about Rose. Such deep waters and she'd dove headfirst right into them. What else would come up?

She put the mug to her mouth, but the coffee was cold. As she walked over to pour another cup, she thought, *hang it all, might as well go all the way.*

...Thinking back on it now, pup, I missed so much of your father's childhood. My obsession with finding Rose pushed it aside. At the time, I thought he was old enough to see to himself. He was naturally so strong. Independent-minded, like you, and I'm not much for motherhood like I said. But when I think now that he was only nine years old on the day Rose disappeared, my heart balls up inside me. If I did it over again, I'd have spent more time with Mason and less time chasing after Rose. Still, there wasn't a chance in hell I'd have let Rose go. But if I had, maybe things wouldn't have ended like this. Well, you can wish in one hand and shit in the other and see which one fills up first, right, pup?

I thought Rose must be alive. If she were dead, she'd have been lying on the roadside that day. But how could she wander off? She was only three—a baby!

I looked in the woods for years and years, with no luck. I set out with a fervor, out there every day. But time went on. I blinked, and Mason had finished high school. I kept going out though. I'd already looked everywhere I could reach in a day trip, so by then I was taking longer trips, going deeper to make sure I covered it all.

One day, I came upon the old Markwell cabin. Would have been, let's see, fall of 1941. If Grandpa were here, he'd argue with me on the year. Never could let me have the dates right even though he was always wrong. I remember because it was just before Pearl Harbor happened.

The cabin was remote. Struck me how far I'd wandered from home on that trip. I camped and hunted, made my way along, looking for my girl. I climbed up that weedy hill until I saw the old cabin's broken windows peek out from behind trees. I recalled when the Markwell family disappeared. They had a boy my age, and we were just thirteen at the time. His mama had pushed into the school room one day and took him home early. That was the last anyone saw of them.

Made sense that the place would be in disrepair after it sat for decades. No way these Idaho winters would allow a cabin built at the turn of the century to stand unfussed that long. And when I got up there, I was right, the roof was collapsing at parts, milkweeds grew up all around it. The foundation though, it was made of rock and mortar, built into the side of the hill, and it stood sure, as did the walls. I stepped closer and got the sense that despite being abandoned, it wasn't empty. I shivered like a goose walked over my grave!

I tried the front door. Was unlocked, but stuck, and I had to throw my side against it to budge it. The door scraped pine needles on the floor inside as it gave, and the scent of dead elk hit my nose. Exactly like when Harold welcomed all those maggots to eat the flesh off a shot-animal's head in order to create a bare skeleton trophy. Saw nothing dead around there, although a family of squirrels skittered around. I put the smell out of my mind. Elk can stink to high heaven for quite a distance, so perhaps it wasn't coming from the cabin at all.

Still, that feeling I had about the place, that it wasn't empty, nagged at me. Was a squatter inside? Somebody making September preparations to ride the winter out in comfort? If so, he was doing a damn good job hiding his presence, because the wood table in the kitchen was covered in undisturbed dust. So was the rocking chair in the living room. Hell, I didn't see a single footprint in the dirt on the floors. Course there were sections where the roof gave in, and the floor was bad off. I swiped a hand across the dust on the table. Just like birds fleeing a tree at gunshot, the particles whirled around me in the air, catching sunlight and bursting with light before falling back to the table. Old-fashioned photographs hung on one wall. I got up close, wiped the dust off the glass. I seen a formal portrait of a beautiful woman and some man who looked roughed up by life. That unsettled me, but I didn't know why. It was just an old picture, like the ones of my parents I had hanging up at home.

There was nobody inside the place, of course. Out the bleary window on the back door, I seen another structure. I wiped the window's grime with my sleeve and looked out. It was a woodshed.

The instant my eyes landed on that old shed, pup, I felt something crawl up inside me and dig a pit in my gut. I knew I was going into that shed, but my caveman voice inside was telling me to run. I shoved that back door open and stepped down the stairs toward it, willing those feelings to skedaddle.

The sun caught me in the eye. It sprinkled light through pine trees, and the dark feeling left. What was I on to? It was so beautiful here. I'd spooked myself! It was just any old shed. Up close to it now, I felt the padlock on the door. Why lock the shed and not the house? I walked around the outside of it, thinking maybe I'd find a window, and I could satisfy my curiosity with a peep, not have to go into the thing.

But it was a shed with no windows, and I was plumb locked out. I reached for a rusted axe leaning up against the outside.

Where had that come from? Surely a looky loo from years ago would have pilfered it. Was it possible nobody had been back to the shed? No. It was so close to the home. Clearly the home had been visited by rocks in the windows from stray kids. Surely somebody must have gotten in here since the Markwells disappeared.

I brought the axe down hard, and that lock gave up on the first blow. It was more rusted than the axe. As I pushed the shed door in, a sliver of sunlight grew and illuminated thick streaks on the dirt floor. I stepped into the woodshed, with that rusty tree feller in my hand still, and something thick all around made the air hard to breathe. I seen nothing too suspect, but felt it. I crouched down. My fingers took up some of the substance making those streaks. I couldn't tell what it was, just looked like stained dirt. By the time I looked up, my eyes had adjusted to darkness. They traveled along the wall until something caught my attention. Dark spots. Black speckles and drips in one area of the wall. I drew up close and touched it.

That's when something stirred from the corner of the shed, and I whirled around. I couldn't make out what stood there. A barrel maybe? Some spades or broomsticks? I moved a step closer.

The shed door slammed shut, and I was left in pitch darkness. I ran to the door, tried to pry it open. Wouldn't budge. I hit it over and over until my hands were damn near bloody. I cried, laid my head against that door, and everything went black...

PATE, IDAHO

July 1989

PATE, IDAHO
July 1989

SIXTEEN

"TELL ME ABOUT John Winton and the Markwells," Syl demanded, bursting into the police station. "Those goddamn portraits, too, whatever the hell it all means."

It was the scripted line she decided on while lying awake in bed all night. She'd wasted the whole first official day of assisting Roger, because she fell asleep in the woods. And that wasn't the end of the world. She wasn't his employee, but what about her reputation? She couldn't leave any room for the sort of comments she knew would come. It had been just like falling asleep at the station.

Yesterday, she went twenty over the speed limit the whole way home from the woods, but the station was closed by the time she drove by it. The Vicky hummed loud, and that's where she came up with this mantra of courage. She shouted it as loud as possible:

"Shit! Shit! Shit! Shit! Shit! Shit! Shit! Shit! Shit! Shit!"

Then dawned a glorious piece of inspiration:

What would a man do?

(He'd feel stupid, same as me, and then he'd act like it was part of the original plan.)

Right, a man would play it off.

Fine, then that's what she'd do too. At least she could try it. Smear confidence all over herself like war paint. Forget war paint, she'd settle for camouflage.

"Look who decided to come in today!" Roger replied. "I didn't realize your *process* was sipping margaritas poolside on day one of a murder investigation."

Hendon and Mac laughed.

Syl cleared her throat, steadied her voice so she could raise it. No to shrill, yes to firm.

"I can't help you out unless I know what I'm dealing with. I've asked you multiple times now for John Winton's case files, and you always hem and haw."

Roger sighed and rubbed his head.

Unbelievable. It worked. Male confidence, the champion of police work today.

"Okay. But look, I need to explain a bit about the town first."

"No. First, the John Winton files, then your commentary."

He nodded like he knew he wouldn't get away with it but it was worth a try anyway.

"Hen, grab the Winton file."

Hendon went into the back room and returned in seconds.

"Well, that wasn't so hard." She was trying to channel the calm, cool, and collected Syl Dixon, but her toes were edging up to the line of anger.

She flipped open the thin manila folder, and what were the first words she saw? Lucky Dog Mine. Her heart did a nosedive over to the side of anger. "John Winton's house is right across from Lucky Dog Mine? Wow, that's so totally unrelated to the Conder case."

Sarcasm isn't helpful right now, Syl.

Roger grabbed his ball cap. "Let's go," he said and walked out in front of her.

"Where?" she asked, not budging her position. "You going to tote me around like some child? When I'm the one helping *you* out here?"

"I'm showing you why they're not related. But if you'd rather stand here and pitch a fit—*like a child*—we can do that too."

Syl sighed.

Once outside, Roger walked toward his truck. But hell no. No more big man sheriff with girly helper Syl Dixon on a string. She came to a full stop and walked toward the Vicky instead. "I'm driving. You ride shotgun and tell me where to go."

Roger dragged behind like a grumpy toddler. She needed to calm the hell down, but John Winton's house in the vicinity of the crime scene kept scrolling across her mind like a banner. And Roger not telling her about it. Keeping it from her. She had no idea if the two cases were related, or if that creepy feeling of being watched played into it, but she couldn't rule the possibility out. Why the hell didn't she just walk away from all this? Why not say no when he called her yesterday morning? She didn't need any of this, curiosity or not.

Her face was hot, probably lighting her cheeks on fire with a nice shade of red. Syl flopped into the driver's seat and slammed the door while she waited for Roger to loaf over.

"Your seatbelt." Roger said, snapping his into place.

Her seatbelt hung untouched. She didn't do seat belts. Sure, it was the law now, but who was the state to tell her she couldn't endanger herself if she wanted to? It was the principle of the thing. People should be able to choose what to do with their own bodies.

Syl held the steering wheel at ten-and-two and squeezed it hard. She breathed.

"You gonna write me a seatbelt ticket, sheriff?"

"Well no, but I don't want you to—"

She turned the music on loud enough to stifle Roger's next words. Her anger felt bigger than just this one thing with Roger, and she didn't understand it. Better not to speak. Plus, right now, if she said anything, it'd come out too emotional, and he'd take it as permission to dismiss everything she'd said.

Been there, done that, got the T-shirt.

God, why did it have to be Barry Manilow on the radio right now? So slow, melodramatic. She hated this shit. Switching the station seemed pointless, but what she wouldn't give for something along the lines of Heart's "Barracuda" in this moment.

Calm down, Syl.

But whenever she got close to calm, the fact of the matter ran across her mind and pissed her off all over again. She could *not* handle offering her time on a case without all the information and without the sheriff's help. Damn, forget help. It was being

108 STEPH NELSON

blocked, that's what really blew her stack. Being asked to help and then being resisted.

Roger rolled his window up and folded his arms across his round belly, like *he* had something to be mad about.

Then he shouted over the music, "Barry Manilow, huh? I hate this shit."

She ignored him.

"Why are your panties all in a twist? Take a right at the bridge, then it's a straight shot." He braced himself, holding on to the door handle as she took the turn. "Dammit, slow down!"

Syl ignored him again. Men could say what they wanted, just like she could ignore them. She sped up.

"Why are you so upset? You need to calm down, Syl."

Shit.

Sure, she'd overlooked the seatbelt comment, held in what she really wanted to say. But she hadn't managed to keep those damn emotions in check. And now she was coming off like a hysterical woman anyway. She slowed the car and turned Barry Manilow down.

"Do you want my help?" Syl asked in the very nicest voice she could find. Sticky sweet, too nice.

"Of course."

"Starting now, I get any information you have. And that includes this backlog of things that for whatever reason you don't want to tell me."

He was rubbing his head again. God, he did that a lot. A nervous tic maybe?

"I'm not trying to keep things from you. I just don't know what you need to know, I guess."

"You didn't think information about a previous disappearance might be useful to me? That it may be relevant that the person who previously disappeared lived in purview of the crime scene?"

Roger flattened his lips so they puckered out. "We're going to the Winton cabin right now. You can talk to his widow. I'll wait in the car. That's the best I can do to solve this situation we're in."

"Alex's death?"

"No! *This* situation." His hand made a sweep between them. He meant them, their fight.

"Oh. Well, it's a start." She didn't expect him to give in that quickly. "You aren't coming in with me?"

"Hell no." Roger's whole body harrumphed, with his arms still crossed over that belly. "Had my fill of the woman years ago when John went missing."

"Was she ruled out as a suspect?"

Roger laughed. "Yes. Mercy! Wait until you meet her. She's a few flowers shy of a bouquet, and that's a generous description. Worst part is she fancies herself some spiritual guru. Really, she's just strange." Getting information from him was like trying to fill a glass jar with a drip every five seconds. So goddamn slow.

"Then how is this going to answer my basic question: Is there a connection between John Winton's disappearance and the state we found Conder in?"

"You don't get it, do you? It won't *answer* anything for you. You'll get to rule it out. That's how you do police work, isn't it?"

She chewed the inside of one cheek, but stopped when she realized she was doing it.

"Here, I'll tell you a bit about it, and you'll see that John's disappearance and Alex Conder are not connected, perhaps even before we arrive at the Winton place."

SEVENTEEN

DOUBTFUL, SYL THOUGHT. Her gut said there was a connection, and while her gut was unreliable at times when it came to investigating, she felt it strongly. There was something here. Had to be.

Roger began. "The Winton's daughter was with John when he vanished, but she had nothing to say about—"

"Like Kyle."

"Like Kyle," he repeated. "At the time, I couldn't tell if she was refusing to talk, or if she was in shock and lost recollection about—"

"How old was the daughter?"

Roger faced her. "How about you let me tell it instead of interrupting all the goddamn time? People around here will tell it their way if you let them. Rush them, and you might not get it at all."

She shrunk in her seat a little.

Roger went on, "Dawn was eight. I thought she knew something back then. How could she not? But she always had this blank face. Said she left the tent to use the bathroom early one morning, and when she came back, John wasn't there anymore. She looked around a bit, but got scared and ran home. After pressing her for a few days, trying to jog her memory, I finally realized she didn't know what had happened. If she did, she must have forgotten. Keep going on this road. It's a ways, I'm sure you remember."

Syl willed the words to fall out of his mouth faster.

"John grew up in Pate, and the cabin Esma's in now has been in his family ever since the Markwells arrived at the turn of the century—"

"Wait, John Winton is *related* to the Markwells?"

Roger gave a scolding school-teacher look, and Syl sank back again, remembering she'd agreed to let him tell it his way. But God, he better tell all of it.

"Mining was dangerous work, and in the beginning, mining accidents were common in this area. Fires—hell, even landslides and avalanches. John knew the area. There's no way he'd get lost in the woods, or even use the woods to run away. I didn't buy that theory."

Like Gran. It was exactly how Syl felt about Gran's disappearance.

"When it comes to mining, the money's in staking a claim. But that was like winning the lottery. Most people ended up working in the mines instead, just your regular old job. John's people worked Lucky Dog Mine. As for whether Esma and Dawn noticed anything happening up at Lucky Dog when Alex Conder disappeared, well, the cabin's quite a distance and not likely they'd be able to see that far. Maybe they could make out a dark spot where the entrance is, but that's it. I don't think Dawn's there often enough, because she works at the hotel. I certainly can't imagine Esma watching out a window. Plus, the Wintons would be the last people to help us catch a killer. They've had nothing but tragedy through the years."

Syl thought of Gran again. Then her mom and dad. Maybe tragedy was less a Winton thing and more of a Pate thing.

"Yes, John Winton came from the Markwells," he continued. "But that's part of the mystery nobody can figure out. They built the cabin where Esma and Dawn live now. One day in the early 1900s, the whole Markwell family vanished. Years later, a lady showed up to Pate with the last name Winton, claiming to come from the Markwells. It was only weeks after Pearl Harbor, where this woman's husband was stationed. He was killed in the attack, leaving her and the baby—John—alone in the world. Tragedy, remember?"

Roger waited to see if she was following.

Syl motioned with her hand for him to get to the point.

"But back in the day, the town thought all the Markwells died. Main theory was the mom had killed them all because she was loony. Now that this Winton lady had returned, it became clear that at least one of the Markwells survived and went on to have children. Not even John Winton seemed to know much about his family though. He was too young to remember anyone but his mom.

"She moved the two of them into the cabin and paid to have it fixed up. Seemed like she had endless cash flow. I was brand new to the police department, a rookie, around the time the place was finally finished. People tried to find out which of the Markwells had survived. Strange thing was nobody could make her speak. The woman refused to tell anyone a thing about her past, where she'd moved from, who her parents were. She just returned to Pate to claim her family's property. She was a mean old woman. Real crotchety. Wasn't long before rumors started that maybe she'd offed them all as a child. Of course, she would have been much too young at the time—or not even born yet—but people will talk. Anyways, by the time John married Esma, his mother was dead and buried and so the two of them took over the cabin."

Syl calculated the math in her head as he was speaking. "John's mother would have died young then too," she added.

"Cancer. Lifelong chain smoker." He pointed again. "Right up there is where the road dead ends. Go ahead and park there." He went on, "That brings me to John. One thing you need to know about John Winton is he was very religious. Zealous even—"

"Real quick recap, to be sure I'm following," Syl interrupted. "The Markwells move here at the start of the century, build the cabin, and then all of them disappear. Years later—sometime after Pearl Harbor, it sounds like—a lady returns, claiming to be a Markwell, but we don't know how she was related to them. It's just her and her young son, John Winton, because her husband died in the attack. This lady dies of cancer before she's old enough to be a grandma, and John and Esma move into the cabin."

Roger gave a single nod.

God, he could have explained it a lot simpler. Syl could tell by the way he squinted his eyes that he didn't remember where he left off.

"John was religious…"

"Right. John wanted more kids, but Esma wasn't able. So, they just had the girl, Dawn. By the time Dawn was walking, they barely left the cabin. Townspeople worried about whether the girl had enough to eat, so do-gooders brought groceries and supplies all the way out to their place. The family never answered the door, so groceries were left on the porch. I checked in on them from time to time, and they always opened the door for me. Known John his whole life even though he was just a baby when I shipped off to war. Esma especially had come from a bad home, somewhere else—Seattle, maybe? I always thought that explained how harebrained she is. Back then, it was hard for me to see them as anything but kids, I guess. I worried about them. Anyways, John spent most of his time in the woods, far, far in. Deeper than anyone else cared to go. The woods, abandoned mines, nobody knows how far in he got. When the girl was old enough to walk, he began taking her along." Roger stopped like it was the end.

"A parent taking their girl into the woods isn't all that weird. My Gran did that. Taught me how to hunt, fish, survive."

"I say 'take the girl deep into the woods' and you hear 'take his daughter hunting.' It wasn't just that. It was their religion, like a ritual. John started to get really weird, and the further off the rails he got, the less anyone saw the wife and daughter. It was like John and his girl were becoming part of the woods, absorbed into them."

Still just sounded like father-daughter bonding to Syl. How weird would Roger think it was that Gran taught her exactly how to get "absorbed into the woods?" What did Roger have against the woods anyway?

Syl pulled the Vicky up alongside a steep hill at Roger's instruction, and he turned to her. "Have fun."

EIGHTEEN

"WHAT ARE YOU going to do the whole time I'm in there?" Syl asked.

"Snoop around your jockey box, I guess." Roger pushed the metal button in front of him, and the lid fell on his knees.

"If everything you've said is true, I'll be quick," Syl said.

"Oh no, take your time. A moment's respite from Tweedle Dee and Tweedle Dum is most welcome." He closed his eyes and clasped his hands behind his head.

Syl got out of the car and looked around. How could there be a cabin here? Was Roger joking? Maybe this was all a big prank. But there was a narrow dirt path leading up, you might call it a driveway. She looked behind her again. Could the Wintons have seen something happen at Lucky Dog Mine?

There was the river they crossed yesterday morning to get into the mine. Lucky Dog was on one side of it, and on the other was the cabin. It was even tighter than the valley where downtown Pate sat. What a weird place to put a home.

She saw a wink of blue paint up the hill when she turned in the direction of the alleged cabin. A car was parked behind the brush above her. A blue Honda, she saw, getting closer. It was as if someone got tired of driving up the path and just quit, decided to walk the rest of the way. But by the time she got to the car, she could see the first of a long trail of wooden stairs built into steep, gravel-covered dirt, leading up to something. About twelve steps in, a structure stood out from between tall pine trees. The woods around it were so dense that if not for the glint of sun on small front windows, it'd be camouflaged. Before stepping onto the warped wooden porch, she realized the windows weren't the only glass catching sunlight. There was a single photograph hung next to the front door. An image of a man. What was even more strange was the picture was torn in half and then carefully centered in a gold frame.

Syl turned around a second time to look across the valley. There was her car, a small dot now. There was the river, like a winding little snake. She scanned up the mountain on the other side of the river again, trying to orient herself in relation to Lucky Dog Mine. The yellow X of police tape over Lucky Dog's entrance flagged down her gaze.

Nobody answered when Syl knocked the first time. After the second knock, she said, "Mrs. Winton, I'm Syl Dixon. I'm helping the sheriff out with a case. I was hoping to ask you and your daughter a few questions."

Shuffling inside, muffled voices. Like druggies flushing dope down the toilet just before a bust.

The door opened fast.

"Can I help you?" It was an older woman. She wore a long, wrinkled skirt and a thin, silky bandanna, wrapped around her head and tied at the back. She didn't quite make eye contact. The woman wasn't overweight, but she obviously didn't get a lot of movement either. She looked like some bird, a turkey maybe, with a small wattle of skin hanging under her chin.

"Mrs. Winton, is it? I'm Syl Dixon. Can I come in and ask you and your daughter some questions?"

"Call me Esma, please." She turned into the cabin and waved a hand for Syl to follow.

Syl was unprepared for what she saw. The cabin was bursting with enough clutter to make Betty Conder look like a neat freak. It was a hoarder's paradise. Thin paths exposed hardwood floors throughout, like trails a huge slug would make. Otherwise, it was walls of crap—boxes, laundry baskets, and brown paper bags filled with stuff Syl couldn't make out at just a glance. The trails through these were a little labyrinth. You couldn't stand anywhere in the cabin except on these cleared paths. How could a home get to this point? She tried to be subtle, looking around without Esma noticing. The main room of the cabin was split by a slug trail into two spaces, the kitchen and the living room, and then another path connected them, like a small cross. Then there was the front door, with windows on each side, both looking out toward Lucky Dog. The kitchen had a table, cabinets against the wall, and an old sink. Syl didn't see a dishwasher or microwave. Just a refrigerator and an old stove. The living room had a fireplace, a couch, and a rocking chair. The slug path of hardwood floors that split the two spaces down the middle presumably led to the bedrooms. And a bathroom, one would hope.

"Dawn's not here," Esma said. "She was running late to meet up with the youth group for a prayer walk. She helps out with the kids. Isn't that nice? She's always running in and out, in and out. Hardly ever here."

"What's her car look like?"

"It's a little blue Accord."

"Like that one?" Syl pointed out to the driveway.

"Oh heavens! Maybe she *is* here. Have a seat." Esma flopped her hand at an exposed corner on an old, rust-orange couch and disappeared down a slug trail. She returned with Dawn. Syl stood up. How in the world did Esma not know her daughter was home? The place was tiny.

"Hi, Dawn, I'm helping Sheriff Mock with the investigation into Alex Conder's death. Did you see anything happening over at Lucky Dog the other day? Would have been Thursday night."

"I'm sorry, I didn't. I work a lot. I'm actually supposed to be at work in twenty minutes, and it's a long drive to the hotel." Dawn smiled. She was quite pretty. Deep dimples and brown eyes that seemed to sparkle.

"You're working today? Silly me, I thought you had the prayer walk," Esma said.

"Oh, not today. Sorry, I know my schedule is confusing."

What did Syl expect these two could have seen on Thursday night? There was no way to really tell if anyone was up at Lucky

Dog from this distance. Still, she had one more question for Dawn. "Did you know Alex Conder at all?"

"No," Dawn said. "His little guy rides a bike to church sometimes, and so I know him a bit, but I've never met the dad."

Kyle, right.

"Well, let me know if you think of anything." She handed Dawn a makeshift business card with "Sheriff Roger Mock" crossed out and her own name scrawled in its place.

Dawn took the card, smiled, and went out the back door. It slammed.

Esma cringed. "She's always letting that door slap!"

Pointing at the seat on the couch again, Esma tried to get Syl to sit down, but the couch was so full of stuff, and Syl didn't even try the first time Esma asked her to. It wasn't even enough space for her flat-as-a-pancake ass. She flexed her thighs in an awkward wall-sit position and pretended it was comfortable and normal. She wasn't staying long anyway.

"Sorry, I've got my projects out everywhere. Hard to care enough to keep the place tidy when it's just us, and Dawn's gone so much. You know what they say about the cobbler's children?"

"They never have shoes," Syl answered, unclear how she was able to follow that line of thinking.

Esma laughed harder than Syl expected and then sat on a pile of papers covering the coffee table across from her. "Yes! And the housekeeper's house is never clean. Dawn's a professional cleaner. She works for the hotel, like she said. You know, the one they're talking about making into a fancy resort? I'm so proud of her for keeping us good with food and shelter. Her father would be proud too... Although, maybe not..." Her face darkened, chin tilted downward.

"John never thought women should work outside the home, but then again, he didn't treat Dawn like a girl anyway. More like a son." She looked up again, eyes concentrated on something just over Syl's shoulder. "No, I think he'd be proud of her. He loved that girl."

Where was Esma looking? Syl carefully turned to see, but it was just a blank wood-paneled wall. No pictures or decorations or anything. Surely someone with pro-level clutter like this would have photos displayed.

"I'm glad you brought Mr. Winton up. Is that his picture outside the house?"

"Yes. Isn't he handsome?"

"Indeed. Why is the picture outside though?"

Esma sighed and stood, turned her back to Syl, like she was cleaning up the projects, whatever they were. Esma shuffled papers, closed books and stacked them on the floor. But then she picked up the same papers and moved them to the kitchen table. It was metal-rimmed Formica like it came straight from the 1950s, also covered with clutter. Open shoe boxes with letters falling out, enough paper to resurrect a few trees, used paper cups, and tools you don't need in a kitchen. Every surface was covered with something. Tape measures (why more than one?), smashed pop cans, candles, unused sticky notes, reams of yarn, old wooden toys, and Tupperware—some of it holding more clutter, some stacked and empty. There was a wooden baseball bat leaning up against the side of the couch.

"That's just in case," Esma answered finally.

"Just in case of what?" Syl had forgotten her initial question about the picture of John.

Esma smiled. "Was there another reason you wanted to talk about John? Or just to find out if that was his picture?"

"Both, I suppose. I wanted to know more about his disappearance, and then I saw the picture and wondered if it was him."

"What could you possibly want to know? It happened so long ago, and there's really not much to it," Esma said in a low voice, then returned to transporting piles of clutter between the living room and the kitchen. She was making zero progress on tidying up, if that was even the goal.

"When you first realized your daughter was back without him, what happened?"

Esma sighed again, louder, as if Syl wasn't understanding something, and she needed more patience to deal with her. "Like I said, it was a long time ago, honey."

She walked over to the kitchen sink and ran the water, but then turned it off immediately and spun to look at Syl. Thighs burning, Syl still pretended to sit on the orange couch. Esma kept pouring out nervous energy, gliding between the living room and the kitchen. Syl was wrong, this woman *did* get movement.

"Why do you want to know so much about John? Why does it matter now?"

"Alex Conder's death." Syl pointed out the front window at Lucky Dog. "I wondered if you saw anything. Would have been Thursday."

She'd already said all of that to Dawn, had Esma not heard?

"No. You can't really see over there anyway. Maybe if I had those special glasses—"

"Binoculars?"

"Yes! Those. But we don't have any. I suppose John did, being a hunter and all, but I don't know where he kept them, and I don't have time to be staring out the window anyway."

What on earth kept this woman so busy during the day that she couldn't look out the window? She clearly didn't keep house.

"No. I can't think about John. It's too painful," Esma said as if Syl were arguing with her.

"I can imagine it was hard to lose him."

Esma made a little "hm" noise and lowered herself to the coffee table again, sitting unevenly, one cheek up on a phone book and the other not. "It's *still* quite hard. I miss him a lot. We were very much in love."

"And how has Dawn adjusted over the years?"

Esma's face tightened up, like Syl had landed on another touchy topic. "You know, years ago, she struggled. But she's an adult now and seems to be handling it better. Has her father's issues with anger though."

Esma was holding something back, Syl sensed it, so she waited her out to see if Esma broke the silence with more information.

"She's very...religious," Esma offered.

"How do you mean?"

Weren't they all religious, based on Roger's account?

Esma sighed, paused like she was combing through her mind to find the right combination of words. It took a long time for her to speak.

"She changed suddenly one day. Dawn was always a good girl, but John was the religious one and, after he was gone, she and I didn't do much about church. She got in with a bad crowd and I don't know if it scared her or what, but next thing I knew, poof! She's the perfect picture of Christian faith."

"That sounds like a great change to me."

"Yes, it is. But, I can't help but feel…"

Esma's voice trailed off, and Syl waited, but then Esma was up and headed into the kitchen again.

Syl had to keep her talking. "If you don't mind my asking, are you not religious?"

"Eh," Esma said and shrugged just one shoulder. "I'm spiritual. But nothing like Dawn. Or John. Promise you won't tell Dawn I said any of this."

Uh, okay. Syl crossed her heart because it felt right in that moment.

"I believe in Jesus as a teacher, and when I first got saved, faith was easy. Uncomplicated, you know? But after John disappeared, I didn't want to go back to it. Was kind of ruined for me." Esma was in the living room now, and she leaned in, whispering, "Are you a Christian?"

"Yes, I suppose so," Syl said, leaning back slowly as Esma got into her personal bubble.

Esma squinted, cocking her head to the side, studying Syl. "Where'd you grow up?"

"I lived with my grandma, LouAnn Dixon, right here in Pate, until I was about six. Then Spokane."

"But you're not the sort of Christian who only reads the Bible, only listens to Keith Green and Sandi Patty, no movies, no alcohol, right? The sort that's certain everyone around you is so full of sin, they'll infect you and send you to Hell; the devil's around every corner. That sort of thing?"

"No. Just a normal person who believes in God."

Syl could have given a more nuanced answer. Truth was, she hadn't been to church in decades, but she didn't want to feed Esma a distraction.

"Don't tell Dawn what I'm about to tell you," Esma demanded. "Can you do that for me? She's in a good spot and I don't want her back with the druggies."

Syl nodded in agreement. Where the hell was this going?

"I have gifts. Special gifts. There's something else though…"

She stopped again, ducked, and leaned across the already tiny space between them and whispered, "You swear you won't tell Dawn this, right?"

God, lady. I said yes.

Syl smiled.

"I've been sensing something lately. Like an energy shift. I don't know exactly what it is, or where it comes from, because it's not always the same. I think it influenced John to leave. People disappear a lot around here. Anyone told you about that?"

"What do you mean? I know John disappeared. My grandma disappeared in the sixties. Do you remember that?"

"Oh hon, I wasn't here in the sixties. John and I got married in 1970, that's when I moved here. And I'm not talking about a few people disappearing. It's a lot of people. Seems like whenever someone new disappears, the energy in the town morphs. I can't describe it very well, but it's as if the town becomes more open to the spiritual realm. People see weird things, dreams intensify."

Syl couldn't take this seriously, not really. But then again, a mummified man who was alive the day before? Kyle dreaming about his dad's condition without seeing it? That howling Syl heard in the forest? Esma might be cuckoo, and that was what Roger hoped Syl would deduce here, but what if not?

"When you say 'disappear,' what do you mean?"

"Poof! Gone. Almost always in the woods."

"Is that what happened to John?"

"I think so."

"Is that why you have his picture up outside?"

Esma waved her hand again, so Syl pivoted even though she didn't want to. This was the closest she'd gotten to answers about the pictures. "Do you think the disappearances have something to do with the Markwells?"

"I'm surprised they told you about the Markwells. Nobody likes to talk about it around here. They want to pretend we live in a normal small town, surrounded by the beauty of nature. People are very proud of their mining heritage. They protect it. Don't want to admit there's a darkness living here too. I think something is coming."

"What do you mean?"

Esma looked at Syl like she was the crazy one. "I can't say exactly, but I feel it."

"Feel what?"

"I don't know." Esma shut down fast.

"Okay, let's talk about your daughter—"

"—Dawn," Esma interrupted.

"Dawn, yes. What did she say when she got home after John disappeared?"

Yes, it was the same question, worded differently, for a third time. Syl Dixon, a woman of endless patience today.

"Nothing. Wouldn't talk about it at all. Said she didn't remember anything beyond getting up that morning and leaving the tent to pee. And then she was running home."

"It's strange that she saw nothing, don't you think?"

"Dawn was a young girl who thought too much about survival and the end times. Put her on constant high alert that something bad was going to happen to us. She was always scared, and it never made sense to me why John would have her living in fear. You tell me. If perfect love casts out fear—that's in the Bible—and if God is love, why do Christians live in fear?"

Sounded smart, but Syl was no expert at stitching Bible verses together to create a mantra to live by. Or unraveling such stitch work.

"Here's my card." Syl handed over another one of Roger's white business cards. "If you think of anything else, no matter how small, please leave a message for me at the station. Sheriff Mock will get it to me."

Back at the car, Syl ducked down to look at Roger through the window. He was stifling a laugh. She opened the door.

"Tell me you solved the John Winton cold case because you spoke with Esma," he said.

"Asshole," was all Syl could come up with.

SPOKANE, WASHINGTON

May 1901

NINETEEN

COMING OUT OF the woods at a dead run, Lily was drenched with rain, skin numb with cold from the wind. The windows of her home were all dark, as if vacant. Where was everyone?

She pushed the heavy wooden door all the way open and shouted into the dark abyss of the foyer like some uncivilized person, "I can't find Margaret! Does anyone know where she is?" What answered was a sense that the home knew what she'd done, and she must approach it more carefully than that.

"Mother?" she whispered as a burst of wind and rain pushed against her back. She closed the door and stood there, dripping on Mother's beloved Persian rug.

Something pressed up behind Lily, but when she turned, it was only the closed door. She was spooked from running through the woods, that was all.

Mother and Father must be out looking. The maid, too, unless she already retreated to the carriage house for the night. It wasn't *that* late, though, was it? She squinted to read the big grandfather clock despite darkness. Midnight. How had time passed like that? Where had she been?

And then, the pressing again. Sharp, demanding, but when she looked back, it was only the closed door. She stared at it, moving closer until her face was only inches away. A puddle formed around her laced-up boots. If somebody pushed the door open from the outside, they'd hit her hard and she would deserve it. She locked the door, scolding herself for being afraid. Of what? A door? As if a door—

Thump, thump, thump.

Lily jumped back and let out a little gasp at the loud knock. Before she could say anything, a voice.

"Miss Carding? You there?" It was Holver, their stable hand.

Upon raising her hand to touch her forehead, she saw her pink dress sleeve was streaked with crimson. "Yes, Holver, I'm here." She tried to brush the blood off.

"Meg with ya?"

"No." Lily blinked. "Is she with you?"

"'Fraid not."

Lily waited to see if he would go away, but then he spoke again. "Mr. and Mrs. Carding will be right glad to have you back."

She felt him on the other side of the door, hanging on, waiting. For what? But then, she knew what it was. Hadn't he spent the past two years sending long looks her way? Didn't she sense his interest in her, and didn't Father too? What, with Father's constant inquiries about how Lily spent her time out of doors. With his shooing Holver away from the house whenever he was there. Holver was muscular, quite nice-looking, barely twenty, and had always been kind to her and Margaret.

"Miss Carding, you need anything?"

"Call me Lily, Holver."

"Lily." He said it slowly. It gave her an embarrassed feeling in her stomach. Like a somersault inside.

Remove your dress.

It was the voice. She walked deeper into the foyer, put a hand on the newel post of the staircase and whispered, "Mother? Is that you?"

She got no answer, but realized the wisdom and took her soiled dress off. Then Lily turned around in the dark. Where could she hide it? The wood stove! She had to remember to light it as soon as Holver was gone.

"I'm all right," she shouted from the living room, as if Holver had asked. Had he? "You best get back out there and look for Margaret." Then she added as an afterthought, "Where are my parents?"

"Miss, would you oblige me and open the door so we don't have to holler?"

"No!" Frantic at first, she ran back to her side of the front door. Then calmer, "No. I'm sorry, I'm not…presentable."

"Oh! Beg your pardon."

"It's all right. Will you find my parents and tell them I lost Margaret about fifteen minutes into the woods? They'll need lanterns now."

"And they have 'em."

Lily rolled her eyes. She needed him to go away so she could think.

Invite him in.

That strange voice again.

"Did you hear that?" she shouted through the door.

"Hear what?"

"A woman's voice."

"Only yours."

"Oh bother, never mind!" Lily was tired and needed to get off her feet, so she returned to the stairs and sat down. Maybe he'd go away.

Ask him in.

"You didn't hear that, Holver? Not a sound of it?" She moved back to the front door.

"Heard nothin', miss."

Why wouldn't he stop calling her that?

Lily flung the heavy wood open, standing there in her corset and bloomers.

Holver was under the porch to avoid the downpour, but still, he was soaked through.

"Whoa, Lily, where'd your dress go?" He averted his eyes.

She took both of his hands in hers and didn't say anything. Holver squeezed his eyes closed, turned his face to the side.

"Holver, look." She pulled him inside.

He resisted at first, and this angered her.

"Don't you like me?"

Holver opened his eyes and seemed to be using all of his willpower to keep them level with hers, but they still slipped down around the top of her corset. "Yes, but wouldn't be right to look. Can't do that to ya."

Of course! What was she thinking? He'd think she was loose, some kind of dirty woman if she kept this up. She let go of his hands. He was already on the way to the linen closet, looking for a quilt. He wrapped it around her, and she sat on the davenport, thinking about how she would have given herself to him. How that would have angered Father and made her feel strong.

Holver brushed himself off, and she motioned for him to sit next to her. He didn't budge. "I really ought to get back out there and search for Meg."

Now he wanted to leave? After she tried to get him to go, and he wouldn't. What did he want from her?

"Sit down," she said, patting the cushion with half-effort. The wild animal inside her returned to its cage, and the prison door closed tightly again. He sat.

"I do love ya, miss—Lily, I mean." He took her hands. "But you know I'm poor. Your pa won't hear of it any time I bring up the topic. Now I reckon if *you* spoke with him, he'd know it's what you want, too."

"I don't imagine it'd do any good. He doesn't care what I want." She looked out at the dark room, not meaning to avoid his eyes, but all the same, not looking at him.

"Well, let's bide our time and see what happens. I reckon we need to find Meg first."

Lily nodded.

"I ain't givin' up, though, Lily Carding."

Her eyes followed him as he stood and sorted himself. He turned to smile at her before he closed the front door and walked back into the rain. She went to the window, pulled the heavy velvet drapes aside to watch him go. Rain streaked the glass so his figure was wavy. He held a lantern straight out in front of him and walked with the confident steps of a boy who'd just won a prize at the county fair. Lily smiled, thinking that maybe she could like a man who liked her the way he did.

PATE, IDAHO

July 1989

TWENTY

SOMEBODY WAS SCREAMING underwater, but there was no water. Only darkness and a glowing light Syl couldn't place. Then the howling started. She was in the woods and a woman lay crumpled on the ground. Someone stood over the body, then a knife, a scream. Syl came to the surface of awake, where she realized it was her yelling. She sat up, dry mouthed and gasping, looking around to solve the mystery of where she was.

Still just Gran's house.

Sweat clung sticky to her ribbed tank top, and the whole area of the bed where she slept was soaked. Like some child snuck up next to her and wet the bed. She looked at the alarm clock. 3:17 a.m., of course.

God, that was a weird dream. Or had it been a dream? It was familiar like a memory, but nothing she remembered from her life. More like thumbing through someone else's twisted family photo albums. Esma Winton was there this time. Her and John Winton, actually. Or she thought. It looked just like that portrait outside the Winton cabin. Made sense. Syl had just interviewed Esma and surely her mind would be trying to process Alex's case while she slept.

She peeled off the saturated tank. Disgusting. She snapped on the bedside lamp and laid the tank out to dry over Gran's old wicker hamper. She put on her yellow terry robe and tied the belt tight around her waist.

She'd had weird dreams before, but this felt real. The kind that stuck with you. The sort you had to remind yourself over and over that it wasn't real. What did it all mean?

Coffee would help. She went downstairs to wait on that old coffee pot and rubbed her eyes, thought about what Esma said.

Something is coming.

She'd tried dropping hints to Roger about Esma's words. See if he'd color in any of the details about the disappearances that apparently included a lot more than John Winton, Gran, and the Markwells. He didn't offer anything. Looked at her like she was speaking a different language. Maybe coming out and saying it would have been a better approach, but Roger was cagey about the whole topic. Syl needed more time to think about it. All of it. Why he'd ask her to help investigate, and then act like she slapped him every time she requested information about the town? Hopefully, the chance to bring it up in a different way would arise.

The dream came back to mind. That howling. How was it possible something so beautiful could scare the shit out of her?

Oh brother, now it wasn't enough to solve a case. She had to try and solve a dream too? Ridiculous.

Sometimes a cigar is just a goddamn cigar. She heard Gran's voice in her head and poured a mug of the small amount of coffee the pot had produced.

TWENTY-ONE

ESMA JERKED AWAKE, her body lurching hard against the sensation of falling. She sat upright in bed, and the clock said 3:18 a.m., and the cabin was lit only by the moonlight that snuck in through her bedroom window. She touched the back of her neck. So wet. Her long nightgown was soaked through, too, all the way from the waist up. The bed felt cold to the touch, wet. She got out of bed to change the sheets.

The dreams were getting worse. More out of control. Sometimes there were people in them she'd never seen before, locations she'd never been to. Sometimes the energy was just... different, and that was the only clue she got. This wasn't the first time she'd experienced someone else's dream, but it rarely happened. Dream hopping felt wrong, invasive. Not only that, but you couldn't control it, you'd just show up on the scene. Poof! That was bad, but the worst part was you couldn't change other people's dreams, so the risk of getting stuck in a worse nightmare than your own was real. One's own nightmares were plenty to handle, and Esma wasn't interested in tromping around other psyches.

Yet, that was exactly what must have happened tonight. She and John were talking in the woods. Then she couldn't remember anything until she was falling from a height. Upon realizing it, she set her mind to fly, but hit the ground, lying prone, face to the side instead. In her own dream, she would have simply flown off, never touched down. Now she was dead, she knew she was, yet she was still aware somehow, still awake. Her hand lay in front of her face, palm down. But not her hand, a corpse's hand, like she'd been dead for years, the skin all shriveled up. John had stood near, watching it happen, but he didn't stop it. He was bending down over her, inspecting.

No clean sheets on the shelf. When was the last time she washed and put them away? There had to be a clean one around here somewhere. She pushed towels aside. No luck. They were probably in one of the stacked laundry baskets, but she wasn't in the frame of mind to go digging through them. She fished what, in the dark, seemed like a flat sheet out of the dirty hamper. It wasn't the right size, but it didn't smell too bad. Probably Dawn's.

John had been so tender in the dream. How long since she'd felt tenderness like that? And what had he said when he leaned over her dead body?

I'm coming home.

Just like Little Esma had said.

Then she'd blinked and come back to life inside the dream. It was something about the feeling she got when he'd said that though. It stuck with her, and not in a good way. The energy wasn't quite right. Maybe she was reading the dreamer's energy instead her own? Did it matter though? If John returned, she'd welcome him with open arms and be so grateful.

After she laid the sheet on her side of the bed, Esma walked toward the bathroom to pee. She was on the toilet when she heard the crash.

Frozen, listening for the squeaky floorboards, Esma waited. Those floors didn't let anyone pass without throwing a fit, and she was sure if it was a robber, the old floor would tell her before she saw anything. But there was only perfect silence. Graveyard silence.

"Oh, don't think that way, Esma! It's just your imagination acting up again," she whispered out loud, hoping it'd make her feel better. It didn't.

It wasn't a robber, and the more she thought about it, the more she realized the sound had come from outside. Probably just some stray animal making a ruckus in the woodshed, right? Or maybe it was Dawn. But what would she be doing out there at this hour? Sleepwalking? Esma finished up with her business, and since she didn't hear anything else, walked slowly back toward bed.

Another crash. Louder.

Esma startled, but now she knew for sure it was coming from the woodshed. Standing in the hall, she faced the back door. Her arms dangled next to her soggy night dress as she looked out the little window there. She had never noticed the way the single-paned window in the door framed the wood-shed perfectly. Dumb thought at a time like this. What could have made that noise? And why was the shed door open? She cracked the door for a bit of fresh air, but got a shiver because her nightgown was still drenched.

Had Dawn left the shed door open?

No. Dawn never went in the woodshed. Wouldn't go in there even if Esma paid her, and Esma never understood that. Sure, a shed could be scary, but not in broad daylight, and surely not to an adult. Didn't matter to Dawn. One time, Esma needed wood for the fireplace, and she asked Dawn to run out there and get some. Dawn screamed at her. It was during Scary-Dawn days, so maybe it'd be different now. Esma had asked back then what it was with the woodshed, but Dawn wouldn't talk about it.

No, Dawn was most definitely not in the shed in the middle of the night, and Esma wasn't going out there in a wet nightgown!

Esma shuffled back toward her room barefoot, listening to the floorboards moan. She peeked into Dawn's room. Dawn was a little blanketed cocoon, her face dark because of the way the moonlight came in through the window at her back. Esma got right up to her face to see if maybe the girl had just gotten into bed after messing around in the shed. Was her heart beating fast? Her breathing harder?

But Dawn was deep in sleep. Esma got distracted watching her for a moment. It was so rare she got to just look at her daughter. Usually, Esma tried not to look at the girl for too long. She didn't want to set Dawn off.

Should she wake Dawn up and have her go look? No. It was a stupid thought that Esma got rid of as fast as it came. Dawn would be mad that Esma woke her, and she'd refuse to go into the shed anyway.

But Esma wasn't going into that shed tonight, door open or not. Tomorrow. She'd go tomorrow, first thing.

After all, maybe Esma wasn't fully awake when she was in the bathroom, when she heard the noise. Maybe she was still dreaming. That thin veil between asleep and awake could be tricky.

Back in her room, she lay down, facing the outside of the bed, and pulled the quilt up under her chin like she'd done since forever. Esma always slept on her own side of the bed even though John was gone and she could sprawl if she wanted. It made her feel less alone. Like she could pretend he was there.

She was just about to doze off, but she rolled over, looking for a comfier position. Esma's eyes fluttered slowly from those final blinks before sleep, and that's when she saw it. A shape under the covers on John's side.

Wide awake now, all sleepiness gone, she couldn't move. The covers on John's side were bulky from the foot of the bed to the headboard, like the quilt covered a head. Esma held her end of the quilt tighter to her chin while her heart stomped like a monster in her chest. Hold still. If only she could be invisible. Maybe there was something wrong with her eyes. Blinking a good couple times, she tried to clear her vision. Maybe she *was* still asleep! She pinched her cheek.

Ow!

Nope, definitely awake. Still, the bulge next to her didn't move. It looked like a bunch of pillows under the covers. A prank you'd play on your mom when you wanted to sneak out. If you didn't have the mom Esma had. If you wouldn't be left alone in a closet for weeks as punishment.

"John?"

Whispering his name out loud made that empty spot inside her grow. She'd said his name out loud more this week than in the decade since he left. It couldn't be John.

No answer. No movement.

Esma had to touch him, it was the only way to know. But she couldn't make her arm leave the warm covers to be mangled by whatever was next to her. Yet, if she didn't act fast, it'd either be her arm or all of her. She could do without one arm, all things told. Esma blinked a handful of times, like it was a magic trick to make the thing go away. It stayed.

Her arm came out from under the quilt in slow motion and moved across the bed until her fingertips touched the blanket where the head was. If it had a head. Her hand froze, holding the quilt, like it was a bandage she had to tear off. Like it might hurt, or be stuck so deep in the wound that it gushed blood. Two quick breaths in and out, and then she'd pull the covers back and face whatever was there.

In, out.

In, out.

Pull.

John's side of the bed was empty but warm.

PATE, IDAHO

January 1962

TWENTY-TWO

LOU RETURNED TO the kitchen table after checking on Syl. She was still fast asleep.

Stranger huffed a big sigh on the floor beside her. He was lying on his side, and she reached down to pet his soft fur. "I know, boy. I know." She squeezed the pen and read over the last few paragraphs to pick up where she left off.

... When my eyes sprung open that day, I was lying on my back inside that confounded woodshed. The door was wide open. Had I made the whole thing up? Did it even happen? That's what run through my brain as I slid down that hill away from the Markwell cabin. I wanted to outrun the fear I felt in that shed. The marks in the dirt and on the walls. The shadow that I swear locked me in like a jailbird.

By the time I came to the river across from the place, my breathing was normal. I looked behind me, and up at that cabin. I started talking sense into myself again. Somehow, I'd knocked that door closed, and then it got stuck and I couldn't open it. It nagged at me that the door was wide open when I awoke, but I decided maybe an animal did it.

Then there was the old, dried blood on the ground and the wall. But why was I so spooked? I seen blood before. Hell, I seen a lot more blood than that every time I gutted an animal I shot in the woods. Maybe the Markwells used the shed for gutting what they hunted. But there was something about that particular moment, seeing it sprayed like that, black dots on the wall. Not to mention scaring the bejeezus out of myself being stuck inside!

I lit a cigarette at the base of the hill, watching the river and enjoying a smoke while I figured what to do next. My eyes climbed up until they found Lucky Dog Mine. You would have had to practically scale the front side of the mountain to get to it. Must have been an easier way to approach it along the side of the hill, but they didn't want anyone to go into that old mine anyway. It had closed down just a few years prior. When I squinted to avoid the sun, I saw a thin liquid pouring out of the boarded-up entrance. A reddish-brown substance coursed its way down the mountain until it met up with the river.

I put out my cigarette, and found the spot miners used to cross the stream. My head was full of questions about what I just seen in that old shed. I slipped over rocks as I made my way, catching myself before my foot plunged into water.

I got right up to the point where that dribble was seeping into the river. It was poison, I knew it right away. Leftover tailings from the mining days. All the old mines spurted that shit. The rust color spun in a little pool as it mixed with the clear water and traveled downstream. Like a devil and an angel holding hands. I looked up at the mine entrance again, but being right underneath, I couldn't really see. For some reason, I thought about all of these mines with holes elbowing deep into the earth. About us, ripping silver from the land until it bled. Poisoning the water, ruining the earth once with the drilling, and again with the tailings. Those dark thoughts gave me a hankering for whiskey to calm the hell down. Good thing I didn't have any. To get my mind off the liquor urge, I walked upstream along the river, away from that poison.

Gleaming silver in the water caught my eyes. Fish. Cutthroat trout, speckled with black spots and a streak of red. They swished along in the fresh water, innocent as all get out. Poor fish didn't even know what they were headed into. Those were the most beautiful creatures I'd seen in a while. But it shot into my mind a different vision of black spots and streaks I'd seen that day. That brought gooseflesh up on my arms and neck again.

You might laugh about this, pup, but in those days, I wore Grandpa's overalls. Had to use a belt to cinch the waist real tight, but they had these big pockets, and that's where I kept my smokes and matches. I was all out of smokes, so I dropped my backpack and sat down. Tried to think on something else. Something other than that cabin.

That's when I heard it.

Howling.

Came from the mountain behind Lucky Dog, I was sure. But I couldn't make out what animal it was. The sound was downright beautiful and haunting. Only thing I could place was that it might be a loon calling.

I stood up, and before I'd thought it through too much, I had my backpack on and I was taking wide steps up the steep mountain.

Alls I could hear was that call, talking to me inside my head, telling me things. Soon, I was close, so close to it. In fact, when I seen how far up the mountain I'd come in such a short time, I looked at my watch. It had been hours and hours! I didn't remember much of the climb at all.

The howling went on. Lonely, sad, asking for help almost. I had to find out what animal made that noise. Maybe it was hurt. Only thing I knew was I had to keep going.

The closer I got, the more my grief over Rose grew. The feeling that I couldn't go on without her. I thought about her alone in these woods and cried. Seemed to get darker the closer I got, but it was still broad daylight. The air felt different. Can't describe it too well here, but I'd never been to that part of the mountain even though it wasn't too far from sections I'd spent lots of time in. If there were trails at all, they were weak. Most were paths only the animals used.

That howl went on and on. It grew louder until I came up over a ridge and to a small clearing. That's when it stopped. Perfect silence. No chipmunks yelling, no wind dropping pine cones from the trees. Just the muffled sound of a small stream in front of me.

That howling again.

Then, I saw a mine entrance in the mountain at the back of the clearing. Who would operate a mine this far into the woods without any roads to it? Wasn't boarded up either.

The howl came softer, more desperate than before, and it was coming from inside that mine.

I had to know what it was...

SPOKANE, WASHINGTON

June 1901

TWENTY-THREE

FATHER FOUND MARGARET'S body a few weeks later, but by that time, it was so mangled from animals scavenging the bones, that the police didn't look too much into it. Father cried at the funeral.

What had gotten into Lily that day? She regretted hurting Margaret, but at the same time, she wasn't sure she could have stopped it, that she could control herself. She had to leave Spokane now, start a new life. A new Lily. She asked Holver if he wanted to leave with her.

"I've some money saved up and been hearin' of silver in them Idaho mountains. It's not too far away. I've a mind to go. But…" Holver sighed and stopped talking. "Can't leave without ya. Never thought you'd want me, so I'd been determined to stay here forever if need be."

"You'd do that for me?" It was so kind, so sacrificial. Nobody had ever done a thing like that for her. Maybe she could truly enjoy marriage. Maybe she could be a better person and leave everything behind. She didn't need money, she could be happy with Holver. A new beginning.

"Course I would."

"I will go to Idaho with you, Holver. On one condition. Make sure my parents can never find us. I don't ever want to see or hear from them again."

HOLVER WATCHED LILY'S tears gather at her perfect chin and then drop on her bosom. She was crouched in that spot on the rock she liked. Holver didn't know if she was looking at the river below or the mountains beyond. The mountains that would soon be their home if indeed Lily came with him.

He sat next to her, feeling the warmth of her at his side. Soon, she'd be his. He'd hoped it would come with some of Lily's money, but he'd take her either way.

"Can you do that for me, Holver? Whatever it takes."

Lily was a looker, that was for sure. Long, thick brown hair. Big brown eyes. Her skin was tanning from the sun, and it gave her a hearty look. When Lily wasn't watching, Holver stared at her chest, which was heaving with sobs.

He could tell her parents a harmless little lie. They'd be so far into the White Pine mountains it wasn't like Mr. Carding could find them on his own. Holver could say they were going to Alaska, the Yukon. Hell, he could say they were going to Mexico, for all it mattered.

Then again, Mr. Carding was a man of means, and he'd already proved to be locked in on his daughter. Would he come after them? Losing two daughters in the span of months might break him and keep him right here. Or it could steel his will to find the one still living. Which way would it go?

"Did you hear me, darling?" Lily asked.

"I heard ya, Lily. You want me to keep your pa and ma from ever findin' us out. Whatever it takes." He repeated her words from before, avoiding her eyes, and instead watching a branch float the distance of the river below, bobbing across white caps.

Holver and his little brother used to throw branches into the river, just before it cascaded and crashed over the falls. Boats, they called them. They were too poor for proper toys. They had the outdoors though. For a second, Holver could hear Jack's voice.

"Look at the boat I found! Let's toss it in. See if it goes!"

Holver had taken the branch from Jack, no bigger than his two fingers in diameter, and hurled it into the river at the top of the falls. The goal was to find the smallest one that could make it through. Big ones could take the beating Spokane Falls gave them. That was too easy. The best boats were free of stubby little branches. Usually it didn't matter though, because the little boats never made it through, they had no staying power. Always disappeared.

"Aren't you happy we'll be together? You look sad," Lily said.

He nodded, but when he looked up, he knew it wasn't enough. Something dark passed across her eyes. It made Holver shiver.

"Yes, yes, Lily. An adventure for sure." He reached over to bring her under his arm and hold her, but she felt stiff next to him.

"When will we go, Holver? Can it be today?"

"Give me the day to think on what I'll say to your folks. We'll go tomorrow, noonday."

TWENTY-FOUR

SHE WAS ALMOST there. Almost free.

Lily waited in Holver's horse-drawn cart outside the estate, grateful it wasn't raining. Holver was still inside, talking with her parents, and he'd been in there awhile. She fretted that something was going wrong. Give her father time, and he could swindle anyone. What if he was telling Holver all the reasons he shouldn't marry Lily? What if Holver listened?

Freedom pressed up against her insides, dancing a little jig and inviting her to join. But she sat still. It wasn't for sure yet, and she couldn't run away with her feelings. She wanted to jump up and stand on the bench of this cart, shout so loud that the next estate over could hear that she, Lily Carding, would be unchained, starting today. Loosed and untangled, she'd be free to run. Make a fresh start. She was excited to keep a home. It would be hers. There would be children. Yes, she would fill a home with children who would love her in the ways she was never loved. Her children wouldn't be selfish like Margaret. No, they'd be kind and loving like Holver. And smart like her. The children she raised would have nothing of this nasty life she'd lived. She'd make sure to never be harsh with them. They'd be poor, sure, but what had growing up with money done for her anyway?

Forging her own path, on her own terms, that was what mattered most. Holver wouldn't get in the way. He was obsessed with striking silver. Getting rich. Fine, let him have it. He'd be away from the house more often, leaving her to conduct her days as she saw fit. She almost squealed with delight, thinking about doing her own washing and cooking and mending. And then she laughed, wondering what happened to the Lily who avoided housework like it was a disease?

It was their *housework, that's why. This will be mine. My whole life will belong to me, and I will love everything in it. I will protect my own.*

But then a dark thought came to her. *What if Holver tries to stand in my way? What if others do?*

They wouldn't. They couldn't. She promised herself right there, sitting on the hard wood bench of the worn-out cart, that she would live her life and be free, come what may.

Father's voice boomed from inside the house. He was yelling, but she couldn't make out what he said. Lily worked the fabric of her dress with her fingers. She looked around.

Father shouted again, and this time something crashed.

Should she crawl under the blanket in the cart and hide? Would Father run outside and grab her, forcing her inside?

Just as she straddled the seat to get into the cart and hide, Holver walked out, straightening his vest coat. He pushed back his long mop of hair. He didn't look at Lily, not even as he mounted the cart and reached for the reins.

"What happened? I heard Father yelling."

"Hiya!" He commanded the horses to move forward, ignoring her question.

"What was all the commotion?"

"Your father tried talkin' me down off it. Offered me money. More money than I'm likely to make as a miner in Idaho. 'Less I stake my own claim."

Lily's shoulders sank. Holver regretted his choice. The dancer inside her retreated to a corner, and the cage door creaked toward shut. She wasn't a prize, she was a duty. But no, that wasn't the way to think. She wouldn't be anyone's obligation in this brand new life.

"Well then, you'll just have to stake a claim!" she said, feeling her weight bounce as the wheels hit potholes in the road.

Holver smiled. "Don't think for a second I'd a gone back on our plan!"

        STEPH NELSON

She looked down at her folded hands. "What did Mother say?"

"Your ma wishes you all her love."

That didn't sound at all like Mother.

"What was Father yelling about?"

Holver pushed his hair back again. "You know how that old man can be. He was madder'n a chased hornet and took it out on a few small tables and vases. Nobody gets the best of Roy Carding."

"Nobody except Holver Markwell," Lily said, looping an arm through his, leaning her head on his bulky shoulder.

Holver smiled. "After your pa threw a hissy fit, he sat down and cried like a baby."

Sat down and cried, just like at Margaret's funeral. Cried for his own loss. Of course, he couldn't be happy for Lily.

Lily watched the mansions go by as they made their way toward Idaho. They passed the rest of the day in relative silence.

The road ahead looked like endless possibilities.

PATE, IDAHO

July 1989

TWENTY-FIVE

ESMA WAS DETERMINED to learn more about that dream. What had been in her bed the other night? Maybe Little Esma knew. She already had the sketchbook out, pens in hand.

> *Dear Little Esma, I'm thinking about what you said about John coming home. Can you help me to—*

ALREADY BEN HELPING. YOU GET THE NEW DREEM I SENT?

Esma set the pens down. The dream—falling, crashing, John staring at her. It had been her dream after all? Why couldn't she control it?

> *That was you?*

I USED MY POWERS LIKE YOU SAY

She started and then stopped, then crossed out a few words, which was exactly what the book said not to do.

> *I'm not so sure the dream helped me.*

And then, as if she'd lost control completely, her left hand gripped the red pen, and her right hand, a slave to Little Esma, flipped back a few pages to the drawing Little Esma had begun. To the lines that looked like stick people but that she had decided must've been trees. Lots of trees. Her left hand hit the paper so hard it hurt, and it finished the drawing where it had left off the other day. Next to all those trees. It looked like a rectangle, but without a bottom line. Then a curve above it. Her hand pushed the pen hard and filled in the space of the rectangle, then stopped.

This is a picture of your dream?

The dream that terrified Esma last night.

YES

What is it?

GUESS IF YOU CAN REMEMMBER.

It looks like it's in the woods. Is that right?

GETING WARMER

Is it the woods by the cabin?

COLD

By Lucky Dog?

COLDER FREEZING!

Esma flushed with frustration. The book said the adult should be more patient. But this wasn't helpful. How could she know what a child's scribbles meant?

Can you give me another hint?

MOONSTEP

Moonstep Mine? The old story about a lost mine in the woods? John used to talk about it. He always wanted to find it, said its silver would be a perfect form of currency during the End of Days, when dollar bills are about as useful as grocery receipts. But what did that have to do with anything? Before she could ask, the red pen in her left hand arrested the page and wrote faster than it ever had before.

MOONSTEP MOONSTEP MISBEHAVE

MOONSTEP MOONSTEP IN THE GRAVE

Esma slammed the red pen down. Something was off, way off. But when she looked, the red pen was back in her left hand, writing. She didn't remember picking it up.

MOONSTEP MOONSTEP HOWL AT NIGHT

MOONSTEP MOONSTEP GRIP SO TIGHT

Stop!

MOONSTEP MOONSTEP SILVER VEINS

MOONSTEP MOONSTEP BLOODY STAINS

Stop it, Little Esma! Stop!

REMEMMBER NOW?

Esma slammed the sketchbook shut. She took deep breaths. The energy was pushy, laughing at her. Her breathing was ragged, fast, but she waited for it to come under control.

She did remember.

It was the chant she and her friends said at recess, but never with the mine's name. She didn't even know about the mine back in Seattle, where she grew up. They'd use another girl's name. A girl they didn't like. Then they'd run a finger up each other's arms as they did it, like tracing veins. Where did that chant come from? It was one of those stupid things you did as a kid. Like saying Bloody Mary three times in front of a mirror, or "Ring Around the Rosie," "Light as a Feather." It didn't mean anything, and Esma hadn't thought about it in decades. There was no way she'd remember the whole thing as quickly as Little Esma wrote it. Yet, something pressed at the back of her mind.

What was the ending? She squeezed her eyes shut, trying to remember. When it came to her, she said it out loud:

"Moonstep, Moonstep, come awake.
Moonstep, Moonstep, soul to take."

TWENTY-SIX

IT WAS DARK, and Dawn was scared. Something was in her hand. Small, dimpled fingers, holding hers. It was Kimmy from the Sunday school class Dawn taught. Where were they? Dawn tried to stand, but Kimmy wouldn't let her.

"Don't leave us," Kimmy said. The girl's red hair looked black in the dark, and she wasn't smiling. Kimmy always smiled.

"Us?"

Kimmy looked the other way, and following her gaze, Dawn saw Stephen holding Kimmy's other hand, Jeff holding his, then Annabelle, Dorian, Mark, Heather, Jason, all the way down a tunnel. Even Emily was there, despite the fact that Emily had disappeared last year. It was the entire kindergarten class.

Dawn heard dripping, slow and tedious.

"Slow obey is no obey." Dad's voice echoed from above. "You know I can't make myself clean."

She had to get away, but Kimmy wouldn't let go. When Dawn looked at Kimmy again, the girl shriveled up. Eyes empty, mouth open. Dawn looked at Mark, and just like that, he shriveled up too. Like dominoes, all the children became corpses. Dawn couldn't get her hand away from Kimmy's skeletal fingers. She pulled and pulled, until she fell back from the effort.

"D? Hey D! Wake up."

Dawn opened her eyes.

"It was just a dream. You all right?"

Monte. Right. She was with Monte. He begged her to take him camping, to show him one of her favorite spots in the woods, and she agreed as long as he swore no monkey business.

"I'm fine." She was still breathing hard. "Sorry I woke you."

"I don't mind. But I was worried. You were thrashing and yelling something with your mouth shut. Bad dream, huh?"

She nodded and her long hair made a whooshing sound on the small pillow.

"Does that happen a lot?"

Dawn didn't want to answer that one.

"Not really."

They faced each other, and Monte reached over and tucked a strand of Dawn's hair behind her ear. His eyes were almost yellow, inches away from hers. She could see them even in the dark. They looked like tiger eyes, with deep golden hues. It was the first thing she'd ever noticed about him. Those eyes.

He leaned in to kiss her, but she pulled back. "What are you doing? You promised."

"I know, but I like you a lot. You like me too."

Sure, but that didn't mean she'd disobey God.

"Can I take you on a date when we get back to town? It's just dinner. Nobody will see us."

A piece of his brown hair fell across his high cheekbone, and her stomach flipped. He was really handsome, and all of a sudden, she felt like maybe she could kiss him. A kiss wouldn't mean anything. It's not like it was sex. Or maybe she was rationalizing it.

Monte pulled her sleeping bag down so the zipper whined in a quick burst and then crawled on top of her.

"No, get off me." She tried to shove him, but he was too heavy.

"It's all right, D. I know it's your first time. I'll be careful."

An animal howled just as Monte was pulling down his boxers.

"What was that?" he whispered, moving off her, propped up on one elbow.

She moved away, smashing herself against the small tent's side, and zipped her bag back up.

"Oh, just ignore it." How could he try that with her? He knew her feelings about premarital sex! She should ditch him, leave him to manage by himself. He was a city boy who didn't know anything about the woods.

Another howl.

"That's pretty hard to ignore. It sounds really close," he said.

"I've been in the woods all my life. It's nothing. Just go to sleep. It won't bother you if you ignore it."

She turned her back to him and pretended to go back to sleep.

Monte sat up, straining to listen.

The sound rang out again, louder than before.

"I have to go see what it is."

"What? No." Dawn whipped around, grabbed his forearm.

She was angry, but she didn't want him wandering the woods at night. Wouldn't wish that on an enemy.

Another howl.

"I'm going."

Dawn pulled hard on his arm. He lost his balance and all six-feet-plus of his bulk tumbled on top of her.

"What the hell, D?"

"Do not go," she said slowly, in her firmest voice.

The thing cried out again.

Monte had gotten away from her and was pulling his shorts on. Lacing up his boots.

"Monte, listen to me. You don't know Pate. You can't go chasing after strange noises in the woods!"

"Shit, where's my flashlight?" he said, feeling around in the dark, his body making a zipping sound against the tent's fabric.

Why wouldn't he listen? She shoved the sleeping bag aside and felt around for her shorts. They kept bumping into each other, Monte looking for a flashlight, and she trying to get dressed.

She had her shorts on now, and her hand felt around for her boots. Instead, it touched the flashlight. She shoved it in the back waistband of her shorts. Maybe if he didn't have the flashlight, he wouldn't—

"Fuck it, I'm going without a light," he said, trying to get the tent door unzipped.

"Are you crazy? You don't know your way around. Let's just go home. I'll come back tomorrow and pack up camp."

He was already outside the tent, standing in silence, listening.

She fumbled out behind him, bending down to clear the tent's opening, and just as she got her balance, the thing called out again.

Monte looked around, like choosing a direction. Then he ran.

TWENTY-SEVEN

"MONTE! WAIT!" DAWN flicked the flashlight on, but nothing happened. She hit it against her hand a few times, and it came on.

He was already way ahead of her. She couldn't see him, but his footsteps crunched pine cones, and she could hear that he lost footing, slid, and then got up and scrambled into a run again. She followed the ruckus he was making, desperate to bring him back to the reality of his situation.

"Monte! Stop!"

He wasn't listening. Hadn't listened the whole time. Idiot. There was no sense yelling anymore. It might just attract unwanted attention anyway.

Dawn took sure steps, holding the light where her next one should be. Dodging big rocks, downed branches, avoiding pine cones wherever possible—it wasn't totally possible, so a few got smashed underfoot along the way. There was a shard of moonlight, but it was dark out. How was Monte navigating the woods so well? A finger of panic tapped at her chest. Maybe she could just turn the other way and run. Flee, like she had that day her dad disappeared. Go crying back to her mom. Back to safety.

Not this time.

Dawn moved uphill, skirting past a sea of tree trunks. The trees were so tight, she had to alternate her eyes between the next uphill step and whether there was a trunk in front of her face, just waiting to block the way. Using her hands to navigate them, she shined the light on bark upon bark upon bark. Dried sap stuck to her palms, and she mindlessly tried to rub it on her shorts.

The howling, the cry, whatever it was, started up again.

She stopped and listened for Monte's loud forest bumbling.

Pine cones crunched. He was close, so she went back to climbing the mountain.

She had a bad feeling about where he was headed. Then her light flickered off.

She hit it against her hand.

Nothing.

Keep going. Stop him.

Another howl.

She slipped on pine needles blanketing the earth, sharp pain in her knees from falling uphill. They were probably bleeding.

Something else was nearby. She felt its presence here even though she saw nothing, heard nothing.

He's always watching you, Dawn.

God was always watching. Not her dad, she reminded herself. She spun around and sat against the hill. Something was definitely there with her.

"Monte?" she said in a weak voice. "Is that you?"

No. Stop it. Monte's ahead, about to run into danger. He isn't here trying to scare me.

She stood, but her legs felt like Dad's abandoned rigs in the backyard. Heavy steel on cinder blocks.

More howling.

She returned to climbing.

It's your sin that's got me so I'm not right with God.

"Shut up!" she shouted. It wasn't her dad, he wasn't there. Couldn't be.

Barely ahead, pine cones crunched. She stopped to listen and wished she'd checked the batteries in that flashlight. The darkness made everything worse.

"Monte?" she whispered.

Again, no answer.

She took a deep breath and said, "Dad?"

Blood pumped inside her ears while she waited.

Nothing. She exhaled.

But there again, pine cones crunching. Someone was taking steps just ahead of her. It had to be Monte.

She picked up the pace even though her thighs burned and her lungs were on fire.

Finally, she recognized her surroundings. The steep hill came to an abrupt halt, and a flat clearing sprawled out in front of her. No animal sounds, only the tiny stream was audible. Ahead, that freaky weird mine.

"Monte?" she rasped out, trying to be quiet.

"D?"

The voice came from her left. She turned and saw him. Somehow, she'd made time with him, and he hadn't gone inside yet. That was a miracle.

"We have to go!" She ran over and let herself fall against his bulk.

He held her loosely, distracted.

"Now!" She pulled his arm at the elbow.

He didn't budge.

She got in front of him, but was no match for his size.

He took a step forward, and she put her arms out, clamping them on his shoulders, locking her elbows, leaning in.

"No! Stay. Don't go in." She leaned her full body weight into the effort, trying to brace him so he couldn't take a step.

He took a step sideways, and she fell to the ground hard.

"Have to see," he said, taking more slow steps. "Gotta know what's in there."

Dawn got up and ran in front of him again.

"You don't. You really, really don't." She grabbed his arm and tried to tug him back. He flicked his arm, and she fell on her knees and cried.

"Don't go in! Please don't."

"Have to," he mumbled, still walking trance-like.

She got in front of him once more. It was her last chance. He was just steps away from the entrance.

The soft blue light inside the mine came on.

She slapped Monte across the cheek as hard as she could.

"Shit! Why'd you do that, D?" Monte looked right at her for the first time. Praise God. He was coming out of it.

Then another howl from inside. Softer, more desperate.

"What *is* that?" Monte stepped past her, took another step. And another.

Dawn put her face in her hands and cried.

He was inside the mine.

She sat down, facing away from the entrance, and sobbed harder than she had in years.

Monte was gone.

TWENTY-EIGHT

SYL PACED AROUND a folding chair at the station, chewing the inside of her cheek. Another person missing.

Monte Shrake's mom had called Roger last night after she couldn't find her son at all that day. She'd called all his friends, and none of them knew where he was.

"We should go look for him," Syl said.

Roger flattened his lips. "New kid in town, lives alone. Don't know him well, but one thing I do know is his mom's overly involved in his life. Could be a lot of things, like a twenty-something trying to get away from an overbearing mother, for one. I don't see how it involves the police at this point."

Mac brought Syl a cup of coffee even though she was already jittery from the cups she had at home. She smiled big at him just to burn Roger. "Thanks, Mac, you're the best cop in this building."

Roger rolled his eyes and motioned with his head for her to come to his desk and sit. But Syl didn't think she could sit still even if she wanted to. She had to be up, moving around. How could they let a missing man go like that? No effort at all? It wasn't right.

Mac stared at her, waiting for something. What? A tip? No, he'd made the coffee—some special brew—and he wanted to watch her take a drink. Creepy, but whatever. She took a sip. It tasted better than any coffee she'd had in months.

"It's amazing. Thanks, Mac."

Mac rubbed his hands together like he was trying to light a fire with two sticks. He smiled, and then spun and walked away.

"God help me. These 'nineties men' will be my ruin." Roger said.

"You know, Roger, you spend a lot of effort pretending like you don't care, like you live in a John Wayne world. I bet you're exhausted at the end of the day."

He waved Syl's comment off. That must be his universal signal for being out of comebacks. She'd won that round, so she smiled, took another big sip of coffee.

"Clock's ticking." Syl looked at her wristwatch. "Maybe we could find this one."

"Maybe Monte simply went on a weekend bender and didn't want to tell his mom."

"Or any of his friends?"

"Who knows."

"I'm going over to his house. Can you give me directions?"

Roger peeled a sticky note and started writing. "Suit yourself."

SYL PULLED UP to the address. There was a gold Beetle in the driveway, but no portraits affixed to Monte's place. Interesting. She knocked, waited. Knocked again, waited more. It was a rundown duplex, typical for a young man barely in his twenties.

The lawn was dead except for patches of feisty cheat grass. The long, thin window next to the front door was made of privacy glass, so she couldn't see into it. If she stretched on her tiptoes she could probably look through the front picture window. She cupped her hands around her eyes and squinted.

"Can I help ya?" The man's voice startled her, like he was the cop and she was breaking the law. He came out the other side of the duplex.

"Yes, thank you. My name's Syl Dixon, and I'm looking for Monte. Just helping the sheriff out with—"

"You're tryin' a find that killer." His tough-guy act seemed to visibly fall to the lawn, lush and green on his side of the property.

He leaned in like they were in cahoots and whispered, "You guys thinkin' it's Monte? Between me and you, I can see it."

"Why do you say that, Mister..."

"Daggerty. Cliff Daggerty." He stuck his hand out and walked toward her like it was a leash pulling him. She shook it.

"I wonder if you could help me out at all." Syl looked past Cliff, suddenly needing to confirm whether he had portraits. Affirmative. At least two next to the doorframe.

"Will if I can." He stuffed his hands into threadbare Carhartt pockets and bent forward a little.

"Have you seen Monte today? This morning maybe?"

"Nope."

"Seen anything out of the ordinary around here in the past couple days?"

"Eh, Monte's always actin' strange. Runnin' round so much, he can't see to his property."

"Other than that, what have you noticed? Any visitors lately?"

He tilted his chin toward the sky and closed his eyes as if she asked him a high-stakes *Jeopardy!* question.

"Just his ma, but she comes by every dern day. Sometimes twice a day, so that's nothing out of the ordinary, as you say."

"Did you see him yesterday at all?"

Chin to sky again, eyes squeezed shut.

"Naw, last time I really recall seein' him was two days ago. It was 'round suppertime when he got in that noisy Bug and left. I was out here, waterin' my lawn. You can tell a lot about a man by how he keeps his lawn. I move my sprinkler 'round all morning to make sure it gets coverage." He said it like *coverge*.

"Well, not even a minute after he left, he swung that jalopy back into the drive and ran into the house. Then he came out again. Didn't seem like he grabbed nothing. Thought that was strange, so I says, 'Where you off to in such a hurry?' He jolted like I'd poked him with a cow prod, and then he says, 'Late for work.' Didn't wait for me to say nothing else, just got into that Bug and left."

"And did he come home late? Maybe you heard him. You know how noisy those young boys can be."

She didn't know if they were, but she knew Cliff thought so.

"Aw hell, they're so noisy! Didn't hear nothin' that night though. Bug was gone all day, and then it came back, but I didn't see him. Just seen that Bug there that next morning, setting in the driveway like that." He pointed to the car.

She thanked Mr. Daggerty and turned to leave, when he shouted:

"Did hear another car pull up that night though. Not sure what time. Can always tell when cars stop over there." He pointed a thumb at Monte's side of the duplex. "Lights flash right into our bedroom winda'. Used to make my Doris batshit."

"Are those pictures of Doris?"

Why not sneak it in among the other questions? Syl walked back over to him.

Cliff turned around to look at the portrait on the house and then gave Syl a hard stare. She asked another question before he could dismiss her. "Was it after midnight? Or earlier, you think?"

Chin to sky, like it was Final Jeopardy and he had thousands to lose. It looked painful. Cliff pulled a hand out of his work pants and started counting on his fingers.

"I don't know. I watch my programs until nine, take a bath, then get in bed. I know it were dark out when them headlights came flashin' to wake me up, but that don't say a lot. I'm asleep by ten every night. Happened sometime after that. Sorry I can't give you more particulars." He said it like *particklers*.

"Well, you could have led with this. Did you see who got out of the car?"

"Naw, couldn't make it out. Do recall it was a lady though. I remember thinkin' 'bout what I'd do if I were young enough for a lady friend to come callin' at that hour, boy howdy."

He waited for Syl to ask what he'd do, but Hell would freeze over first. She thanked him and left.

PATE, IDAHO

January 1962

TWENTY-NINE

ONCE MY FEET stood on that clearing, I wiped sweat off my fore-head and walked over to the mine like a goddamned fool. I took the lamp off my satchel and lit it. Standing at the black entrance, I felt something dark. I'm not overdoing it to say it felt like death. Then something spoke up inside me, made my heart beat fast and my mind sharp. Told me to run. Run for my ever-lovin' life. But my feet were going toward the mine. Lots of times in my life, I could have made a better decision, could have stopped what was coming, but this wasn't one of them. I was moving my own feet, sure. But stopping would have been like dying of starvation while sittin' before a feast, or letting your throat crack and dry out while holding a bucket of drinking water in your very own hand.

Inside the mine, the howling went on. Came from deep within. There was this blue light, so I followed it like a dupe. I kept stepping, until I came nose up to a huge silver vein. The sort prospectors dream of. Biggest lode I'd ever seen or heard of! But this was no ordinary silver ore. It made that whole damn cavern glow.

I couldn't take my eyes off it. Looking into that vein, I seen I was lost in the spiritual sense. That I'd always be lost and no amount of saving or finding could fix it. Despair and fear came. Like embers that'd always smolder inside me, no matter what. Then these embers bursted into flame. The flame singed my feet and burned up my legs, scorching as it took me over, an inch at a time. I couldn't move. When it had swallowed my neck, it stalled just under my chin.

I was about to plummet into deep despair when a woman came to me. Not a real woman, I suppose, but I'll get to that. She put that fire clean out, breathed life into me. Promised to let me see Rose. She asked me if I wanted that. I said yes. I could have said no. I should have, pup. The minute I said yes, she changed. Became misshapen and hideous. She opened her mouth and it grew, took up her whole face, and out came that haunting call I'd followed. I covered my ears. Was afraid they'd bleed.

Next, I seen myself covered in blood, smiling. I felt the power of killing, the way taking life could make me stronger. The way it fed her. All the veins in my body lit up, it was almost magical looking, glowing, and I would have marveled if I weren't scared shitless.

"That's not me!" I hollered. "I'm no murderer!"

Her laugh pounded inside me. Doesn't matter, she said. You will be. Like the ones before you.

I couldn't pull my eyes away from that silver vein in order to shake it. I was hooked in like a trout on a line. All the fear and dread she promised to remove came back stronger. It seethed, gathered up power inside me like I might erupt and gush out an entire civilization's worth of terror. Felt like I was carrying all that darkness inside me, and truth be told, I was, in a sense. In my blood runs all the things my ancestors had done wrong. The potential that I could do those things too. That Mason could, and down the line.

Then, in my mind's eye, I saw that dribble of poison leaking out of Lucky Dog. The brown liquid turned to bright blood as it tangled with fresh water, forming putrid sludge. Left alone and naked to do its thing, it floated through the river until it sank out of sight. I seen it settle at the depths of Great Pine Lake. It slept there, waiting for someone or something to dare to disrupt it, so it could attack with its poison. Whatever poison didn't make it to the lake bottom, came ashore with the river current. There, sunshine baked it into flakes of fine dust. And then the wind, pup. I seen the wind carry that poison dust to small lungs playing, sleeping, crying for their mothers. I cried out, but couldn't stop it. It went on and on and on. Babies became mothers, who birthed babies who became mothers. All the while, blood was being shed, and the earth was dying.

I thought of you, pup, and that's what finally gave me the strength to look away from the glowing vein.

When I ran out of the mine, it was night. A whole day had passed and only the deep, dark woods surrounded me.

I never did tell Harold about finding that godforsaken place. He'd think I was crazy.

The image of blood-poisoned water, and the cycle of things birthed in us that we can't control, haunted my dreams at night. Something had happened to me in that mine, and I felt like it was my job to keep it in, whatever it was inside me. I never knew for sure that anything was different until one morning when I came down the stairs to start the coffee.

It was a warm summer day, and already the temperature had climbed, so I didn't need my robe. But when I reached the kitchen, I realized my smokes were in that robe, and so I went back to fetch them. I shuffled past the spare bedroom and heard something behind the closed door. It sounded like a laugh.

It was Rose's old room. I didn't have the heart to clear it out after she died, and so it had sat, door closed, for almost a decade.

The light was off inside the room, and the curtain must have been drawn, too, because the slip of space below the door was black. I touched the door handle and then scolded myself. My imagination was running away with me again.

I stepped away to get my smokes.

Another laugh rang out. This time I heard the squeak in it.

I stopped, and that's when I felt a blast of cold that made me shiver so deep, I felt it in my guts.

Something tapped on the floor from inside the spare bedroom.

I knew the sound. It was Rose's dolls. She used to hold them up and make them dance. Porcelain feet hitting the floor.

I put my hand on the knob again and held my breath as I gave it a little turn, opened the door slowly.

The light of the hallway illuminated a sliver against the floor and wall of the dark bedroom.

"Rose?" I whispered, my voice cracking.

Nothing.

My breathing quickened. I wanted to slam that door and never go in again, but I couldn't. I had to know who made those sounds.

"Rose?"

I reached for the light switch. Nothing happened. Of course, the bulb would be burned out. We hadn't been in that room for so long.

Then I heard quick shuffling on the floor over by the small bed.

I came close to it, stepping so my slippers wouldn't clack on the wood floorboards.

The dust ruffle shimmied.

Maybe it was a mouse, something explainable.

My fingers touched the dusty scalloped fabric and I lifted ever so gently.

Two glowing silver circles against pitch darkness stared back at me.

I swallowed a scream. Forced myself to stay put.

Then I did something I'm sure makes me insane. I reached in to feel if it was real. Maybe I was just seeing things. My hand touched soft curls and I pulled it back.

That's when I did scream. I dropped that dust ruffle and ran out of the room, slamming the door behind me...

PATE, IDAHO

1905

STEPH NELSON

THIRTY

BY THE TIME Holver noticed Lily acting odd, she'd birthed him two children. Owen was three, and then there was the girl, Katie, two years old. They'd lived in Pate for four years.

It was always dark when Holver ended his shift in the mine. Walking out of Lucky Dog, he felt the sharp, cold air, and the first thing he noticed was his house across the river. A place he'd built with his own two hands. Holver grew up in Spokane, so he understood snow, but winters in the mountains were much harsher, and he knew he needed a large fireplace when he built the house. Good thing he was more than a stable boy, although he didn't let this on to very many people. He was nothing like other men, strutting around as if they were something special, better than they actually were.

Holver never let others see what he was capable of. That's how they controlled you. Let them think you're weak, a buffoon even. That way, you were free to act as you wanted, and nobody was the wiser.

He waved goodbye to the other men he worked Lucky Dog with, and Percy Burgh waved back. Percy always arrived at the same time as Holver—before sunup. From outside the mine, the little house looked like a bright orange blaze. Lily liked going to bed early, so usually the place was dark when he got off shift. She had the fireplace going this time. Holver had made a trade for the supplies needed to build it. His stash of whiskey for the mason's rock pile and mortar. He'd sworn off the whiskey when he married Lily.

The blaze worried him as he slogged toward it in the dark. It was too much for the small hearth and it was a God-awful waste of good firewood. What was Lily doing?

Holver came into the home, stomped out his boots and worked to set his helmet and lamp down by the front door. There was no supper waiting. Lily sat in the wooden rocking chair, staring out the front window into the darkness he just came from. The fire shone bright on her right side, with the dark side of her facing him.

This wasn't the first time Lily had been strange. A fortnight ago, he'd woken up to her coming in the front door at an ungodly hour. He'd rubbed his eyes to be sure he wasn't just seeing things, but he wasn't. She wore her night dress, and crept into bed smelling of pine. Real strong, like she'd been rolling around in it.

That next morning, she had been pouring cups of flour into a bowl to make bread when he was on his way out to Lucky Dog.

"Why'd you go out of doors last night?"

She'd given him the sort of laugh that made him feel small. "I didn't!"

"You did. I saw you darken the door after midnight. What were you doin'?"

Lily faced him, with flour all over her hands and apron. "Holver, that's ridiculous. I didn't go outside even a step yesterday. Let alone at night!"

"You were in your night dress. Smelled like trees when you come in."

She laughed hard now. "You've been dreaming, dear! Quite realistic, I suppose, but just dreams, nonetheless."

Tonight, he stood over her, between her and the fire so that his shadow cast across her and put her in total darkness. His eyes worked best in the dark anyway. What, with being underground from before sunrise to after sunset.

Lily's brown eyes were red and swollen all around.

"Fire's too big," he said.

"The light will bring her home."

He squatted as close to the blaze as he could, in order to break those logs down somehow.

"Bring who home?"

"Katie." Lily said from behind him. "She's gone."

"What d'ya mean?"

Still looking out the window, Lily said, "She wasn't in her bed this morning. Owen told me she got up in the middle of the night, but he fell asleep and doesn't recall anything else. If she sees the fire, she'll be able to find her way back."

"I don't believe a word of it. Where've you got her?" He was walking around the place, looking under blankets and furniture.

"Why would I hide her from you?"

THE FIRE WILL *make it right.*

That's what the voice had said to Lily, so she obeyed and built the largest fire she could manage. It was done, now she just had to wait.

Holver went out the back door with a lantern and Lily stood to follow.

"Katie!" His voice cracked over by the shed. A raindrop fell on Lily's face, and when Holver looked up at the sky, staggered rain hit his face too. She went inside to get a shawl and returned to stand in the rain and watch.

Holver stumbled around the woodshed, and around the house, shining the lantern on every inch of earth to his name. Shouting Katie's name. Lily knew it wouldn't help, but she figured her husband had to try.

Lily stood there in the back doorway, her arms folded across her chest, shielding her eyes from the rain. Holver was climbing the small, steep hill behind the shed now, big boots slipping on soaked pine needles, which caused his knees to collide with the wet mud more than once. Rain pelted him now, drenched the ground. Lily stepped back under the roof's small eave. It didn't keep her out of the rain, but it helped a little.

She watched Holver finally reach the small meadow atop the hill, look back at her from the considerable distance, then disappear behind the shed, away from her sight.

THE MEADOW WAS flat except for a small mound at the edge, where it became the forest again. Behind the shed, a shovel had been tossed beside a fresh pile of dirt. Holver looked back to the house, to Lily standing down there, immovable in the doorway, blanket wrapped around her shoulders, watching him. He then ducked behind the shed and took up the shovel.

"Forgive me, Lord," he whispered and then dug into the dirt.

Katie wasn't buried deep, so he had her above ground in minutes. The rain did most of the work washing the mud away. He held the lantern high. Her face was shriveled up, making her look near to a skeleton. Like she'd starved to death even though she'd only been missing one day. She weighed almost nothing when he removed her to make a deeper hole, give her a proper burial.

He piled needles on top of the makeshift grave. Wasn't like he could go into town and get her a headstone. People would ask too many questions. Questions he could never answer.

He peered around the corner of the shed and saw that Lily had gone back inside, so he made his way down.

Removing his boots and shaking off his hat as he entered the back door, Holver said, "Can't find Katie anywhere." Then he took Lily's chin, forcing her to look at him. "What happened to my girl?"

Lily pulled her face from his grip and started crying. "I don't know! She was my baby girl, I looked for her all day, and so did Owen."

Holver grabbed her by the arms. "You take her out of doors on one of your midnight romps? Did you hurt her?"

"No! Never! Why would I do that?"

"You don't remember things right, Lil. Been months and months now of you actin' crazy."

She put her face into her slim hands and sobbed. "I didn't hurt her! I could never! She was gone, Holver. Gone when dawn broke. Already gone..."

PATE, IDAHO

1910–1911

THIRTY-ONE

IT WAS A Sunday when Pate's first snowfall of 1910 arrived. Holver was on his way out the back door to chop wood. He expected snow this soon. Lily was in her rocking chair, where she'd spent the better part of the five years since Katie died. By now, Holver was used to coming home and seeing her set right there, and no supper.

"I'm with child," Lily said, like you'd say, "Pass the butter."

Holver looked her way, didn't say a thing, and then went out. His feelings toward Lily hadn't been the same since Katie died.

That evening, Lily was in the bedroom, brushing out her waist-length hair. She braided it, wrapped it up under a nightcap, and then got into bed. He stood there, watching her, but she didn't seem to notice him.

When Lily didn't get up the next day, Holver went in to check on her. She was in bed still, but her eyes were open.

"Lil?"

Nothing.

Sometimes she slept with her eyes open. It bothered him, but he'd just roll over in bed and face the wall instead of staring into her dead-open eyes. Holver thought maybe she was actually dead this time. He put his finger under her small nose but felt hot breath.

Maybe she was sick. After all, being pregnant usually tired her out in the early days. But after three days of her not even getting up to eat, he was sure something was wrong. He fetched the doctor, who came along, swinging his medicine case.

Doc examined her, but left his medicine case at the entrance, and so Holver opened it. You never knew what you might need. Penicillin would be nice to have around the house, for one. Holver wasn't a thief, but he liked to be prepared. Life started him off with no advantages, and so he'd learned to make his own, just like his pa taught him. He helped himself to a few other things and had it closed by the time the doctor emerged, saying Lily seemed fine. Your typical early-stages pregnant mother. Doc thought maybe there was some grief over losing Katie mixed in there.

Holver took Lily a cup of tea every morning and made sure she ate every day. He even took her to the outhouse when he got home from the mines. Owen was eight years old and independent, able to get himself to school.

And then, spring came, and like Lily was waking from a single night's sleep, she stirred when the first forest birds cracked their song from the trees. She heaved her large belly out of the bed, changed out of her night dress, and spent the days outdoors gardening, harvesting berries, and tending to the apple tree that Holver had planted the year he built the house. She added irises and roses around the perimeter until the whole thing was surrounded by gardens upon gardens. Holver didn't mind that one bit. Those were good days.

Lily seemed bigger than normal with this child, though, and Doc came to check up on her. "Might be two babes, but won't know until they're here. Should be any day," he'd said. That old coot didn't even ask about the missing medicine. If Holver had known he was such a dupe, he'd have swiped two bottles of penicillin instead of one.

"I don't want more babies," Lily said after the doctor left.

"Too late for that. Babies are comin'."

"I'm afraid, Holver." Lily sat up best she could, and he saw she'd been crying again. "Afraid I won't be able to protect them."

"From what?"

She shrugged. "There's this voice inside that tells me what to do."

"What sorta stuff's it tellin' you?"

"Sometimes nothing too big, but other times, it tells me to do things that don't make sense."

"Stop listenin' then. Just stop."

Lily nodded, laid down, and went back to sleep.

The babies came, and Holver trudged through the snow, coming home from work one night. The winter's chill cut through his warmest overcoat. It wasn't time for snowshoes yet, but it'd get there soon enough. The glow of firelight against pure darkness made him stop in his tracks. Lily had that fire blazing again, confound it.

Owen slinked out from behind a tree.

"Been watching for you, Pa," he said, teeth chattering.

Holver startled and saw the cloud of warm breath from Owen's words.

"Son, you'll freeze your tail clean off out here."

Owen looked at their home behind him. "Pa, something happened."

"JOE WASN'T IN his bed this morning," Lily said. She was awake, although groggy. "I don't remember. I don't remember anything..." she cried. What would Holver think?

She had gone to the cradle that morning, and when she saw Joe missing, she picked up Jake, the other twin. She looked into the child's face. Did he know what happened? Surely, he saw the whole thing. Lily had held the baby so his face was even with hers and squinted to see if she could divine anything from it.

"What did you see, darling? Tell me, please," she whispered.

Now Jake cried, and Holver went to his cradle when he saw Lily wasn't making a move to soothe the baby.

Lily suddenly noticed Owen's absence, and a bolt of fear ripped through her. "Where's Owen?"

"Done sent him to bed."

She relaxed.

Holver bounced the child in his arms. Lily could tell he was angry, but she couldn't move herself out of the chair. Couldn't face baby Jake tonight.

"Holver, remember how I told you sometimes I hear a voice?"

Jake was really taking off now, a droning scream that Lily saw raked Holver's nerves. "And I said stop listenin'. What of it?" he asked over the noise.

"Yes, I've been trying that, but lately I'm not awake much, and I don't remember, so I don't know if..."

"Lily, you need to stop listenin' to what you're hearin' in your head. Ain't real. The kids, they're real. Our life, that's real."

"I don't trust myself," she whispered.

"You gotta stop listenin'. It's lyin' to ya. You gotta be stronger. Control your fury."

She looked at him now. What did that mean? *Control your fury?*

"Kids need their mother," Holver said, handing Jake to her.

Lily's sobs came in heaves.

THIRTY-TWO

LILY WAS TIRED. So very tired even though she was in bed. All she'd done for days was lie in bed. The bedroom window allowed weak sun to streak through thin curtains. She tried to sit up, but the room spun. It wasn't worth the effort, so she lay down again.

Sheer darkness met her eyes the next time she opened them. Holver was snoring beside her. Sleep found her again, although she didn't remember dozing off. The light woke her. She tried to stand, but her knees wobbled, and she dropped back onto the mattress. The springs sang out.

What day was it?

She looked through the small window and saw snow heavy on pine. It was drafty in the room, and her teeth chattered. Lily hated the winter. Why had she come here at all? To this place where winter consumed most of the year.

You have to get up.

It was the voice. Cursed voice. She couldn't listen to it. She wouldn't. She wanted to get up though. Maybe just this once, she'd listen. One leg, then the other, until both bare feet touched the cold slats of the wood floor. She leaned forward to put weight on them. They trembled from the effort once again, but she braced herself with a hand on the bed's brass headboard. There was the door handle. A few more steps and she could open it.

Thoughts of Katie and Joe came, and she felt numb. Had Holver done something to them? No, Holver wasn't the one with a violent past. He was a good man. He was nothing like her, and yet, how could she hurt her own children? Then again, how could she have hurt Margaret? She couldn't stop herself, and then it was over in a breath. Lily whimpered, and tears wet her face. She was alone with this blackness inside. Except not alone, because there were still two other children she was supposed to care for. How could she continue like this? Holver tried his best, but he didn't understand. Nobody did. Nobody ever had. All Lily had wanted was to make her own way. To live life on her own terms, to have children and take care of them. Protect them.

Her hand squeezed the cold brass so tight, her knuckles turned white. Her whole body wavered like she might collapse.

Holver opened the door.

"Lil! What're ya doin'? Here, let me help ya get back in bed. You're sick again." He put the back of his hand against her forehead. "You don't feel feverish, but take it easy. Rest. I brought you tea and a piece a bread. You'll feel better after you eat somethin'."

Lily sat on the edge of the bed and took the cup and saucer from his huge hands. Holver knew best these days, and she was grateful for his help. The porcelain clattered, but she had a sip, a few bites of bread, then fell asleep.

Lily was surrounded by darkness. It was damp. Cold. She heard a dripping noise, but what could it be? Then a baby screamed. She couldn't see in the dark, but she felt dirt between her fingers. Rock along the wall. She stood up, and a blue light shone all around her. It lit up a tunnel, and she couldn't help it, she had to walk deeper into it. One foot in front of another until she tripped over something. On her knees, she saw what it was. A baby. Joe! It was Joe, but he was like a skeleton. And Katie, laid out next to him, a skeleton too. Then the Katie skeleton sat up and said, "You were supposed to take care of us."

Lily screamed. She woke up to the sound of a baby crying. Screaming, in fact.

She was in her bed, like usual. It was still daylight outside. The house was quiet. Children must be at school. She rolled over to Holver's side of the bed to look into Jake's cradle. He was fast asleep.

There was no screaming baby at all, she must have dreamed that too.

She spun from the exertion it took to lean across the bed. By the time her head found the pillow, she was asleep again.

PATE, IDAHO

July 1989

THIRTY-THREE

LUCAS'S FACE BARGED into Syl's brain right as she laid her head on the pillow. God, it was going to be one of those nights. She'd been doing well, keeping her mind so busy it didn't have time to harass her with Lucas-thoughts.

(You should call him.)

Can't. I'm working a case.

(No, you're getting ready for bed.)

But she'd already dosed herself, and in less than ten minutes, she'd feel like she was under a comforter made of lead.

Where would she begin even if she did speak with Lucas? What, after so many weeks of radio silence?

Sorry, I probably never should have had children. You understand, right, five-year-old?

Pointless. He was too young to understand and too old to slip a quick call in without existential questions like, "When are you coming home?" pointed right at her.

Still, his face.

The way his little forehead always screamed to be kissed between the eyebrows. That face would thin out soon and produce acne, and then he'd be in the world of dating, and growing facial hair. Then SAT tests, college applications, and—

Syl squeezed her eyes shut. Fine to think about him, fine to miss him even. But fast-forwarding his life like this only tricked her into thinking she could still be a part of it. That door was closed, she'd seen to it. Syl rewound the mental tape to the forehead image and recalled what that spot of Lucas's head felt like against her warm lips. Memories of him as a baby were all she had a right to. That time frame when she'd been a real mother to Lucas. As long as she kept her mind there, she was fine.

Syl turned to look out the window, but with the bedside lamp still on, it was a black square. Like a mine entrance. She understood why Roger had cracked, left Lucky Dog in such a hurry that first day. He was an odd bird, but Pate's mines were creepy. Even so, she couldn't dismiss the thought that he was holding back information. But what could she do? You can't make a man speak.

When will these sleeping pills kick in?

Syl took out her French braid and shook her head. Her hair expanded into a huge lion's mane. She rubbed her scalp to relieve the tightness. It'd frizz her hair out even more, but who cared? Nobody here to see it.

God, and that howl. The woods felt more active than anything she'd known before. Why *were* those mines so creepy? Was it because so many men had died? They were essentially burial grounds when you thought of all the miners who were trapped inside and never recovered. Early blasts they couldn't outrun, cave-ins they couldn't escape. The job was full of danger, and death was almost an inevitability.

Just then, something moved outside, down in the yard.

Syl flicked the lamp off to get visibility, so she wasn't in a fishbowl if someone was out there. She walked over to the window to see what it was. She waited there in just her tank and underwear, and a shiver of cold went through her body. It was unusual to get a chill, because up here in Gran's room, it was extra hot during the summer.

All she heard was the whirring of the box fan she never turned off. All she saw was her own reflection in the window. The shape of a tiny teenager with crossed arms, waiting for her life to start. She'd spent all of her twenties on the kind of living that earned most people wrinkles. You'd think smoking, refusing sunscreen, staying up late, and getting up early would do it. If not, a steady diet of Frosted Flakes and coffee might. Yet, she still looked like a kid.

Syl squinted eyes to blur her own reflection, find the shape of someone more like the person she knew was inside—

There, again, a flash of something down by the barn.

What was that? If it weren't moving around, she'd wave it off as the moon's reflection on some yard ornament, and get into bed. Instead, she put on her robe, grabbed her gun, and went downstairs. It had to be an animal, trespassing onto land that used to belong to its kind. Animals had no sense of property lines, and why should they?

As Syl stepped out into the clear night, a showcase of stars amassed against a liquid navy sky. It looked like an open treasure chest, some mythological god bragging about their diamonds to the mortals below. Her arm felt heavy holding the gun. Sleeping pills were kicking in. She'd have to fight against them to stay alert.

Syl kept the gun's safety on. She wasn't exactly in the frame of mind to handle a live gun, but it'd be a perfect threat to any teens messing around.

"Hey! This is private property. Pick a different way to unleash your anger at the world!" Syl shouted into the quiet night. Then she felt woozy.

Gran's house wasn't exactly downtown, but it wasn't in the boonies either. It was on a corner lot, and cars lined the streets on both sides of the house and barn. Streetlights were sparse, but existent.

"Did you hear me, asshole? Get out of my yard!"

Still no reply, no noise.

But then two small, glowing orbs appeared from the far side of the barn and ducked back immediately.

"What the fuck," she whispered as her brain tried to understand it over the course of one or two seconds.

A cat's eyeshine?

(Too big to be a cat.)

Cat standing on a pile of logs.

(No pile of logs next to the barn.)

A deer?

(Deer would have run off when you yelled.)

Could it be a big cat? Like a mountain lion?

That was where she landed, a mountain lion, but it didn't help her confidence in the situation. She removed the gun's safety, just a flick of the finger, then almost lost her balance.

Shit, she was in no condition for a confrontation. What if she just hallucinated the whole thing? Best thing to do would be to go inside and wait until morning.

Instead, she took steps into the yard, then looked at her feet. No shoes. Gran's yard had gone to pot, thanks to the renters. Where grass used to be, now it was weeds and rocks. Two steps in and the soft arch of her foot found the long, dry spike of an old weed.

"Shit!" she yelped, reaching down to remove the sticker from her flesh.

The barn door was open from when she made a running start at Gran's clutter earlier. She thought she closed it, but she must not have. Not all the way.

She needed shoes. Shoes and a flashlight.

(No, you need to get your ass in bed before the sleeping pills have their way and you spend the night out here with your mountain lion.)

Forget shoes, she'd just take a quick look in the barn. Her eyelids were heavy.

Syl opened the barn door wider, but it was dark inside. She stood hidden behind the door, listening.

Silence.

The minute she walked inside, her foot hit a wooden crate, and she let out another small cry.

Shit, why'd she do that? What sort of detective shouts out their position to a potential intruder over a stubbed toe? Her hands groped around in the dark. Gran's crap was everywhere. There was no way she'd be able to see anything or even move around in the barn without a flashlight.

Syl's eyes were like iron curtains now. She could barely keep them open, let alone focused. Wouldn't adrenaline help keep her awake? Too bad the damn sleeping pills don't work like this at 3 a.m.

If anything productive was going to happen in the barn tonight, she needed a flashlight. She closed the door tight this time and shuffled inside, unsure if she could make it through the kitchen. Where was the flashlight anyway?

The couch called to her on a deep level, so she pointed her little body at it, climbing onto the cushions and landing with one arm and one leg hanging off. Good enough.

SYL WOKE UP and looked at her wristwatch. Goddamn 3:26 a.m.

Instead of going up to her bed, she found her shoes and a flashlight, and went outside. Darkness still settled over the mountains, and the stars sang with light. But at least she was sober.

Were there any tracks? Any sight of big cat tracks would settle it. She'd call animal control and be the town hero who saved all the small children from a hungry mountain lion. But there were no animal tracks, just her own tiny bare feet marks all over the place. The dirt was soft. It would give if anything stood on it.

Syl whisked the flashlight around the property, but still saw nothing. How could a mountain lion be so quiet?

Maybe it was a person, and they hid behind boxes in the barn.

(A person would leave at least one left foot and one right foot mark. It'd be shoe tread.)

There'd be animal tracks if it was a mountain lion!

Then she remembered what Kyle said. His dad in a dream with silver, glowing eyes, and glowing veins.

She was certain of two incongruent things: No way this intruder could be human, but also, it *had* to be human.

THIRTY-FOUR

ESMA HAD ANOTHER bad dream.

She woke herself up crying, quite hard based on what the bathroom mirror told her. Her eyelids were puffy. They squished like tiny water balloons when she pressed them, it was like she'd been crying for hours.

She never woke up at the three o'clock hour, and now she'd done it twice this week. What was going on?

Esma sat on the toilet, thinking about the dream. It had been dark, and in the woods. There was a mine, but that was probably because she'd been thinking about old Moonstep Mine so much, thanks to that unnerving chant Little Esma reminded her about. Either that, or her daily view of Lucky Dog out the front window. Mines were a part of life around here. But there had been a lady there, some old-fashioned pioneer-looking lady. She was covered in blood. Then John showed up, and he walked Esma through the woods and back home together. They were happy.

New tears stung her eyes. Coming out of the bathroom, she noticed Dawn's door open, so she peeked in. Dawn's clean room bore into Esma's soul, asking if Esma was ready to die. She hated tidy spaces! They were so empty, so blank. The energy bothered her. Dawn wasn't home, and so Esma went to close the door so it would stop sending her all those death signals. As she was about to pull it shut, something made her linger instead, silencing the voice of death. How could Dawn get rid of so many things? How did it not feel to her like erasing the future? Forgetting the past. None of her toys or stuffed animals were out on the shelves, no reminders of the girl she used to be before Scary Dawn and then Jesus Dawn took over.

"Dawn?"

Oh, what was she doing? Dawn wasn't home.

The wood flooring was cold on her feet even though it'd probably reach eighty degrees later today. It was late July, and they were coming up on the warmest days of the year in Pate.

Esma walked to the front window to double-check that Dawn's car was gone. Then she went into Dawn's room even though she wasn't supposed to.

Dawn's dirty hamper showed the new peach-colored Bloomsday fun-run T-shirt on the top of the pile. She couldn't remember what day Dawn wore that one. It was her favorite, so maybe yesterday? The girl was probably working a late shift.

Esma sat down on the edge of the made bed and looked around the room. When she turned on the nightstand lamp, the red shade made the room feel moody. A little angry, actually, but not too bad. Sometimes colors affected Esma's read on the energy, and she had to differentiate between the color red feeling angry, and the actual energy in the room being angry. It was the color this time.

All this thinking about John in recent days, longing for him to come home, brought life into clear focus. It was too fast. You can't wait to grow up and be an adult, and then you take a couple breaths, and you're an old lady.

He misses you too.

Esma picked up Dawn's navy-blue diary and felt the cover's canvas fabric. The bulb in the lamp hummed.

All of these little events, experiences that added up to touchstones that made up a life. Until what? It's over? Poof! Just gone? Time for new humans to inhabit the space on the planet that others used to hold? That Esma used to hold?

She was crying again, and so she couldn't see through the tears to read the diary, but she saw a lot of prayers Dawn had written inside. A few copied Bible verses. That was really all the girl thought about now. But Esma knew there was someone else inside there. Where was the Dawn who saw what happened to John that day? Esma closed the diary and stood. The full wastebasket called to her—not audibly, Esma wasn't that crazy—but now the urge was overbearing.

She sorted through Dawn's trash, pulling out grocery receipts, an empty tube of mascara, and a brown apple core. Esma scattered them across her shining wood floor, and she sat next to it, legs out in front, touching each piece and coming up empty. It was all just Jesus Dawn stuff. None of it was anything like what Dawn kept around when John was alive. But what did she expect? A piece of trash with a clue leading to John's whereabouts after ten years? Ridiculous. But where had John gone, and why didn't Dawn remember anything?

She felt John's presence then. It held her, like he was there and could feel her pain.

I'm coming home.

The energy felt the same as in the dream. They were happy, surrounded by hope. She had spent the day focusing her thoughts on John, him coming home, like Little Esma said. She had to see him. If only to ask what happened to him all those years ago. It had felt cold and empty all around her earlier. Now, though, she felt him.

"John?" she whispered. "John? Is that you?" Esma put the wastebasket back together and looked around to be sure everything was the way Dawn left it, then she walked into the kitchen to look out the front window. If it was John, which she hoped it was, surely he'd be out front on the porch, right by his portrait. Then she could decide if she'd let him in, based on how he seemed. But who was she kidding? She'd welcome him inside as long as—

A crash in the woodshed.

It was the same loud bang she'd heard a few nights ago. She spun and walked toward the back door, pulling on her boots and walking out, catching the door before it slapped.

Esma felt John's presence stronger now. Also stronger was her longing for him, unlike anything she'd known before. The night was a bit cooler, and a single owl called out as she approached the shed. Esma held the rusted handle and rubbed her thumb against its ridges, hesitating before going in.

What if she opened the door and it was nothing again? It was always nothing, but she couldn't handle that this time. This time, it had to be *something*.

She pushed the door open slowly and introduced the darkness of the outdoors to the darkness inside the shed. It smelled rotten in there, like an animal had died. Did they have a mice problem?

There was a silver flashlight hanging just inside the door by the jamb. Oh, let the batteries be good. It worked.

"John?" she whispered, walking inside.

Breathe, Esma.

"John?"

She felt movement, but didn't see it, so she shined the light in the direction it was coming from.

There he was, hands over his face. He wore big, clodhopper boots. But when he lowered his hands, she knew it was him.

THIRTY-FIVE

SILVER GLOWING EYES. Syl had to know what the hell it was. She went back out to the barn a third time in twenty-four hours. It was daylight now, and she needed answers.

Wings flapped from up in the loft, and Syl's mind went right to bats even though she knew it was pigeons. They'd broken in through a small window and made their ever-loving home in the loft this summer, but she hadn't made a move toward stopping it. Should have. Now pigeon shit coated the simple wooden stairs leading up to the loft. Maybe she'd just light the whole barn on fire instead of actually sorting through Gran's things when the time came. That was the way to solve a thing Syl Dixon-style: avoid whenever possible, and if not possible, create some chaos in your wake.

Could whoever—whatever—was on her property last night have been hiding up in the loft? The stairs wobbled and creaked as she set foot on them, like they might break even under her scant weight. Her shoes would be covered with bird shit when this was all said and done, but it was the last thing she could think about. As soon as she got up high enough to peek into the loft, she realized it was full of boxes, and tiny. Also, there was a line of crows perched where the pigeons usually were. That was weird, but unimportant. Unless someone was sitting on top of these boxes with their head in the rafters, they couldn't hide up here. How was the loft bearing up under the weight of those boxes in general, let alone if you added a person to the weight? She shooed the crows away and came down the stairs.

Fishing poles lined the inside walls. Nets, snowshoes, some old hunting rifles, and boxes full of... Syl didn't even know what. Parts of old fans, mismatched shoes, handbags, and little veiled hats she was certain Gran never wore, not even in the 1950s. There was crap everywhere. Not to mention all the furniture. Her old white wood bedroom set, including the canopy bed, leaned up against the back wall. The old-fashioned TV that she watched cartoons on. The sort that you had to walk up to and turn the dial in order to change the channel.

What was she looking for here? What did she expect to find?

There was all this mining crap, probably Grandpa's. She was no mining expert, but some of it seemed unique. There were really cool rocks, agates, and small, polished stones. Helmets, lamps, pickaxes. Bookshelves full of classic children's tales and atlases. Fold-up maps. It's not like Gran and Grandpa ever traveled, but maybe they imagined they would someday.

Syl groaned out loud and rubbed her eyes. Then she reached for an apple box, with the name of a central Washington orchard on the sides. The lid made a sucking noise as it came off. Inside was a brown leather photo album. She went from knees to crossed legs right there on the sawdust-covered floor and opened the album.

It was blank, so she turned the page.

Blank.

Another, blank.

What the hell?

Finally, she got to a page with a picture of a beautiful woman. Her mother. Gran had hung her parents' wedding picture up in the hallway when Syl was small, so she knew what her mom looked like. She turned the page of the photo album. Another sea of white space stared back at her. Another page, and then more pictures of her mother. Three more blank pages, and Syl came across one of herself as a child. A black and white photo. She was in a dress, sitting on a little rocking horse. Far in the background was Gran, as if the photographer was taking a shot of Syl, and Gran just happened to be in the frame. Gran wore her favorite green housecoat. Syl recognized it even in black and white because of the grid pattern with random cherry prints. Her salt-and-pepper hair hung long and draped over her shoulders. No shoes. Gran only wore shoes when she went into the woods. Gran was smiling at something off to the side. She looked happy. Gran's handwriting said "June 1961" at the base of the picture. The summer before she disappeared.

Syl stared at the picture, at Gran. Did she know something back then? On the day the photo was taken, was she worried about what was coming? Had she heard that howling in the woods?

She came to the end of the album and that was it. No other pictures. Another album had more pictures in it than the first, but about every third or fourth picture was missing from its slot. Those were all of Syl, just her. Her as a baby, her as a toddler, a small girl. It was as if someone went through all the photographs and removed everything but the pictures of Syl and those few of her mother. But why?

She brought the two albums into the house and set them on the kitchen counter. Enough sorting for the day. Even though it wasn't quite nine in the morning, she was emotionally exhausted and came to exactly zero conclusions about what could have been in the barn that night.

Starving too. She poured a bowl of Fruity Pebbles and opened the refrigerator to get the milk. When she pulled her head out of the fridge, something streaked around the corner into the living room.

What the fuck? She looked around for her gun, but it was still on the coffee table from when she crashed out on the couch early this morning. Syl set the milk down.

Was there really something there, or am I making scary shit up again?

(You'll have to go see. You know you won't be able to settle unless you do.)

She tiptoed over to a kitchen drawer, pulled it open slowly, and found a butcher knife. Taking a few deep breaths, she peeked around the shared wall to see into the living room. There was the wood stove, the plaid couch, and the big front window that looked out at a quiet summer day in a seemingly normal small town. Bare walls, like the rest of the house. God, it was nothing. The insomnia was starting to mess with her waking hours now. She had to figure out how to—

A crash in the kitchen.

Syl grabbed the gun and hid behind the wall on the living room side now. How had whatever it was snuck past her? She listened. It sounded like her bowl of cereal got knocked over. Had a cat gotten in while she was outside in the barn? A cat? Or a bigger animal? She thought of the mountain lion and dismissed that right away. Ridiculous. A really clumsy burglar (cat?) with silver eyes, maybe silver veins? Good God, get a grip.

Hearing nothing else, she slowly stuck her head around the corner.

Nothing.

Except her cereal bowl was upturned. It wasn't broken, but what could have knocked it over?

She cleaned up Fruity Pebbles and poured another bowl. She ate slowly, on alert, trying to figure it out. Finished, she tipped the bowl and drank the colored milk, and set it in the sink, along with the spoon. A jolt of cold out of nowhere rushed across her back. Was she coming down with a bug of some sort? A warm bath would take the chill off her bones. She flicked off the kitchen light and went upstairs to start the tub.

THIRTY-SIX

WHEN SYL PUSHED open the door to Pig Out Place, Pate's only real diner, the smell of bacon and coffee hit her nose. Dishes clinked in the back.

Roger removed his reading glasses and folded the newspaper to find her standing where the waitress usually planted.

Hendon had told her at the station that Roger was having a late breakfast.

"Can I join?"

"Can't stop you."

Syl sat down when the waitress came to take her order. Her name tag said, "Josephine."

"Not Jo?" Syl asked.

"Josephine."

"Everyone around here gets their name shortened. How'd you avoid it?"

"I'm annoying about it. That's the trick. Won't answer unless they say it right. What's your name, darlin'?"

"Sylvia."

"Syl," Roger interjected.

Josephine glared at him and said, "Well, *Sylvia*, what can I get you?" She poured Syl's coffee.

Syl straightened up like she was a Very Important Person. She'd already had breakfast, but what the hell.

"Eggs Benedict, with cheese sauce instead of hollandaise. Wheat toast."

Syl looked at Roger's plate and saw egg whites, oatmeal, and a bowl of fruit. She winced. "Egg whites?"

Roger tapped his chest. "The heart thing, remember?"

"Didn't seem to bother you when you got into the Conders' donuts the other day."

"Eh, win some, lose some."

"Why don't you ever eat at home? Can't Mary cook?" Syl smirked into her coffee like it was the only one that understood her clever joke. When she looked up, Roger wasn't smiling.

"Easier this way. Lets Mary sleep in."

Why did Mary need to sleep in when she was basically a retired housewife? Syl's food arrived, and she spread strawberry jam on her toast.

"Why are you eating the toast first? Who does that?" Roger asked.

She shrugged. He rolled his eyes.

"Since we're here, want to recap where we're at with the case?"

"Why not? It's either that or read about Gorbachev ending the Cold War." He folded the newspaper and took off his reading glasses.

Syl picked it up and flipped a few pages. "Or hey, how about the release of that new Japanese Game Boy toy?"

He rolled his eyes again. He was really channeling teen angst today.

"Where do you want to start this exercise in futility?" he asked.

"A bit further back than Alex's murder." Syl shifted her weight in the diner booth and green vinyl groaned. She wasn't going to tell him about the thing with glowing eyes in the barn, no way, no how. But despite her resolve, it was really all she could think about.

Roger slit his eyes and flattened his lips. "Oh-kay."

"Let's just speculate for fun. See if something pans out."

"Or not."

"Or not," she agreed, and Roger introduced jiggly egg whites into his big yapper.

Gross.

"Let's start with the Markwells. They disappear, and that seems to set off a string of disappearances. Esma told me a lot of people disappear. Plus, she said other odd things happen."

Like beings with glowing eyes that have no footprints.

Or cereal bowls mysteriously falling off countertops.

Roger took a break from shoveling food into his hole to rub his bald head. He sighed.

"Yeah, so people disappear."

Maybe this was her chance to push him on what Esma said.

"Esma said something is coming. She was vague."

"And clearly, Esma is the most reliable source we can think of."

"Fine. Is there a connection with the people who disappear and the photographs on homes?"

The answer was yes, it had to be, she just wanted confirmation. And context.

"Can't say."

Syl sighed. This wasn't helpful.

"Kyle said something strange when I interviewed him. I didn't mention it at the time because it was only something from his dream. His dad, mummified, and with silver glowing eyes and glowing veins. Despite that he didn't know how we found the body."

"I'm sure he heard through the grapevine about the shriveled body. Probably made that other shit up. Too much TV."

"I asked Betty about his exposure to information specifically, and I don't think so. But set the mummy part aside. What about glowing eyes and veins? Ever heard anything like that before?"

Roger took another bite and looked out the window. He seemed to be trying to come up with something. Syl wondered if it'd be the truth or another deflection.

"When I was a rookie, just fresh back from the war, my first call was to the Buckley home. Young family, said someone was coming into their kid's bedroom at night."

"And…?" Syl prompted.

"It was nothing. Didn't see any proof of forced entry through the windows or doors. Dismissed it as the kid's imagination. Parents never saw anything either."

"Did the kid stop complaining about it?"

"No."

"Did the kid know the person?"

"Claimed it was his buddy's older brother. Coached their little league team before the guy disappeared."

"Any other details?"

Here was Roger again, making her drag things out of him.

He cocked his head to the side and took a bite of oatmeal. "Used to appear at the kid's bedside and whisper 'C'mon Ricky, show me that cannon. Throw it right over the bump.' Ricky was a pitcher. Went on to play in the minors."

Not pertinent.

"How about the glowing?"

Roger took another bite and then rubbed his head. God, what was it with him?

"Maybe sounds familiar, can't say for certain. But the boy was terrified of everything in his room. Finally, the parents removed it all except the bed. That worked. They thought he was imagining things. Making up stories about shadows he saw in his room."

"Any other situations like that?"

"Not exactly."

"All right, John Winton, then. Why do you think—"

"You need to get off it with the Wintons. You interviewed them yourself. Nothing special about that case." He sawed a huge piece of cantaloupe in half with a flimsy diner knife, struggling with it until he finally picked it up with two fingers and took a bite.

He was dodgy whenever she mentioned John Winton, but then again, he'd been responsible for investigating that one. Maybe she was banging on a nerve.

"Was there any real-life connection between Alex Conder and John Winton? Same school? Anything?"

"We all went to the same school. Only one school in Pate."

"Just humor me about the Wintons, Roger. You asked for my help."

He sighed and looked sideways at the ceiling while he chewed. "Same school, but different years. John was older."

Syl cut into her eggs Benedict.

"John never had a real job, and Alex always worked construction, so no connection there."

"It's a small town. Surely John and Alex would have known each other somehow."

Roger heaved a slice of canned peach into his mouth, slurping it like a spaghetti noodle. "It's a small town, but it's been ten years since John disappeared. You always forget that part. How does what happened to Alex a decade later have anything to do with John?"

"Just my gut feeling."

"That what they teach at the academy nowadays?" *Slurrrp.* Another peach.

No, it's how sort-of detectives sort-of find killers.

PATE, IDAHO

January 1962

THIRTY-SEVEN

MORE TIME PASSED since I seen those glowing eyes under Rose's bed, and I decided I must be crazy. I needed to get out of town. Thought it was my grief swallowing me whole and turning my mind into mush.

And then, just like an answer to prayer, I read in the newspaper about jobs at a new Spokane air base. Women were keeping the production line running while our boys were at war. "No experience needed! If you can read, you can work on airplanes," it said. I still recall that.

Well hell, I thought, I can certainly read, and most of all, it was my ticket out of town and away from my pain, away from what I saw in that God-awful mine.

I couldn't convince your grandpa to leave with me. Mining was all he knew, and he said he was too old to start a new trade in Spokane. But there's plenty to choose from over there, I'd said. Much safer jobs that pay more money. We fought over it, and he told me to go on without him. He didn't think I'd do it, but he didn't have all the facts about the situation either.

Grandpa took the Greyhound from Pate into Spokane to visit me once or twice a month. Those were good days. We sat outside the base Quonset, smoking cigarettes on my break. I missed him, but I didn't want to go back to Pate.

A girl I worked with had just inherited a rig from her dad who died. She didn't know how to drive it, never got a license, which was crazy to me. All the same, one night I drove it up to Sandpoint with her. We went square dancing. This was the one time since Rose died that I couldn't say no to whiskey, and we both drank so much we all but fell over. Me being a mean drunk, I started to poke fun at her because she couldn't drive. Was foolish, and I didn't know her very well, so I didn't know what she was capable of. She got red-hot angry. This girl was big, real scrappy, and she smashed a glass on the bar floor and then ran hard at me. I had the presence of mind to move to the side and put my foot out so she tripped. I was trying to be funny, make the situation better. I didn't mean for it to happen. But she went headlong into a barrel full of whiskey and broke her neck.

I killed her, pup. She was dead because of me. I thought of the words I heard inside Moonstep Mine. That voice saying I would kill people, that it was in my blood. The deep thrumming of pain and shame came on me in force, as if I hadn't gotten a breather at all. I was afraid of the law now, too, so I hitched a ride south to Pate that night. Nobody at the bar knew us, and nothing came of it. Never told Grandpa about that gal, but he was so tickled pink I was back, he didn't pose any questions.

Christmastime that year came and went. One day, I had the wood stove roaring. I was taking down the Christmas tree, trying not to step in the dry pine needles that had fallen off the poor thing. I'd gotten the ornaments off and was heaving it up to toss out back by the barn, when I heard singing out of nowhere. Faint, couldn't quite make out the song. But then I did.

"Twinkoh, twinkoh, iddoh star..."

My stomach dropped into my socks, and I closed my eyes. How foolish of me to think it had all been in my head. To think I could run away from of it.

I already had the tree in my grip, and it was dripping dead needles and tinsel every second I stood there slack-jawed, so I went on with my task. On the way out the back door, I passed through the kitchen and tried not to drop needles into the plates of cookies I'd made. Pup, maybe you'll remember how every Christmas I make too goddamn much. You'd think I'd learn, but no. I hoped Harold would take the extra plates to the mines with him that morning, put them in the break room. But he forgot.

When I returned to the kitchen through the back door, the plates were empty. Every last cookie had vanished.

The singing started up again.

I got a shiver, but I wasn't too afraid. If it was Rose, she was stealing cookies, for Christ's sake. Wasn't like she wanted to hurt me.

I put a foot on the stairs. Despite the little pep talk I gave myself, my heart hollered at me, swooshing blood in my ears. I wondered if I'd explode from the blood pumping inside. I took one step, then two. The singing stopped. I stopped. Waited.

The singing started up again.

Twinkoh, twinkoh, iddoh star, how I wonner wha' chew are.

The same first verse over and over. It was the only part of the song Rose knew.

And then I saw the door was cracked open. Harold must have gone in there. I sure as hell didn't know why.

I pushed the door open and reached to switch on the light, but once again, it didn't come on. This time, I knew I'd changed the bulb.

Good thing I was smart enough to put a flashlight in that old spare room after the last go round. I flicked that on and moved the light around.

Steps padded behind me and out the bedroom door.

I followed as quickly as I could, but when I got down to the kitchen, I saw nothing.

It was nothing.

The singing had stopped, everything was back to normal.

Exhausted, I dropped my bones into a kitchen chair and pulled out a cigarette. I laughed at myself. Making things up like that. But my chuckles soon slowed as I remembered the cookies and what I had seen in Rose's room, and what I had felt beneath her bed.

My brain buzzed. I tried to make sense of it. It was real! I seen something under that bed, goddamn it.

I walked back up the stairs and into Rose's room. Something drew my attention now that the light was on. An old oval-framed black and white photograph of Rose hanging on the back wall.

It was the only one I had of her. Had it taken just before she disappeared.

I put the flashlight directly on that hanging portrait, and there was Rose in the chair, with a little pull toy at her feet just like the day she sat for that picture. But there was something else that most certainly was not in the picture before. She held a star-shaped Christmas cookie in her little hand...

PATE, IDAHO

July 1989

THIRTY-EIGHT

"JOHN!" ESMA PULLED down the oil lantern from the rafters, lit it, and set it just inside the shed on an old stump John had used for chopping wood. She ran to the corner where he was crouching. John didn't seem to know her. She tried to touch him, but he moved away. What an ordeal he must have been through!

"It's me, it's your Esma." She tried again to touch his arm, and this time he allowed it. She felt the linen material of his shirt. He looked so worn out. His eyes were a shiny silver color, different than she remembered. Were they glowing? Weird. Where had he been for ten years?

"You look really good." She brushed his long hair off his forehead. "Can you speak, dear?" She wanted so much to hear his voice, but he struggled a bit as he tried to reply.

"Never mind, you just relax," she interrupted his attempts. "You must be exhausted. I can run you a bath, and you'll be back to your old self in no time."

But that was something too. He looked exactly like his old self from ten years ago. Reaching out to comfort him, Esma caught the brown age spots along her exposed arm and all over her hand. She compared her hands with his. John's were dirty, but didn't seem to have aged much at all.

"Where have you been? Inside the fountain of youth? You look incredible! Like the last time I saw you."

Up close, she studied his face. This was most certainly John, but something about his jawline seemed different. He was probably just clenching his teeth, so those jaw muscles stuck out a bit more than she remembered.

Esma went on talking despite that he hadn't replied. "Wait until Dawn sees you're back. She'll be so excited."

Esma pulled him up, trying to get him to his feet, but he twitched and made a funny noise.

"Are you hurt? Don't you recognize me? It's Esma!"

He cocked his head to the side, as if to study her face. Her heart danced, and the energy was like a rush of love, a pool full of stuffed animals she could jump into.

"Es-ma?" His voice was scratchy, but he said it! He said her name.

"Yes! It's me. I've missed you, dear. And I have so many questions for you. Did you visit me the other night in our bed?"

It seemed like John was still trying to figure things out. He looked all around the shed, and then at her. She didn't need him to talk, not really. It was enough that he was here.

"I knew it was you! I've been trying to send out the sort of energy that would call you back to me. I thought I'd just hear your voice and speak with you across the distance. But look! You're back in the flesh!"

His eyes narrowed, like he didn't approve of what she was saying, and all at once, she remembered how John was. So religious. He'd consider all of this witchcraft, just like Dawn would. Esma explained it in a way he'd understand.

"I mean, the Lord showed me a vision of you and told me you'd return. He said I just had to ask. 'Ask and you shall receive,' like the Bible says, right, John?"

"I...want..." John managed, but then stopped. He seemed so exhausted!

"Who? Dawn? Oh, she's off somewhere. Probably a night shift at the hotel. You can see her later. Gosh, you'll be so proud of her. She's a hard worker, just like you always thought she'd be. And—"

"Moonstep."

"Moonstep? John, what do you mean?"

"Mine."

"Yours? What's yours? I'm here, and I'm yours!" Esma buried her head against his chest, and felt again all the love she had for him.

"Moonstep... Mine."

"Oh." Esma pulled back and looked at him. The Moonstep Mine talk was really starting to dampen the energy.

"Moonstep Mine's just an old story, John. Is that where you've been? Looking for it?" She laughed softly. "That's what you've been doing all these years? Everyone knows Moonstep Mine isn't a real place. There's no unclaimed silver in a lost mine. Can't be. Wouldn't prospectors have found it by now?"

"It's—"

"All right, hush now," she interrupted him. "Forget whatever all that talk is about. Look, you're home now. Here in our shed."

He looked straight ahead, gave no answer.

"Come into the house! I'll get you some coffee." She pulled his arm, but he yanked it back with force. "Don't you want to come in and get settled?"

He didn't answer.

Of course! He loved this shed and spent most of his time out here. Sometimes with Dawn, sometimes not. Made sense that he'd feel more at home here.

"But I want you with me inside, where I can keep you close forever."

He wouldn't budge, so she sighed and let it go. She could never talk John out of his ideas, even if it made no sense for him to stay out here. Maybe he needed to ease into things. Dawn most definitely wouldn't come into the shed, but maybe she didn't need to know he was back yet. That would mean Esma could have John all to herself. Not that she wouldn't want to share him. Not *exactly*.

"Know what? You're right. You always know best. The shed is a perfect place for you." Esma smiled. He always loved her smile.

She nudged her head under his chin, and they sat like that for a while, until she really did feel the energy shift. A cold blast, absolutely frigid, like the shed had transformed into an arctic cave. And there was the start of a headache at the back of her head too. She hadn't had a headache in so many years!

"I'm going in to get a sweater, dear. I'll be right back. Don't go anywhere."

The sun blinded her when she walked out. It was already daylight, but how could time have gone that fast? Dawn could be home any minute! She ran inside, and lucky for her, Dawn was fast asleep in her bed. The girl must have come in very early this morning, since she hadn't been home as of three o'clock. Esma released a big sigh. She was dead-dog tired, and her head was really hammering now, so instead of getting a sweater, she found her bed. She really wanted to get back out to that shed, but she fell asleep instead.

THE SOUND OF crows woke Esma up.

Don't leave the bed. Stay here for days and days.

What a silly thought to have. With John back, there was no way she'd stay in bed all day. How did she even stay away from him for this long?

The cabin was empty now. Dawn must have gone to work.

The shed door creaked as Esma opened it. She had a flashlight, but it didn't matter because there was nothing in there. Nothing at all. No John. No trace of him.

She went into the house and looked around, then walked out to the front porch and took down his portrait. How could he leave her a second time? What was wrong with her? Was she that terrible to be around?

"John?" She called his name one last time, and then hung the portrait inside the shed.

He was gone once more.

THIRTY-NINE

ROGER TOOK HIS time returning to the station. He even stopped for a six-pack of Coors.

He'd recently given up drinking, so his ticker could have a better chance. Today, however, he needed a beer. He really wanted a cigarette, too, but Mary would smell that, so this was the lesser of two evils.

Alex's death was cause enough for a beer, but now he was dealing with the John Winton disappearance all over again too. God, he'd botched that one up, but how could he go into the woods to look for the man? Now there's a new kid missing, but what should he do? Cordon off all of the public land to keep people from going out into those damn mountains? He couldn't protect this community, and usually he could hide it, but the failure was starting to take its toll. What if he cracked in front of Tweedle Dee and Tweedle Dum? Even worse, in front of Syl Dixon.

Mary would understand a beer slip-up.

When he pulled into the station's lot, Syl was waiting by his parking spot. She stood on tiptoes to peek through his rig's high window and found the six-pack taking cover on the passenger-side floor. Her eyes widened. Roger pretended not to see her expression.

"Join you?"

He shrugged. He didn't care who was there or who wasn't.

"Well, a six-pack isn't enough, and the station isn't the place to drink it," she said. "Let's go to Emmy's. You can get beer if you want, but it's whiskey for me today."

"It's not even lunch time."

"I think we've had enough of a week to warrant whiskey with lunch."

He spit his gum out, unwrapped a fresh piece, and said, "Just don't tell Mary. Get in."

WALKING INTO EMMY'S Saloon made Roger think of Alex, of all his friends over the years, so many who moved away as the mining industry closed down. Those who disappeared. A few who had died. The place was filled with last night's smoke, a haze that never seemed to clear out. Then again, Oscar never opened the windows, either. Might do this place some good if he did.

Oscar was in his spot behind the bar and threw a hand up to signal hello as Roger walked in. Roger gave a two-finger salute back, then looked around for a table, somewhere away from any hubbub. Although, the most he saw were a few sad drunks, already head-down at the bar. Still, he wanted isolation.

Syl went directly toward Oscar at the bar, then a few moments later, turned around with two shots of amber liquid. She was serious about the whiskey. Roger thought he should stick with beer, but just one whiskey wouldn't hurt. Couldn't let her think she could outdrink him. She was always looking for a leg up. They called it *equality*, but really, women wanted special treatment.

Roger listened to the sound of Johnny Cash's voice crackling in the cheap saloon speakers, the Man in Black declaring that he "fell into a burning ring of fire." At least someone had good taste in music around here.

Syl met him at a corner table that glowed red from the neon R of the Rainier Beer sign above. "Why'd you choose the table in the red-light district?" she asked, squinting at the sign.

He wasn't really in the mood for jokes, which was a shame, because beneath the sign, Syl's face was red like she'd spent two weeks in Hawaii without sunscreen. The perfect setup for a lobster joke.

"If you don't like it, then pick another table."

She looked around like she was considering it, but then sat down and pushed a shot at him. He tapped the small glass bottom of the drink on the table while she downed hers.

"What's this about, Roger?"

Roger shook his head and drank the shot whole. Damned if he'd let her mother him. He raised a finger so Oscar would bring another round.

"Used to come here with Alex every Wednesday night."

"Why Wednesday nights?"

"Not sure, it was just the night we met up."

Oscar arrived and lined up two more for each of them. Roger went on like he hadn't just decided to keep his trap shut a few minutes ago. The whiskey was already coursing through. Proof that he hadn't had any alcohol in months.

"But it's been awhile now since we did that. I'd quit the booze and we stopped hanging out once I wasn't coming to Emmy's anymore."

"Must be hard to know everyone around here and watch this happen."

Well, shit. If he didn't change the subject now, he was in real danger of being mothered. "Any luck finding a trace of Monte Shrake?" It was his attempt to reroute the conversation even though he'd given up hope that they'd find anything else out. About Monte, about Alex, about any of it. He'd lived here long enough to know how things stood. Still, it made him feel like he was doing something to have Syl running around like she gave a shit.

Syl rolled her eyes.

"That good, huh?"

"Not a goddamn trace. Was with some girl the last night he was seen. Neighbor filled in those details. Very colorfully, I might add."

Roger gave a chuckle. "Maybe the kid just wanted to get away from his meddling mother."

"Yes, but there are easier ways to get away from your mom. Staging a whole forest disappearance seems like overkill."

"Although around here it'd be a good way to be sure nobody comes looking for you. So many fucking disappearances. Can't keep up."

Roger threw back another shot and looked down at five empty glasses and four still full, waiting on deck. They were like rabbits multiplying. Had Oscar brought more without him noticing? He lined up his and her empties like a boundary between them.

"Ah yes, the disappearances again," Syl said. "What are we talking? Two a year? Three?"

Roger smirked. "Try more like fifteen to twenty a year. Some years more, some less. Depends on the town's population. Ultimately, though, it all depends on who is stupid enough to go into the woods, chasing that goddamn howl."

He was saying too much.

Syl leaned forward. "I heard it. I heard the howl. Sounds like a loon call, but—"

"It's no loon. Loons call back and forth to each other."

"Usually at night."

Roger put a finger in the air and shouted, "Pepsi next round, Osc."

He finished his last shot and wiped his mouth with the back of a hairy arm. He was saying too goddamn much.

FORTY

HOLY HELL, SYL thought.

There was something batshit going on, and Roger knew about it. So that's why all the head rubbing and grunting. Blocking and ignoring. Why the hell did he ask her to help figure this thing out and then not get her up to speed? This old question burned again, she felt it on her cheeks, but she couldn't get ahead of herself.

Tread lightly. Be an unassuming, adorable girl, so you can get the information you need.

"What do you think that sound in the woods is, then?"

Roger sighed.

"I know what the stories say it is. Never cared to find out for myself. Not about to take my chances out there if guys like John Winton can't hack it."

Patience, slowly.

"Out there?" Syl said, cocking her head to the side to invite him to speak more.

"There's supposedly a lost mine around here. Called Moonstep Mine. Thing is, there's no record of it. But prospectors found claims all the time back in the day, and many of them were kept secret out of fear and greed. These mountains are vast, so they often forgot where their own claims were. Thing is, nobody ever bragged about finding Moonstep. Nobody knows where the name came from. Just sort of always was. Or never was. Nobody's even sure it's real."

All right, enough with what nobody knows. What do people know?

"Nobody's sure it's real?"

Old Sheriff Cummings would be so proud of her mirroring tactics. Maybe she could be a good investigator, after all.

"Can't be sure it's real if nobody returns to talk about it. Story's simple, far as I know. Doesn't make it believable though. There's something inside the mine. Whatever it is, it calls out to people. That's the howl. Some people are better able to resist it than others. Always surprises me who can withstand and who cannot."

"You're thinking of John Winton?"

"Must be what happened to him. But why he couldn't resist and Dawn could... It's baffled me for ten years."

Roger took a sip of Pepsi.

Syl had heard that call too. But it was easy for her to walk away. In fact, she wanted to get away from it.

"Why do you think some can resist it?"

"Don't know the answer to that one, either. Like I said, never felt compelled to walk too far into those woods to find out for myself."

Syl wanted to ask who else had been seen going into the woods and then disappeared. Was there a pattern? A sort of person more susceptible to following that call? Had anyone ever returned?

Instead, she said, "You don't want to find out for yourself?"

"Hell no. What if I'm attracted to the call? They say Moonstep Mine is more active during some times than others. It's been quiet for a lot of years until recently. Last time it was active to this extent was when I just got back from the war."

"More active?"

"Like a high time. A time when not only are the disappearances happening, but..." He took a drink of Pepsi.

He sighed and did some work rubbing his head.

She couldn't push now. He was aiming to tell her something important, and she couldn't fuck it up. Even so, waiting on him was like stabbing yourself in the eye with a letter opener.

"...Reappearances too."

"Reappearances?"

Mirroring was supposed to be easy, but Roger made it exhausting.

"As in people coming back."

"People are coming back?"

Roger looked around, as if to make sure nobody was listening.

"Well, not like 'case-closed' or anything. More like the missing people... They reappear. Not always permanently. And not always chronologically. Sometimes you'll get someone from seventy years ago reappearing while someone who went missing a week ago doesn't show."

What? Syl had been following along until this. Now her mind was in free fall, trying to reach for a branch, a rope, anything on the way down.

"What does that mean?"

"That's all I know."

Roger was like a door moving toward closed, but there was still a crack open, so she pressed.

"Wait, you think we're in one of those high times right now?"

Esma had said something was coming.

"Don't know. The state we found Alex in says something weird is happening, although a shriveled corpse is a new one to me."

"People hang up portraits of their missing loved ones."

Roger nodded.

"Why?"

Roger waved her off. "That's all I got. Done talking about it. You have any kids?" Roger changed the subject so abruptly, she flinched.

She straightened up in her seat. God, of all the topics to jump to. This one? "It's complicated."

"It's not, really. Either you have offspring or you don't."

"How about you, Rog? You have kids?"

Roger smiled. "Indeed. Both are grown and flown. Your turn."

She closed her eyes and sighed. "I'm too sober for this."

"Oscar!" he shouted. "Tequila for the lady. Make it a double."

Syl drained her Cuervo and then said, "I had a husband, I have a son. I left them. It's that simple."

"Well, that actually sounds complicated to me."

She closed her eyes again. Chewed her cheek. "It's your typical sob story. Got pregnant way too young, and the father was someone I liked, but I guess not enough. Stuck it out for a few years, and then left like a bat out of hell. Thought being on my own would be better than seeing up close the monumental failure I am as a mother."

"And is it?"

"Is it what?"

"Better?"

Syl didn't owe him any information about herself. Oscar was there with another shot of tequila, and she downed it. Then she folded her hands on the table and stared Roger down.

"Sorry," Roger said as he took a sip of pop. "Kid's in Spokane, right? It's just an hour and a half away."

"No. He's in Florida with his dad now. Better for Lucas in the long run anyway. Carl, that's his dad, is amazing. Like he was born to be a father. Lucas is better off without me screwing things up for him."

"Well, you know that's not true," Roger said. "You should go see the kid."

Syl flattened her lips and said, "The only place I'm going is to the ladies room, and when I come back, no more talk about my personal life."

She swung open an old metal bathroom door. All kinds of dicks and f-words were carved into the paint on the stall.

What mattered here wasn't her fitness as a mother, it was that Roger knew a lot more than he originally let on. It was guaranteed he knew even more.

PATE, IDAHO

January 1962

FORTY-ONE

A FEW DAYS *after the incident with the Christmas cookies, seeing Rose holding one in that portrait, I took to bed. It was the flu, and I was drenched in sweat with a fever.*

I saw Rose there in my dreams. Heard her laugh.

Days later, when I opened my eyes, it was night. I was lying in my bed, looking square into Grandpa's face, but I could barely see it in the dark. He was sawing logs like usual, so I rolled over.

Rose was there, staring at me with those glowing silver eyes.

"Mama?"

She was sort of flickering like a light about to die, like her veins were electric, and I could see through her skin. And in my delirium, what came to me was her body looked like one of those family trees. You know, like you see with royalty? Who was born from who. I reached to touch her little dress, to make sure she was really there, but my hand went through. She wasn't really there. Was I imagining her? I rubbed my eyes and opened them again to see her face pressed right against mine, her head tilted to one side.

"Mama...camp? Go...woods?"

I could barely find my voice. Barely calm my breath.

"Not tonight, sweetie. Can you get back in your room?" My voice was sweeter than molasses, I made sure of it, because for the first time, I was scared of her.

"No...bed. Woods!"

Something metallic caught the moonlight, and I saw our little hatchet in her hand. The one we kept by the wood stove.

She toddled around the foot of the bed to where Grandpa was.
"No," I whispered. "No, Rose!"

I pushed Harold's shoulder, and he jerked awake, but he didn't have time to defend himself.

Rose, or whatever that thing was—it was really just a glowing light on Harold's side of the bed—landed the edge of the hatchet into his arm with more force than any three-year-old could muster.

He hollered and pushed at her, but his hands went through like mine had. He grabbed the axe.

She disappeared.

This wasn't my Rose at all. Somehow, I knew that, deep down. Just couldn't admit it. I knew what to do. I should have done it much sooner, but better late than never, as they say. I moved to get out of bed. Problem was, I was dizzy from being sick.

Her little feet came quickly behind me. I had to go faster.

I made it into Rose's room.

There was the oval portrait on the wall, without Rose in it.

I reached up for it, but the dizziness hit me hard. The walls wiggled, and I passed out.

The first thing I seen when I came to was Grandpa sitting next to me on the bed. His arm was in a makeshift sling. It was covered in bandages. Not much time had passed because it was still night.

"Lou, been waiting on you to wake up. Didn't want to leave you here, being sick and all, but I need to get the sheriff."

"Won't solve it."

"Somebody's in our house. Attacked me!"

"It's Rose." I stared at the ceiling.

"Our Rose? What the hell, Lou."

"Can't explain it, but I think it's her ghost. Been happening for a while now. Although, she's never been violent before. Usually she just runs away scared."

"That's crazy talk. It was a burglar breaking in. Got me in my sleep. That's what happened."

"All right, then show me the broken windows. Busted locks? What did the burglar take? Or did he just come in, attack you with our stove hatchet, and then leave?"

I started to sit up, but the room spun from the exertion and that damn flu sickness. I heard laughing inside me.

"How in Sam Hill could it be Rose?" Harold asked, scratching his head. He looked out the bedroom window.

"Don't know, just is. Somehow, she's connected to that photograph hanging in the spare room," I started to explain, but Harold just looked at me like something had ripped the common sense straight from his skull.

I stumbled into Rose's room again. It was quiet, and the curtains were shut, but I hadn't shut them.

I came up to that old portrait and saw my girl beneath the glass where she should be. I lifted it off the wall. Her face was contorted in a smirk. Cherub cheeks and soft smile gone. It might have been the last picture of my girl, but it was the only idea in my head.

Harold held me as I took the stairs, slowly, constantly checking to see if Rose was still in the picture.

She was.

We approached the wood stove, and he opened the door. I slammed the frame down on the brick hearth, and the glass broke. I pulled out the paper portrait. It had changed. The photograph was the way it should be. Smiling, sweet girl, with a wooden pull toy at her feet.

Shit. Was I crazy? Would I really destroy my only picture of Rose?

Then she was gone, no longer in the picture, and I looked all around us until I saw her once more, standing right there in front of Harold, with that goddamn hatchet again.

No way she was getting him again, so I tossed the picture into the fire and watched it coil up into the flames...

PATE, IDAHO

September 1915

FORTY-TWO

WITH THE HORSE and cart, it took Lily about two hours to get into town. But today, it was just too pretty out. So, she decided to walk down the hill instead. Being alone in the woods was invigorating, and it gave her that old, wild feeling she used to get while sitting on the rocks that overlooked the river in Spokane. This was the way the boys went to school, because it was so much faster.

It had been five years since they'd lost Joe. Five more since Katie died. Lily still got sick and stayed in bed every time the snow fell, and she struggled to remember anything at all. Still, she'd come to accept what she had done to Katie and Joe, like what she'd done to Margaret, except without any recollection of the events. She wanted to move on from the guilt, but she couldn't, and she was mindful to keep herself away from Owen and Jake, lest there be another lapse in her sanity while they were around.

She had stopped listening to the voice in her mind, and so far, it seemed to be just the trick. Jake was six, and Owen was thirteen. Lily was with child again, but she hadn't yet told Holver. Maybe if she didn't tell him, it wouldn't become real. The very last thing she wanted was another child, and this had her wondering if she could get out of it somehow. But the only thing her mind could conjure was much too dangerous, and she was chicken. Leaving Pate after the birth was another option. Holver would see to the child just fine. Probably marry another woman real quick.

Holver always said Lily had fury locked inside a cage, and it snuck out when she didn't mean it to. But now Lily knew it wasn't fury inside that cage, it was her. Just plain old her.

All she needed in town today was fabric to make herself a new dress. Holver didn't want her spending that kind of money, but she didn't care. She thought she'd make a fresh start here in Pate, that she would be a different person, but then Katie happened, and she knew she'd never change. Never *really* change. Turns out, she wasn't all that different from Father—all this violence inside. But at least he'd never killed anyone.

Once she realized this, Lily started squirreling away any coins she got ahold of, just in case she needed to run again. During the spring and summer months, she sold flowers from her garden in town, but Holver had no idea. He'd take her money from her if he knew. If there was one thing Holver Markwell was fixated on, it was earning money. But he was careless with it, too, or maybe just no good at figures, so she'd taken a bit here and there, over these fourteen years as well—just in case.

Of course, now Owen knew where her stash was located, which was a liability. Last week he'd snuck out of the house behind her, and she'd led him right to the spot where she buried the money. A branch had snapped beneath his feet, and she caught him. She had been livid, but he looked so scared that she softened right away. He began crying, and she warned him to keep it secret from Pa, or else.

So far, he'd done it.

As far as she knew, at least.

The town seemed empty today. Lily pushed open the door to the general store and placed her order. The store merchant said he had the brown calico at home, but none in the store, and could she return in an hour or two? When she turned around, Ruthie Burgh was right there, like she'd been waiting all day for Lily.

"Holver disappear, Lily?"

"Pardon?"

"I'm wondering if Holver's disappeared like so many in town have."

Lily narrowed her eyes, but didn't answer.

"Well, what mine's he workin' then?"

"I'm sorry, I don't understand."

"Percy's wondering which mine's got Holver now."

Percy and Holver worked together at Lucky Dog. Or, so Lily thought.

"He's at Lucky Dog," she said, but as it came out, she knew it was a misstep.

"Beg your pardon, Lily, but Holver ain't been at Lucky Dog in years. Thought maybe he'd gone off into the woods, like other prospectors. Most don't return."

"He's over at Twilight now!" She smiled, touched her forehead. "Don't mind me, little out of sorts today." It was the first mine that came to her.

"Oh my. That's quite a distance from your place. He take the horse every day?"

"I suppose he does."

"Odd," Ruthie said. "Why leave Lucky Dog? Owners not treatin' him good?"

"I'm not too sure his reasons. You know how men can be."

Ruthie looked at her, waiting for more explanation.

"Now, if you'll excuse me," Lily said and moved around the woman before Ruthie could get another nosy question out.

Holver is lying to you.

It was the voice, shouting inside her head the minute she stepped out onto the dirt road.

Lily walked farther down Main Street, as fast as was prudent without raising any suspicion, but she wanted to run. Run as far as her legs could take her, and then she'd start life over again. A wave of nausea came over her.

The baby.

She was still chained.

Find out what Holver's been doing.

Lily kept walking, ignoring the voice. She wasn't ready to go home, so she went to the river's bank, just under the bridge. She stood at the edge of the water, watching the afternoon sun bring sparkles up on little currents, and she cried.

Holver still brought money home. Where was he getting that money if not from mining at Lucky Dog? He wasn't taking the horse anywhere, so whatever mine he worked had to be within walking distance, but most of the mines were closer to town. Only Lucky Dog was within distance for them.

Lily walked back to the store and canceled her fabric order. The storekeeper's assistant was confused, said the fabric would be here any minute. She blamed herself, saying she'd made a silly mistake and couldn't go home with more fabric they didn't need.

Then, she walked into Emmy's Saloon. The floor was dirty, as if nobody bothered to sweep up after a rowdy night. It was empty, too, except for a few drunks and some whores, alert and ready to work. She found the barkeep with her eyes and said, "Har Baker around today?"

The few heads present turned at the sound of a woman's voice.

Let them think what they will about a respectable woman walking in. Emmy's Saloon was the only place to find the man who sold what she wanted to buy, and it was the one thing the voice said she'd need.

PATE, IDAHO

July 1989

FORTY-THREE

SYL STOOD IN the mountains, trees heavy with snow all around. The sun shone bright, and the sky was clear. She wore snowshoes without any boots, just bare feed strapped in. How were the straps not hurting her skin? Not only that, but she was naked except for Carl's white tank top and her underwear, yet she wasn't cold. She trudged up the incline until it flattened out into a clearing. Before her was a big dark cave with a black entrance. A mine. Framed photographs hung all around the rock opening. Someone spoke inside, or maybe it was an animal, she didn't know. The snow crunched under her snowshoes with every difficult step she took. She watched her feet move like they weighed twenty pounds each, but she ignored the resistance and took another step. Then another.

When she looked at the mine again, there was a car blocking her way. Emergency flashers were on, but the car was turned off. She came up to the trunk and popped it open. There lay Esma, curled into a fetal position. Esma's eyes opened fast, and she tried to speak.

"I can't hear you, Esma, I'm sorry," Syl said, annoyed that the car was in the way of the mine's entrance.

Esma opened her mouth wide, as if to scream, but words didn't come. Syl felt something cold constricting her throat. She couldn't breathe but didn't know why. Just as she went to close the trunk, Esma's voice broke through.

"Don't go in there."

"I have to."

"Don't look."

"Don't look at what?"

"I'm in your dream," Esma said, suddenly distracted and looking around.

"This isn't a dream."

"Yessss it issss." Esma's hissing turned into the sizzling of fire, and her body went up in flames, which quickly extinguished. Her charred body, black and burned, lay back down in slow motion, resuming the fetal position. Her black arm reached up and closed the trunk door. The car disappeared.

The noises inside the mine grew louder. Syl had to get in there to see. She went inside the mine, and standing with her back to Syl was a woman with long, salt-and-pepper hair. A quilted knee-length housecoat, arms limp at her sides. The woman held a lit cigarette between two fingers.

"Gran!" Syl shouted, but the woman didn't respond. She was looking at something against the rock and dirt wall.

Syl resisted the urge to run and instead slowly stepped over to her.

"Gran, I've missed you," she said to the woman's back.

"Pup, you should go."

"But I just got here."

When Gran turned around, her eyes were huge, and glowing silver. Veins lit up, pulsated throughout her body as her face stretched into a smile that didn't seem like Gran's at all. Her hands clutched Syl's neck. Gran's mouth opened, and she sucked the air out of the mine. Syl tried to scream, but could barely breathe.

Syl sat straight up in bed. The clock said 3:39 a.m.

What sort of insane fucking dream was that?

PATE, IDAHO

September 1915

FORTY-FOUR

LILY COULD TELL herself all day long that she wasn't stuck, but she was. She could pretend there was another way to make this work, but there wasn't.

If Holver lied to her about going to Lucky Dog every day, what else had Holver lied about?

Lily rocked back and forth in her chair, looking out her front window as if her freedom would ride up on a saddled horse and whisk her away.

It was the next morning, and Holver was already gone for the day. Despite this new information, Lily couldn't get herself out of the rocking chair. Poor Owen and Jake had taken pieces of stale bread for their breakfast. They barely looked at her when they left for school. And now she felt the weight of cold steel on her lap. Har Baker had shown her how to operate the Colt .45 after he gleefully took her money. It was more than he would normally receive because she paid for his silence too.

Her life was better now than it had been in Spokane, but still, she was stuck in this home with children she loved but couldn't protect—

(Katie! Joe!)

She couldn't even finish the thought, because their faces broke through and new tears ran down the worn trails she'd been wetting all morning. She loved her children. More than she had loved Margaret.

Right now, she needed to know what Holver was doing. That was what mattered.

Follow him.

The voice was strong today, but it was also making a lot of sense. Despite this, she wanted to fight against it. She didn't trust it. Didn't trust what happened when she was sick or asleep. She'd been quick to listen to it yesterday and bought that six-shooter. Now she had to slow down, think rationally. Maybe she could find proof of Holver's lies around the house. Figure out what he was up to, enough so that following him made sense. Then she'd be doing it because of logic, not because the voice told her to.

Something was strange about all of it. Lily squeezed her eyes shut. No matter how she tried to reason it out in Holver's favor, the nearest mine was five miles away, and it'd take him two hours to walk there because it wasn't a straight shot. And she'd told Ruthie Twilight Mine! Why couldn't she have said Fog Mountain Mine? Or Drummer? Either of those were closer than Twilight!

Well, she'd find proof then. She'd look around the house. If she uncovered something suspicious, she could always follow him tomorrow. There was no rush.

Or Lily could just ask Holver about it. Tell him what Ruthie said and watch his response.

Immediately, she dismissed the idea. If Holver was hiding something from her, surely it was because she wouldn't approve. But then again, Holver had never been anything but kind to her. Even after Katie. After Joe. It stood to reason that he would be understanding and give her a rational explanation.

No. She'd trust herself this time. Find something to act as proof of his deception and then follow him if necessary.

Lily put her hand where the new child was growing. She was in prison here, but where could she go? Not back to Spokane—what would her parents say? Especially since she hadn't spoken to them since she ran away.

She turned over quilts and looked inside cupboards. Nothing out of the ordinary.

Holver had stopped prospecting on his days off. Staking a claim and becoming rich had been his original plan, hadn't it? And yet, that dream just silently died. What would make an ambitious man like Holver suddenly content to work another man's mine without so much as a whimper of complaint?

She went into the woodshed and looked inside canisters and jars on the shelves. That's when she realized she still had the .45 in hand. It had been a rash move, buying the thing. She moved crates around, turning them over until she found an old fabric bag with drawstrings. She put the gun into it and cinched the strings tight. She then grabbed a barrel of sugar from the shelf—a barrel that Holver never opened—and dropped the bag inside.

PATE, IDAHO

July 1989

FORTY-FIVE

WHEN ESMA OPENED the shed door the next day, John was in the corner, exactly where he'd been before. She lit the lantern.

"You're here! I was so worried you'd gone. That maybe you'd just come to tell me you were still alive, but not to stay. I didn't know. But look, here you are again!" She threw herself against his chest and almost knocked him over. They sat down together, side by side.

His eyes were really shining today. John's eyes were blue, and it was probably just the way the lantern was hitting them.

"What happened to you all those years ago? Where have you been for a whole decade?" Had she already asked that? Did she look desperate and pathetic asking it again?

He began shaking. Then his lips smacked open, like they'd been glued shut by sticky saliva. "Moonstep—"

"I'm sorry I asked, dear. Let's not talk about it anymore."

She wanted to know where he'd been, but not if it drudged up all that Moonstep talk again. Unbelievable. Any talk of Moonstep threw the energy off. Maybe it was best if they just focused on moving forward. Yes, the future. They'd talk about that.

He stopped talking, but was worked up, and speaking much better than before. Maybe it was his energy that felt so heavy. Esma wanted to be there with him, but his energy was affecting her own. Making her tired. Her headache had died down in the cabin last night, but now it was starting up again. This, after years and years of no headaches at all. How frustrating.

"She lied," John said.

Who lied? Who was he talking about? It had to be Dawn. Maybe Dawn lied about what she saw the day John left. Made sense. She'd always felt Dawn had seen more than she was telling anyone. Esma supposed she'd be upset with Dawn, too, if she were John.

"I'm so sorry. I don't think Dawn meant to cause any harm. She was just a little girl back then."

Esma laid her head on John's shoulder. "You're here now though. Let's focus on the good and think of ways we can spend our days together. I'll need to clean up out here and make it nice for you, but you know me—awful at cleaning. I can't get Dawn to do it, because she won't come out here at all. Gosh, there's so much to tell you, John. You might not recognize our Dawn, but it's all right because she's serving the Lord, and I think you'll see that and be so proud of her. She's just so—"

"Could not get away."

John was still trying to tell her about this thing that had his energy roiling around like a volcano. Why wouldn't he just let it go?

"Now, now, dear. It's all over. We're here together. Isn't that the most amazing thing? You and me reunited after so many years apart." She pushed his long hair off his forehead.

He grabbed her wrist and held it tight. Then he brought those glowing eyes closer, and she felt a deep shiver start down at the back of her neck and scramble all the way down her spine. The energy was really off. She wanted to be with him. It was all she'd wanted for a decade! But could she stay in here, in the freezing cold, with his energy going crazy like this? With those eyes almost blinding her? She had to push through it. Sure, maybe it was uncomfortable, but she had to stay with him. What if he left again?

She wriggled her wrist free and gave a nervous little laugh. "John! Please don't." John had never grabbed her before, never laid a hand on her in that way. What had made him do that?

John looked at her and then turned away, staring into the shed at who knows what.

"Well, how shall we spend our time together? I can go in the house and get your Bible. We can read it together."

John was fiddling with something on the ground, on the other side of his body. Esma couldn't see what it was, and when she tried to look around him, he blocked her view, hiding it.

"What have you got over there?" Esma laughed and reached across him. He batted her hands away.

Oh well, he didn't want her to know. Maybe it was a gift for her, and he was waiting for the right time to give it. She could play along. No reason to spoil the surprise. "All right, all right," she said, smiling, but unable to ignore the freezing cold. She'd forgotten her darn sweater again. Who needed a sweater in July?

Esma got up to get one, and he took a handful of her skirt.

"Stay," he said, his face drawn and sad.

"Aw, that's so sweet, dear. I want to stay with you. It's all I've wanted for years and years, and you know I'm not going any-where, but I need a sweater, or I'll catch my death out here."

Esma was relieved to go, but why did she feel that way? John was all she'd wanted, but these headaches and the cold were too much. Was the universe pulling her away from him? Why would that be happening after the universe brought them back together? She got into the cabin and immediately felt better.

PATE, IDAHO

September 1915

FORTY-SIX

BEFORE HOLVER ROSE the next morning to go wherever he went that was not Lucky Dog, Lily was already in her rocking chair, looking out the window at the apple tree. Its leaves were starting to turn.

Beneath her dress, hidden from view, Lily held the small pouch she'd found under a loose floorboard in the kitchen the day before. The spot looked crafted, like maybe Holver designed it as a hidey hole when he built the home. The pouch was the leather one she'd made for Holver their first year in Pate. She hadn't seen it in ages, but there it was, bulky in her hand, and when she'd opened up the drawstring, her jaw dropped.

Glowing silver rocks. Galena.

Maybe she hadn't been born to the mining life, but she knew a thing or two by now. She was sure it was galena. But how did Holver come upon it? And if he'd been secretly prospecting, why hadn't he staked a claim? Why the secrecy?

"You spooked me!" Holver said when he saw her in the rocking chair.

"Sorry about that." She stared out the window.

Owen and Jake were asleep, and school wasn't for a few more hours. She'd written them a note to say she'd gone out early to collect firewood. Holver always put it off until the first snow, and then he'd spend all day on a Sunday stockpiling the shed from dawn until dusk. Of the two of her boys, Jake had a more suspicious nature. But he was still so young, he wouldn't question it. Owen was trusting—too trusting, in her opinion. After all, he was on the brink of manhood. She worried he'd be taken advantage of. Plus, the boys knew how cross she grew whenever Holver put off chopping the firewood. It could make sense that she'd help this year.

"Well, I'm headin' out," Holver said, grabbing his helmet and headlamp. "See ya at supper?"

"Yes."

Lily watched him shuffle down the hill a few steps, and then she went into action quietly, so as not to wake the boys. She put on boots, her coat, and brought along a few apples in case she got hungry. Then she wrapped a handkerchief around her head, secured it under her chin, and set out.

She hung back as Holver went down the road a bit, then crossed the river at the log bridge, as if he were going toward Lucky Dog. It was the same way he went every day, but now that she was behind him and could see more, she wondered: Why weren't there other men out here at this time? She looked up at the mine, and from this angle, she noticed another trail leading out the opposite way Holver always went. That route was hidden from their property. No way she would have seen it otherwise. She had to be out here, inspecting the mine entrance from a distance. The route he took every day wasn't even the way to Lucky Dog! He was simply going into the woods. How long had he been lying to her?

The anger she'd pushed down bubbled up, and her breath quickened. Her heart was a team of horses, thundering down a dirt road. She picked up the pace, careful to avoid anything that might give her steps away.

Holver swiftly climbed through the woods, like he knew exactly where to step. Like he'd done it a thousand times before.

Lily crouched behind a huge boulder when she saw him slow down and take a look around. They'd been walking for hours. She felt faint. There was a steep hill ahead, and he climbed it, disappeared over the top. She took the hill slowly, hiding behind trees the whole way. Once she could see over the top, she stopped. It was a clearing. An absolutely silent open area. She took another step, but her feet crunched too loud against the quiet. She shuddered. Should she turn back? No. She'd already come this far and wouldn't return home until she saw what he was doing.

The problem was that Lily still hadn't seen anything out of the ordinary so far. Well, besides that Holver wasn't working in a mine like he said he was. She tried to peek over the ridge to get a view of the clearing, but she had to keep enough distance so as to stay out of sight. There was a stream and what looked like a mine at the back. Pine trees lined the perimeter.

Then she heard the sound of metal against the earth. Holver was digging with a spade. He hadn't brought a spade along, so he must have kept one here. She took a risk and poked her head up again to see. He was burying something, and then that something caught the sun and glimmered right at her, blinding her.

Silver! He had more silver, and he buried it up here! She was just about to turn and go—she'd seen plenty to know Holver was not who he said he was—but right then, he walked into the mine. What was he doing in there? She snuck up over the ridge even though every step she took sounded like a flock of birds taking flight. She hid behind a pine tree outside the mine's entrance.

"I been planning to offer all of 'em!" Holver shouted. "You need to give me more silver. It's a big cost to me, in more ways than one."

Silence.

Had Holver gone mad? He was talking to himself in the dark!

"First, I gave you my best one, my Katie girl. You don't even know how that hurt me. Or the show I had to put on for Lily."

Lily covered her mouth before a gasp could erupt.

"I gave you the baby after that so you'd know I was serious."

The trees around her spun. She stumbled backward the way she'd come, but it was noisy. Sickness lurched inside her, but she couldn't get sick here where it was so dead quiet. He'd hear it. She took careful steps until the birds sang again. Then she bent over to vomit.

It hadn't been her!

She hadn't hurt her own children. Hard sobs tried to come out, but she covered her mouth to tame them.

No time to feel too relieved when she just found out Holver had murdered her babies. Rage rocked around in her bones, like it did the day Margaret died. She tried to calm herself down, but her body shook and demanded she pour out tears for Katie and Joe all over again. The children would never come back, but it was something to know she didn't murder them.

Holver had.

Why? And how was it she couldn't see he was capable of this. Especially since she'd grown up with Father, seen evil in herself. You'd think she would recognize it.

Holver came into view even though he was still yards away.

Lily ran down the mountain in the direction of home, slipping on pine needles and catching herself, until she finally took a tumble that threw her skirts open.

Blast! She was too loud. Standing up, she rubbed her rump, hoping the baby hadn't been hurt.

She cared about the baby. It was a revelation.

Lily placed her feet more carefully than before as she ran. Soon, the nausea would come on if she didn't stop and eat. But she couldn't stop. Not yet.

After making her way down for a while without hearing Holver behind her, she decided it was probably safe enough to eat something. After all, what good would it do if she fainted, and he came upon her? She sat on the earth, facing downhill with her back against a huge boulder. The sun told her it was around noon. Apples didn't seem substantial enough, but she pulled one out anyway. The trees were so tall that a slight breeze made the tips sway. Pine cones dropped like light rain. She was halfway through the apple when she heard his steps again.

"Somebody there?" Holver shouted from above her.

Lily held the half-chewed bite in her mouth and wiped her face with her coat sleeve. She blinked, feeling like he could hear everything down to her eyes opening and closing. He was closer than she thought.

"If I find you out, I'll gut you. I swear it!"

Lily placed her hand over her mouth again, just to be sure no noise came out. She willed her breath to slow.

He was just a few steps up the mountain from her, but thankfully that huge rock was between them. The forest floor crunched hard under his boots.

He stopped on the other side of the boulder and panted like a grizzly bear. She held her breath while they both listened to the trees groan. Then a small doe appeared far off to her right, and Holver grunted.

"Damn deer had me goin," he said to himself and then walked in the direction of the doe.

Lily waited until she couldn't hear his footsteps anymore. And then she waited longer. Now to decide whether to follow him to see what he was up to next, or just run home.

PATE, IDAHO

July 1989

FORTY-SEVEN

SYL WAS STEPPING out of her jeans to change for bed when she heard something down in the kitchen, scratching against wood. She came out into the hall to inspect, but it stopped.

She waited, and it started up again. It was definitely scraping, like claws against a cupboard. What the hell?

She started down the stairs, but stopped halfway when she saw something.

Bare feet. Strong legs. Green housecoat. Salt-and-pepper hair. It was Gran.

Syl's limbs went numb, her legs weak. Like all the life had gone out of her and what was left was a shell that couldn't compute the view in front of her eyes. It was impossible. And yet, what had Roger said?

Some reappear. Not permanently though.

She got a shiver of cold, and wrapped her arms around herself in a sort of hug. It felt like an hour passed where Syl stood statuesque, staring at the backside of the woman she'd so missed all these years. It was probably only seconds. What was she doing? She squeezed her eyes shut and then opened them to bring herself back to reality.

"Gran?"

Gran turned around, bracing herself against the kitchen counter as if she might fall at any moment.

Her eyes shone silver.

Syl took a cautious step down. This wasn't really Gran, was it? How could it be? Look at her. She was straight out of the sixties. If, *if* it were possible that Gran returned, she'd be much older than this.

Syl tried to make sense of it. She didn't know what this was, but it *wasn't* Gran. Couldn't be Gran.

At the bottom of the stairs, she went for the light switch next to the back door, keeping her eyes on Gran at the sink. She had to turn away to find the switch, but then she flicked it on and spun around. Gran was gone.

Syl rushed over to the green phone on the kitchen wall, picked it up and realized she didn't have Roger's home number memorized. He wouldn't be at the station at this hour, either. She slammed it down and ran upstairs for her address book.

This thing looked like Gran, but it wasn't *really* Gran. Again, two incongruences swirled around in her mind. She was in the same situation she had been the night she saw the glowing eyes at the barn.

"Roger, I saw her," Syl said into the phone, without a greeting. She twisted the curly cord around her finger mindlessly.

"Saw who?"

Roger's TV was loud in the background. The *Gunsmoke* theme song.

"Gran! I saw Gran! When I came downstairs, she was there. Standing in front of my sink. You said something about reappearances. I need details."

Roger sighed. "I'm coming over."

Syl paced the kitchen while she waited. Then she realized she was in her underwear and ran upstairs to put jeans back on. Before she came down the stairs, she bent to see the kitchen in full view. No Gran.

ROGER TOOK LONGER than seemed reasonable. Nowhere in Pate took an hour of drive time. She chewed the inside of her cheek, then scolded herself for doing it.

A knock at the door.

God, finally.

She swung it open and there was Roger, holding a brown paper bag. "I brought us a snack."

She craned her neck and opened her eyes wide, as if the sheriff were completely daft. "Are you kidding? I just told you I saw my goddamn probably-dead grandmother in my kitchen, and your first response is to stop for a snack?"

"Sandwiches. I hope you like turkey. Diner was out of ham for the day. You gonna let me in?"

She stepped aside, and he went for the kitchen table.

"You saw her in here?"

Syl nodded, hugging herself again.

Roger looked around the room. He opened drawers. He looked at the walls, the outside of the refrigerator.

"What are you looking for? She's not in the fridge!"

He turned around and gave her a sarcastic smile.

Then he pulled a metal kitchen chair out, and it dragged across the linoleum with a screech. He sat down, reached into the brown bag, and pulled out a sandwich. White paper fell open. He lifted the bread to confirm salami and took a huge bite.

"Roger, what the fuck?"

He gave her a "What?" look, with his chipmunk cheeks full of salami, lettuce, and Italian bread.

"I know you know what's going on. You didn't want to tell me. That was fine up until now."

It wasn't, not really. But she'd already tried to get him to tell her more. It's what she'd been doing since the first moment. She tasted metal in her mouth. Damn it. The inside of her cheek was bloody.

She went into the bathroom for a tissue, then realized it was too much blood for a Kleenex, and dabbed it with a washcloth instead. Roger was mowing down his sandwich without a care in the world. Tears stabbed at the back of her nose as she stared at herself in the mirror. Had she ever felt this frustrated before? Why wouldn't he just come out with it? She opened her mouth wide to stretch her face and push back tears. It was a weird trick, but it usually worked. She went back into the kitchen.

With sandwich in hand, Roger was looking through one of the photo albums Syl had brought in yesterday. "Here's your issue," he said. He tapped the photo of her and Gran.

"An old picture? That's my issue? Goddamn it, Roger, if you're trying to piss me off, you win the world championship."

He swallowed his bite, removed the photo from behind the plastic cover, and brought it to the kitchen table.

"She look like this when she appeared tonight?"

"Yes. Exactly."

"You need to burn it."

"Why the hell would I burn the only picture I have of my grandma?"

"You sure it's the only one?"

"Yes! I'm positive. Been looking through the boxes in that damn barn like it's my full-time job. These were the only albums. Most of which are empty, by the way."

"Lou was smart. Must have missed this one though." He reached into the brown paper bag again and handed her a sandwich. "Eat."

"I already ate, Roger! What's a picture got to do with a fucking ghost in my house?"

Roger gave a little head nod at the box on the counter. "Fruity Pebbles doesn't count as food. Eat."

"I'm going to take a bite, and then you're going to *stop* eating and tell me everything."

"Fine by me."

She unfolded the thin, white paper to a square sandwich, cut diagonally. She shoved most of one half of the sandwich into her mouth and then motioned with her hand for him to begin.

"Impressive bite," he said as he set his sandwich down and brushed his hands together.

"What do you want to know?"

"Stop being coy and spill it!" she yelled through her bite, spraying bread crumbs on the word "spill."

Roger rubbed his head and sighed.

"My sister disappeared when I was ten. She was older, by about two years. My parents were ruined. My dad got it in his head that the woods were to blame. He heard stories of hunters who'd said there was a noise in the woods, a howling call. He grew obsessed with finding out what it was and set out just a few weeks after Winny's disappearance. He never came home."

FORTY-EIGHT

ROGER TOOK ANOTHER bite of his sandwich, and while he chewed, Syl understood something. Like a curtain parted to show her behind the scenes of Roger's mind. He was coping. He had brought food because it'd help him get through the telling of this story. She wanted to be mad, to kick and scream and throw plates against the wall. He'd been holding on to knowledge this whole time. Thing was, she didn't have the energy. She went to the fridge and got out a bucket of fried chicken she bought the day before, dropped it in front of him.

"Do you want coffee?"

"If you're making it." Roger continued, "When Dad disappeared, Mom really couldn't handle life. It was just her and me at that point, and I took care of her. Until I left for the war. When I got back, she met me at the Spokane airport, looking like a new person. Radiant. New dress, new hairdo. A smile I'd not seen in years. 'Wait until you see who's waiting at home,' she said. I'm sure you can guess what comes next." He took another bite.

"It was your sister and your dad. With glowing silver eyes. Maybe some lit-up veins."

"Right."

"Dad was in a suit. The one he wore on their wedding day. He had a good twenty years shaved off from the last time I'd seen him. Winny looked the same age as when she disappeared. At first."

Syl stared at him.

"They come out of photographs. That's your cut-to-the-chase. If there is more than one photograph, they can appear at different ages, but only one at a time."

"What are they? Ghosts?"

"Depends. Close to their photograph, they can be lifelike. Touchable. But the farther they get from the photo, the more like a ghost they are. They can't get through walls or doors or anything like that."

"Are they dangerous?"

"Can be. In our case, my dad was exactly as he had been, except for those silver eyes. Never really made a wrong move. My sister, though, she had scared my mom a few times. My mom began recognizing Winny around the house based on photographs she'd taken. That's how she figured out the connection to the pictures. After that, she kept all of Winny's images in one room with Dad's, and that was her 'visiting room.' It contained Winny a bit."

"Until…"

"Until Winny tried to put the dog's collar on Mom while Mom slept. She'd passed out on the couch in the visiting room, and when she woke up, Winny was choking her, demanding to take the dog on a walk."

"Holy shit. Why wouldn't your mom be more careful? Get out of that room before falling asleep?"

"Mom wasn't in her right mind; I thought that might be obvious by this point." He took another bite and then spoke around the mash of sandwich. "Wasn't as bad as other stories I've heard though."

"You know other people who have experienced this?"

"Of course. I've taken all the calls for help over the years. Some real bad ones."

"Does everyone reappear? I mean, if they die of natural causes, can they come out of pictures too?"

"No. Only the ones who disappear in the woods. The ones who find…"

He took another bite.

"Moonstep Mine," she said.

"Moonstep Mine."

"So, why don't people just burn the photographs of missing loved ones? Avoid the whole mess?"

Roger took the picture of Syl and Gran, and walked over to the gas stove. He lit the burner and held it high above the flame.

"No!" She ran to him, grabbed his arm.

He gave her a there's-your-answer look.

"Because it's too hard to let go," she said quietly, looking at the picture like it was precious.

"Bingo. There's hope for you as a world-class detective yet," Roger said. "And she's your grandma. Imagine your spouse, or worse—your child—disappears. You going to go burn all memories of them as a first reaction?"

She cleared her throat. "What happened with your mom?"

"She made the mistake of telling me what she figured out. I burned all the pictures in the house. Ones of her, even ones of me. Never let my photo be taken to this day. Last thing I want is to return and hurt my loved ones. No way. Bury me in a pine box in the old cemetery and be done with it. That's how I want to end up."

"So, people around here know about this?"

"Most do. Nobody talks about it, as you know. They hang photographs outside when a loved one goes missing so that when a high time comes, the loved one won't be in the home, you know, strangling them in their sleep or something. A couple portraits have already disappeared around town. People bring them inside when their loved one reappears. They consider it special, sacred almost, to get to live to see a high time. They only hope their own loved ones will be one of the few who reappear."

"And that they'll be less like Winny and more like your dad."

Roger nodded. "Grief is the ultimate blind spot. People are so sure *their* family members would never hurt them."

"How often does high time happen?"

"Only once every few decades or so. No set schedule."

"Why? Why does it happen?"

Roger balled up his white sandwich wrapper and reached into the fried chicken bucket, pulled out a leg. Syl remembered the coffee and went to pour two cups.

"Best I can figure, the mine, or the thing in the mine, needs to recharge. Then when it's at full power, it can send down little messengers to collect more souls. I know this is true because people who have been killed by their reappeared loved ones have been known to reappear, too, as if they went missing in the woods."

"What makes a high time end? How do we stop it?"

"Not sure. I suppose the thing in the mine gets tired, worn out, and it just stops. Haven't figured out why it would stop. Thought on that for lots of sleepless—"

A rustling on the far side of the refrigerator made Roger stop talking.

The woman in the green housecoat stepped out into the center of the kitchen. "Pup?"

Roger and Syl looked at each other, eyes wide. He gave her a don't-you-dare look. She ignored him.

"It's...me...Gran." Gran stood there, slouching a little. Then she went on, "Pup...I...tried..." Her words were forced, coming out of her mouth like thick sludge. Like it was unnatural for her to speak.

Syl started over, but Roger put his arm out to block her. "Don't. It's not her."

She pushed Roger's arm away and glared at him. She wasn't his child.

Syl approached Gran and took her hands. They were warm, as if she were truly there.

Syl couldn't help it; she hugged Gran. Tears came, and a dam broke inside Syl, expanding the emptiness of growing up without her parents, without Gran. Feeling like she never really belonged anywhere, to anyone, how it made her unable to really love. How she was set up to fail as a mother because of it. Embracing Gran should have made it better, been a comfort, but instead it was worse, more desperate, like a monster inside Syl had been freed, and it was hungry for the childhood years ripped away from her. Angry about how things turned out. Syl couldn't let go, but Gran didn't hug back.

"You," Gran said, looking at Roger over Syl's shoulder. Syl blinked and touched her forehead. Were all those dark feelings really living inside her? And why was it so cold in here?

"This…on…you…"

Gran shoved Syl aside with force and went for Roger, but he moved to the stove in what seemed like one leap. He fumbled with lighting the burner and held the old photograph up in a victorious gesture. The flame purred as the image dangled like a dry leaf.

Gran wasn't in the picture anymore. It was just Syl, smiling in that navy-blue dress.

"Lou, I'll do it. You know I will. It's the last one of you."

Gran seemed to hesitate and then took a step back. Her veins glowed, and silver moved like blood through them. She looked at Syl, softening. "My…letter."

"What letter? Gran, you didn't leave a letter."

That really pissed her off, because she charged past Syl and pounded against Roger with her small frame. The photo fell on the floor.

This thing was stronger and faster than Gran ever was, even in her peak fitness. Although, how easy would it be to cling to her, looking for answers to the longing Syl had just felt? She understood why people took the risk, but Roger was right. This was not Gran. It wasn't.

They were on the checkered linoleum, Gran on top of Roger, her mouth opening wide—so wide that it stretched across her face, just like in Syl's dream.

Syl scrambled to the floor and got the photo.

"Stop!" Syl shouted, holding the photo over the open flame.

Gran's head swiveled to look, her body still straddling Roger. "Pup, it's me. We can be together."

The air seemed to leave the room when she spoke. As if she was pulling in all the oxygen, again like in Syl's dream. Syl choked, gasped, looked at Roger. He gasped harder than her. Like he was suffocating.

"You're not her." Syl's tears fell as she said it, then she dropped the photo on the burner. As it shriveled, Gran disappeared. Both Syl and Roger took big draws of air.

PATE, IDAHO

September 1915

FORTY-NINE

RUN HOME.

That was what Lily decided. She didn't care where Holver was off to next; she wanted to get herself and the children out of there. Especially after Holver said he wanted to sacrifice the boys too.

It was just about two in the afternoon when their home appeared through the trees. Owen and Jake were still in school. She crossed over logs in the river, but instead of going up to the house, she went around the side of it, bracing herself for another run through more woods. She was exhausted, hungry, and her feet hurt, but she had to do this. Had to get the boys and leave this godless town today. They would go to Spokane. Maybe she'd confess to Margaret's murder, make things right. But how would that help her boys? Her boys who had barely made it this far in life, whose father had planned to kill them and sacrifice them to... What? She didn't know. He was receiving silver for it, that she knew. The thought burned hard inside her.

Most important thing was to get her children to Spokane. To fall on her parents' mercy. Maybe they would be so thrilled about having grandsons that they'd help her build a life. Feeling stuck had new meaning to her now. Anything was better than life with someone who could kill her children.

When she opened the door to the one-room schoolhouse, she wasn't thinking and busted it open like a stickup. Most of the kids jumped.

"Ma! What are you—" Owen started.

"Have to take my boys early today. I do beg your pardon, ma'am," she said to the school teacher, whose mouth gaped open.

Jake spoke, "Ma, what happ—"

"Hush, boys! Not another word now."

She shuffled them out and ran toward home, but another wave of nausea came on. Before the climb over the hill, she bent over, breathed, vomited.

"Ma, eat something." Owen handed her a piece of bread leftover from his lunch.

She took a bite. It did help, a little.

The boys didn't ask questions, only ran alongside her, ahead of her at times, but she shouted, "No! Stay back, by my side." She didn't want them to come upon Holver suddenly. Her corset was soaked with sweat.

Finally, Jake said, "Ma, you're scaring me."

She didn't have any breath in her lungs to explain. It'd all come out later, when the horses were breaking hard toward Spokane. When they were safe.

Approaching the house, Lily crept up to see if she could tell whether Holver was home or not. Probably not. He never came home before dark, but she'd spooked him, and what if that sent him home early out of paranoia?

There was no sight of Holver inside, and Lily saw no signs that he'd been there. Everything was just as she'd left it. She gathered what she could, packing what was light and important. She told the boys to pack their things too.

"What's this all about?" Owen asked.

"Where's Pa?" Jake asked.

They both stood there and watched her. "Get your things, I said! Hurry!"

When they didn't move or respond, she changed her tone, softened it. "Don't you worry about Pa."

Jake again: "Why are we leaving him behind?"

"It's a surprise. We're going to visit your grandparents in Spokane today. I'll tell you more about it on the way." She forced a smile, hoping it'd be enough to put them at ease. Just a fun little adventure, nothing to worry about. "You boys go wait in the buggy. I'll be right along."

They walked toward the front door, and she whisper-shouted, "If you see Pa, don't tell him about Spokane."

She caught two confused looks on the boys faces, but they went out and followed her instructions anyway. Lily was about to follow right behind when she remembered the six-gun in the sugar. The voice had been right in telling her to buy it after all! She had to get it; who knew what they might run across on the road. And after all, she'd never be unprotected again.

"Ma, you're actin' funny. Didn't know we even had grandparents."

"Jake! I told you to wait in the buggy with your brother!" She turned and shoved a small bag at his chest, pushing him off balance a bit. "Take these with you. Be a good helper."

He straightened and went out the front door again.

Lily walked into the woodshed.

There he was. Holver.

"Holver!" she said, jarring to a stop.

"Lily, why you in a huff?"

He was wiping that pearl-handled blade against his pants, like he always did in the evenings by the fire.

"Oh, I was just coming out for some firewood," she said casually, walking toward the sugar barrel.

"Firewood's over there."

She stopped and closed her eyes, with her back still turned. Soon it would be the dark of night, and then what? She had to move fast.

"Oh, silly me. Don't come out here often enough, I guess," she said, turning around.

Did he know about the gun?

Holver kept mindlessly wiping that blade, and she was reaching for a log when Jake burst into the shed.

"Pa! Ma's crazy again. Says we're going to Spokane. Seeing grandparents!" he shouted.

Holver smiled and rubbed his stubble. "C'mere, Jake."

"No, Jake, don't go to him. Go back to Owen!"

Jake looked at her, rolled his eyes, and sauntered over to Holver.

Holver stood facing the boy, with a large hand on Jake's shoulder.

"All those months in bed and you still thinkin' they'd listen to ya?" His eyes were fixed on Jake's face, but he was speaking to her. That's when she saw a blackness in his brown eyes, like the sky with no stars.

"Sleeping pills I stole from the ole doctor came in right handy for your tea. Not that you needed any help. You're crazy and dark-hearted all on your own."

Jake stood there smiling at Holver. How he loved his dad, but he was too young to understand any of this! Seeing Jake like that brought tears to Lily's eyes. She had to help him.

Then there was a flash of metal as Holver cut Jake's throat with one quick flick of the bowie knife.

Lily screamed and Jake fell to the floor, blood rushing from his neck so fast it made her think of the Spokane Falls, where Father's mill had been. Where her life had been hell, but now seemed like a refuge. She pushed out a loud, savage sound that surprised her, and then backed up toward the sugar barrel and the door. Holver looked at the boy's body.

"I'm goin' to be rich," he said to himself, squatting as the blood throbbed out little Jake's tender neck.

Lily felt behind her for the sugar barrel, removed the lid, and reached inside. Her sweaty fingers sifted granules of sugar until they found fabric. Then strings. She pulled the neck of the bag open. Sweat mixed with sugar and made her hands sticky.

"What's going on in here?" Owen shouted, barging into the woodshed.

FIFTY

"OWEN, GO! RUN!" Lily cried before Holver could say anything. "Whatever your Pa told you about me isn't true! Look what he did to Jake!" She pointed at her baby, the third one Holver had murdered.

Owen looked at Jake and sobbed.

"Aw, boy, you know I'd never do a thing to hurt Jake. Who been hurtin' the rest of ya this whole time?" Holver took a step toward Owen.

"Ma," Owen said between snorts and sobs, wiping his nose with the back of his hand.

Lily's mouth fell open. He'd been planning this the entire time. Drugging her, keeping her sick, and then poisoning the boys' minds against her so he could prey on them. So he could get rich. She played into it too! Stayed away from the boys, thinking she would hurt them. Took away their only real protection in doing it. Fear tried to take hold of her, paralyze her. But instead, rage stood up inside and shoved fear right out of the way.

"Holver Markwell, stop right there." Lily pointed the Colt .45 at his face. She reached an arm out for Owen like a net, trying to scuttle him behind her, but he moved past her and toward Holver instead. Then he stopped, as if he wasn't sure who to trust. The worst of it was Owen was in the way of her clean shot, but he couldn't see it because he was facing Holver. At least he was still out of Holver's reach.

Holver put his hands up in surrender. "Look, Lil, let's be civilized. You don't have to go all crazy about this." He made a just-go-along-with-it face at Owen.

"Owen get out of the way. Your father is dangerous." She took a step to the side, to get Owen out of her line of fire. The gun trembled in her hand. It wasn't enough, Owen was still in the way. Holver crept toward Owen, just a small step.

"Owen, ask your father to show you his knife."

"You know you can't believe a thing she says, boy. She ain't even awake half the year. You seen how she gets."

"Owen, darling, look at me," Lily said, keeping the gun pointed at Holver.

He obeyed and turned his face, and she regretted asking him to do that. Holver could leap across the shed and grab him. But if he did, she'd take her chances with a shot. She had to. Lily spoke fast. "I haven't been the mother you deserve. But do you see that Jake's neck was slashed with a knife? Do I have a knife on me? Anywhere around me? Is there blood on my hands?"

Holver moved to hide his hands. She snapped her face back at him. "I'll shoot you. You don't know what I'm capable of." She still didn't have a good shot.

He laughed. "You think I don't know you killed your own sister? That you murdered her in cold blood? You threw your dress in that wood stove and forgot to light it. Hell, even before that, I saw the blood on your corset. Ain't been one moment where you been ahead of me. And actually, that's what sealed the deal for me. Figured you were just like me. Couldn't help what was living inside you. The darkness. The will to survive. To come out on top."

"Owen, you run. Run right now to my stash. You know where it's at in the woods. Take everything I've got, and get on a train out of here. Go anywhere. You're free, and you have enough to get by until you can find work."

She could hold Holver off while Owen got away.

"Owen! Don't pay her no mind! She's crazy! Kilt your brother and sister. Kilt Jake! She's tryin' to set you up so as to kill you too."

Owen seemed unable to think clearly. He cried again and moved closer to Holver. Owen's movement still didn't provide enough space to hit Holver square in the chest, but now, Lily could wound him real good.

Lily changed her strategy with Owen. He didn't trust her, that was clear. But if she didn't get him out of this wood shed, he wouldn't live through the next few minutes. She had to say whatever it took. She'd explain it to him later. After Holver was dead and gone.

Lily took the shot at Holver and hit him in the leg.

"Dammit, woman! You *are* crazy!"

Owen stepped in front of Holver to protect him from Lily.

Lily moved the gun slightly until it was pointed directly at Owen, and with tears in her eyes, she said, "I'm crazy. He's right. If you don't leave this shed right now and run to get all my money, I'll find you and kill you, like I killed Katie and Joe. Like I killed Jake. Like I'm going to kill your Pa."

Owen yelped like a hurt dog and ran out of the shed. She refused the feeling of relief, but with a dip in the tension, her hands were shaking even more than before.

"Now what, Lily?" Holver moved to sit on the ground, grunting from pain. "You gonna run off to Spokane?" He was sweating, and blood pooled from his leg, swirling into the halo of blood around Jake's white face.

"Doesn't matter, you won't be around to find out." She lifted the gun to Holver's head.

"You got no money, and ya just sent Owen after your stash."

She reached into her dress pocket with her free hand and showed him the leather pouch. "That's all right, dear. I have yours."

He laughed. "That ain't enough to live off. What you gonna do, beg after that?"

She smiled and watched him writhe in pain for a minute. This was the moment she was waiting for. The moment where he'd see that all he'd done was in vain.

"No, dear, of course not. I meant I found *your* stash. By the stream, near that mine."

Holver let out a cry that sounded like a growl. "It's my mine! You evil witch! You can't steal it from me! Moonstep is mine!"

Now Lily really laughed. "Don't care about the mine. I don't need anything more than what your buried stash can give me. Thank you, Holver. You finally gave me my freedom."

She cocked the gun.

"Freedom to run to Spokane and into your ma's arms?" He spat at the ground. "Your parents been dead since the day we pulled off in that buggy."

Lily stumbled backward until her back touched the sugar barrel again.

"What...? How...?"

Holver smiled that big smile, and then gave an exaggerated shrug. "You told me to."

"I did no such thing!" she shouted, trying to show strength, but it was hard to hold the gun steady with her shaking arm.

"'Whatever it takes' were your exact words."

"I meant you should lie to them! I meant to make something up so they couldn't find us."

"What can I say? I like a sure thing."

She walked toward him with the gun aimed at his head.

"I've got a sure thing for you, Holver."

Lily pulled the trigger. Through a cloud of smoke, his head slammed backward against the wall. Once he was gone, she stared at him. Her world had changed so much and all in one day.

A third child, dead and gone.

She lost what she thought was a man who loved her, who turned out to be a murderer.

Her parents! All these years they'd been dead.

She dropped the six-shooter on the dirt floor and rushed to cradle Jake's head. She wet his face with her tears. She cried for all of them. For Katie, Joe, and Jake. She cried for Margaret, too, and all the ways she'd done wrong in her life. How could she ever—

"I can't let you get away with this." Owen's mousy voice came from the shed doorway.

She turned and looked at the double-barrel shotgun aimed right at her. Tears covered his face. He wiped his eyes with a forearm and went back to steadying the heavy gun.

"Where did you get that? Put it down, Owen," she said, but he only stiffened his aim at her chest.

"Pa bought it, said we might need it someday. When you came for us."

"Darling, it was *him*." Sobs came out of her. The rage had dried up and now, so close to freedom, her strength was gone. She felt sixteen years old again, afraid, the way she'd lived her whole life.

"He lied to you. He found Moonstep Mine, and he was killing you children in order to get rich."

"That sounds crazy, Ma. You're crazy!" he shouted. Spit flew from his mouth as his chest heaved out sobs of his own.

She took a slow step toward him, as if to tame a wild animal. "Listen to me, dear—"

Owen pulled the trigger, and a big *ka-boom* rang out.

Lily opened her eyes to see that she was leaning up against Holver's dead body. She touched her chest, where a circle of blood-soaked yellow gingham was expanding by the second.

She looked into Owen's face, and her last words sputtered out in sprays of blood, "I'm so sorry."

PATE, IDAHO

July 1989

FIFTY-ONE

ESMA WAS INSIDE total darkness. All was quiet. She couldn't see her own hand in front of her face. It was just like when her mom locked her in the closet. She screamed, cried out, and then heard a voice she knew. It sounded far away, but she knew it. Low, stern. No, not stern. Strong.

Slow obey is no obey.

"John!" she shouted. It was John's voice. He used to say that to Dawn all the time. She tried to stand, but couldn't pull her rump off the ground. Esma placed her hands flat against the dirt and pushed to lift herself up, but nothing happened. Above her head, not even inches away, her hands hit some sort of ceiling. Cold earth fell on her, rolled off her bandanna and onto her lap. This wasn't the closet, and Esma sighed in relief at that. She ran her hands along the ceiling. More dirt fell, but something brushed against them. Roots, maybe? She pulled a small one down, and it gave, came loose into her hand. Why wouldn't her eyes adjust to this darkness?

She punctured the small root with her fingernail and brought it up to her nose to smell. It had no scent. She was dreaming. Had to be dreaming. She dropped the root and sat still, imagining herself bursting out of whatever underground cave this was. It didn't work, so she pictured herself above ground in the July sunshine.

Nothing happened.

She thought about digging out and landing in her own bed, waking up.

Again, nothing.

This was someone else's dream. But whose?

You must love discipline.

John's voice again, muffled.

Someone was crying.

"John! John! Can you hear me? Please help me."

She felt around to see if there were side walls in this space. There were. Dirt surrounded her, and there was no way out. Esma whimpered and held her knees to her chest, laid down on her side that way. Her heart beat against deep silence. Then she heard another heartbeat. It was slower, stronger.

Rule your spirit!

"John? I can hear you. Are you there?"

A girl cried. It sounded like Dawn.

"He can't hear you when you're down here, you know that," a boy whispered. The voice was old-timey. She couldn't see anyone.

Esma sat up, crossed her legs again.

"Who are you?"

"Silly, you know who I am."

"No, I really don't."

"Jake. Name's Jake."

"Jake who?"

"Hush. Listen to your ma's heartbeat. It's the only thing that works to make it better."

She heard it, thrumming like she was inside a womb. Something about focusing on it made a little doorway in Esma's mind open, the way it does sometimes when you visit other people's dreams. You just suddenly know things. Esma knew two things. Dawn was scared, and John was hurting her.

"Focus on the sound," Jake's voice brought her back to Dawn's dream. "Want me to count heartbeats with you?"

"No! I want out of here."

You know I can't make myself clean.

"John!" Esma yelled. It was John's voice again.

"All right, the worst part's here now," Jake said. "Just think about your ma and focus on counting. 1, 2, 3, 4, 5..."

FIFTY-TWO

ESMA SAT UP in bed and gasped. It was only midnight by the alarm clock. She had been in Dawn's dream, and how terrifying! Her scariest visit to a foreign dream yet. Why was Dawn dreaming about John hurting her? He loved Dawn, his only child.

A slimy finger wormed around her mind, and once fully awake, sitting up, she couldn't swallow another moment of denial. John had hurt Dawn badly and probably more than once. But how could he? Dawn was everything to him. So much that sometimes Esma was jealous of her. Of their relationship. Did Esma know about this somehow? She smacked the side of her head repeatedly, and tears came hard. She must have, because if the realization came in a dream, and it did—in a side moment disconnected from the substance of Dawn's dream—surely her subconscious could confirm or deny it once and for all, even if her conscious memory had no clue. Maybe Little Esma knew.

In the kitchen, Esma turned on the light. It flickered, then hummed on. The bulb needed to be changed. Did Esma really want to know the answer to this question? She wiped her eyes. She was weak, running out of strength to believe, to fight for John. She'd waited ten years for him to return, and now this!

What if the headaches were due to her subconscious knowing John was hurting Dawn?

It was an intrusive thought, and she didn't like it. Her headaches were exactly what would have given John opportunity. Esma completely disappeared into her room whenever they came on. Even now, it was her headaches keeping her away from him, out of the shed.

The kitchen light flickered again, but stayed on. She'd ask Dawn to change out the bulbs next time she saw the girl. Where was Dawn? In fact, Esma had been so single-minded about John returning that she couldn't think of the last time she had a meaningful conversation with Dawn. Always trying to keep secrets from her.

Esma pulled out the sketchbook from under the loose floorboard, and held both pens in her hands. She moved the blue pen to paper to ask these questions about John, get some finality about her suspicions, no matter what the answer may be. But instead, the red pen slammed paper hard, and her left hand wrote.

TOOK YOU LONG ENOUGH.

It came like a slap across the face.

What?

SUCH A DESPERATE LOST PUPPY! YOU DIDN'T EVEN SEE HOW HE HURT HER RIGHT UNDER YOUR NOSE.

Tears came in a rush again, found routes along the sides of her nose and into her mouth, But she wouldn't let go of the pens, not even to wipe tears.

How? How did this happen?

STUPID, IRRELEVANT QUESTION. THERE'S ANOTHER QUESTION MORE IMPORTANT.

Nothing was more important right now. Esma stiffened, pushed down the urge to run away and hide, to wallow in her failure as a mother. She had to stay here. She deserved whatever Little Esma had to say to her, and more. Yet… Esma put the pens down and flipped back a few pages. Something was off. Why was Little Esma's spelling so much better now?

Little Esma, tell me the name of our dog again.

WHO FUCKING CARES. YOU TELL ME SOMETHING.

This wasn't her inner child. This was someone—something—else.

You're scaring me.

ANSWER MY QUESTION AND MAYBE I'LL LET YOU GO.

Esma tried to let go of the pens, to bring her hands up from the sketch pad, but she couldn't. Her body was heavy, like weights she couldn't lift. She was stuck, held in place.

WHY ARE YOU SO SMART ABOUT SOME THINGS AND SO FUCKING STUPID ABOUT EVERYTHING ELSE?

She could only cry. No answer was good enough for this question. The asker was right. Absolutely right. Then Esma's left hand wrote faster than she'd ever written before, completely out of control.

YOURE MINE YOURE MINE YOURE MINE YOURE MINE

The sketch pad slammed shut on its own and the light bulb went out. The force of the book closing pushed the kitchen chair over on its side.

Esma hit the floor with an elbow and a hip. The pain felt right, like one step closer to making this all better. She was shaking, unsure what had just happened. Who had hijacked Little Esma? No time for that, other things were more pressing. Where was Dawn? She hadn't been in her bed when Esma came into the kitchen, but the girl had been dreaming. How odd. Esma had to find her, apologize, hold the girl forever and never let go. But first, she had to confront John.

When Esma passed Dawn's room on the way out the back door, her heart pulled, like wanting her to go inside. Esma sat on the bed in the moonlight and let the tears run. Something white poked out from under the nightstand, so she reached down and pulled it out. A Polaroid image of Dawn and a boy. A very handsome boy indeed! On the bottom, someone had written "Monte + Dawn."

Who was Monte? Had Dawn found a boyfriend? How exciting! But then the pit returned to her stomach. She had no right to Dawn's happiness. She put the picture back where she found it.

Ducking out of Dawn's room and into the hallway where she could see out the back-door window, a figure stood between the back door and the shed. A sliver of light from inside the shed made her want to cry out. She forgot to close the shed door! Esma pressed her back against the wall, out of sight in one quick motion. But why was she hiding? If it was John, she was on her way to confront him anyway. Still, something inside told her to stay. But no, being afraid of him was an indulgence she did not deserve.

She opened the back door and walked outside, down the stairs. He stood against the dark of night, so she could only see those creepy glowing eyes. She shuddered, wanting to flee, to run past the shed, over the hill. Run until she got into town. Find Dawn. Leave this place together.

"Hi, honey. I thought you didn't want to come into the cabin," she said carefully, buying time, wishing she'd grabbed a kitchen knife or something.

John took slow steps toward her. Once within reaching distance, he towered head and shoulders above her. His energy was so dark, she swore it felt evil. But even so, Esma's courage grew. He had never hurt her before, but he might after this. She'd deserve that too.

"I know what you did to Dawn."

John cocked his head to the side, curious, as if inspecting. He didn't say anything.

"You hurt our daughter."

"Had to."

The flicker of courage gave way to rage. Esma ran at him, beat his chest with her fists.

"How could you?! You evil motherfucker! I hope you die. I hope you rot in Hell!"

John grabbed her by the bandanna in her hair, ripping some hair with it, and pulled it off.

Esma fell to the ground on the same elbow as before, and a sharp zing reminded her of the pain. Good, good, yes, pain. She'd take all the pain coming her way. She sobbed, wailed, and screamed. Spit flew out, strings clinging to her chin, but she didn't care, didn't wipe them away. He was right there, and if she turned, it'd be those two glowing orbs. She turned.

It wasn't just the glowing eyes this time. His whole body was lit up with a silver glow, everything from his cheeks to his fingertips. Where his shirt was open a bit at his neck, veins glowed under his skin. Where his thin clothes covered skin, she could see the veins as a blurry silver haze underneath. Esma let out a scream so razor sharp that it hurt her throat.

"Still don't get it, do ya?" John asked.

Esma was curled up in a ball on her side. Pine needles poked the skin through her nightgown. More pain, yes good. Maybe this was her end. That would have been fine, except she wanted to make things better with Dawn first. If only that. Everything else, whatever John did to her, she didn't care.

"Still askin' all the wrong questions."

What? John sounded like *not*-Little Esma. Why?

John gripped a fistful of Esma's loose hair and pulled her a few steps toward the shed. She wriggled, kicked at his legs, and scratched his fingers to loosen them. He brought the full weight of his strong arm down against her face, knocked her so hard she blacked out.

ESMA WOKE UP in the corner of the woodshed, huddled in the exact same spot John had occupied on her visits before. A faint light shone from the oil lantern. John stood over her, glowing. Esma's headache came on right then, starting in her face like her eyes and nose were being sucked outward, as if a heavy blanket dropped over her head.

"John, I loved you."

Esma tried to keep her voice soft and even, so as not to set him off, but it quaked and wavered still. The pain in her head consumed any open space in her mind and suffocated rational thought. How would she live long enough to see Dawn again?

John pulled out a pearl-handled bowie knife and ran it across his pants, as if he were sharpening it.

"Where did you get that?" she managed, suddenly distracted. "I've never seen it before."

It was the thing he'd been hiding from her earlier. The thing she thought was a surprise gift for her. How stupid she was.

"John, please talk to me." Esma reached up to touch the fabric of his pants, and he moved so she couldn't. He smirked and turned his face toward the knife. It was her chance.

She lunged at his knees like a wild cat and knocked him to the shed floor. The knife tumbled out of his hand. She climbed on top of him, straddled his waist, punched, cried, spit flying as she shouted, "You devil! How could you hurt our little girl?!"

John threw Esma down on her back and pressed both his hands on her chest. Like one long chest compression, and it was hard to breathe. She gasped, trying to bring air into lungs collapsed by his weight.

"John, no! Stop!"

He had the bowie knife again and held it at her neck with enough pressure to bring just a drop of blood. The warmth of it ran like a collar around her neck to the back. She tried to kick, but he was immovable.

"How could you?" she sobbed.

It would be over in seconds, but still, she wasn't ready. She had to make it right.

Esma growled and screamed in his face, "I'm not ready!"

The suddenness of her scream threw John off his focus. Esma tried again to wriggle her arms free of the weight of his thighs, but he hit her across the face. Then he leaned in close, so close that she felt the sour heat of his breath on her skin. His mouth opened so wide that it filled his entire face. She tried to scream again, but there was no air. She was tired, sinking. And in her final moments, she projected her last intention out into the world, pictured it like her life force shooting up into the sky of stars, where it would act as a searchlight to find her daughter.

I will see Dawn again. I will do right by her.

Then her vision narrowed until John's shape, the man she had once loved, was surrounded by dark edges, fading away. She was dropping through the floor. There was beautiful Dawn with a ponytail and dimples, then as a small fry, then a baby. It was Esma's wedding day, John's face, so full of hope. Woodstock, her prayer of salvation. Carmen the mutt. And then, her mom. Mom's smile, and what her hugs might have felt like if Esma had ever experienced one. There was no hate or fear or abuse. She just held her mom and watched all of that dirty black energy separate itself from her and float away. She was whole, and loved, and healed, but she kept falling, falling, falling, until it all went black.

FIFTY-THREE

THE KITCHEN LIGHT was off when Dawn got home around 2 a.m. She'd taken extra shifts at the hotel, even helping with the front desk in order to stay busy and avoid thinking about what happened to Monte. Of course, she mostly just feel asleep during the night shift.

She flicked the light on, but nothing happened. Bulb must be out.

The light of the open shed door caught her attention. Something wasn't right. Had someone broken into the shed? Why in the world would anyone bother? They had nothing of value, and especially not in the shed.

"Mom?" Dawn whispered.

Mom wasn't in her bed, so Dawn looked closely out the back-door window. Mom's bandanna was on the ground in front of the woodshed. A white scarf, glowing in the moon-light, colorful flowers all over it. Mom wore it every day.

She'd need to go check out the shed. Find Mom. The thought was a cold stone dropped inside her stomach. She retched like maybe she'd vomit, but nothing came out, so she walked back into the kitchen and sat on a chair, trying to catch her breath. Checking the shed was inevitable, but fear paralyzed her.

What if Mom's in there? What if she had a heart attack or passed out? Move, Dawn! Go now!

Dawn reached into a bag on her bedroom floor and pulled out a flashlight, then went outside.

"Mom?" she whispered into the vast space of their property. The only response was a soft breeze in the pine trees. It had been hot today, but cooled off significantly, and while she wasn't chilled, her work uniform felt a bit sparse.

After a few steps through the night, she was face up to the open crack of the shed door. She peeked inside, but didn't see anything except the lit lantern on a stump.

Slow obey is no obey.

Dad's face came to mind. His hot breath, the belt, his trousers loosening...

She shook off those thoughts and pushed open the door. It creaked slightly, and she stopped, couldn't look. Maybe she couldn't go in there after all. Maybe she didn't need to. She could just call the police. But why? If someone broke in, they were gone now. Then again, where was Mom? Calling the police was—

"Dawn?" a man's voice called from inside the shed.

She froze, unable to move at all.

"It's me," he said.

It couldn't be him. It wasn't possible.

She opened the door all the way and first saw her mother lying on her back, mouth open wide, face shriveled—or mummified, more like. She was dead. Mom was dead. Dawn's breathing was erratic now. She wanted to run, but had to go to Mom. Then she saw him. Suspenders, big boots, and long, unkempt hair. It definitely looked like her dad. She slammed the door shut and stood outside, trying not to hyperventilate.

With her back against the door, she slowed her breath. So many thoughts hit her mind at once. Her mom! Dead. Sobs grew inside her chest, asking for permission to erupt into gushing tears, but she pushed them back. Not now, she had to figure out what to do. That man. It wasn't Dad. It couldn't be him. There was absolutely no way. It looked like him, and yet... Dawn felt a realization curling around her mind. It looked like Dad, yes, but even more, it looked like someone else she'd seen.

WHEN DAWN OPENED the door a few minutes later, she held a little gas can that Dad kept by the fuel tank alongside the woodshed.

Nobody was there, so she set it down outside the shed and went to kneel down by Mom's body. Mom, gone! The horror of it outweighed her fear of the wood shed. Tears finally overpowered her, and she touched Mom's face, feeling the leathery hardness of dried, stretched skin.

That's when her eye gravitated to the old picture leaning up against the wall of the shed. The man and the woman. Except only the woman was in the portrait now.

Not-Dad was suddenly at the back of the shed, despite that he wasn't there even seconds before.

"You're not my dad."

He took another step, and she saw a bowie knife. She scrambled back to the shed's door to grab the gas can.

"You're him." Dawn motioned to the old portrait once she was out of his reach. "I used to stare at your picture while my dad beat me. Used to think it was him in the picture, that he could never die. That he'd always been, and always would be— that he'd live on forever and ever. Then I thought maybe he was living through me because I was so bad. I tried to be good, to keep him from bubbling up inside my anger. Only later did I learn it was our distant relatives, Holver and Lily Markwell in that picture. You. Not my dad."

The resemblance was uncanny. Holver was the same age in the picture as Dad was when he disappeared. They could be twins. He must have fooled Mom into thinking he really was Dad.

Dawn had learned about the Markwells quite accidentally through a friend in school who was obsessed with their disappearance. She didn't bring it up with Mom because she didn't want to encourage Mom to think about Dad more than she already did. Dawn's heart gaped when she thought of how excited her mom probably was, thinking Dad had come home, and how this *thing* had tricked her and then killed her. How Dawn could have prevented it if Mom only knew how much Dad looked like Holver.

He took slow steps toward her. "I ain't gonna hurt you."

Dawn sloshed gasoline inside the shed. She didn't know why burning it down made sense, but she knew she wanted to be rid of that torture chamber. Never see it again. If whatever that monster was inside the shed got caught in the blaze, even better.

That's when Holver disappeared. She looked at the portrait, and there he was, next to Lily, but holding the bowie knife in one hand.

Dawn placed her foot on the stump, where the oil lamp was lit and glowing.

"Goodbye, Mom. I love you," she said, and then pushed her foot so hard that the stump fell over and glass broke. Hot flames licked up from the ground and traveled fast, washing over Mom's body. The last thing Dawn saw before she slammed the door was that old portrait burning.

The Pate Fire Department was on high alert this time of year. Dawn was counting on them. Wildfires tore up the mountains on a regular basis, especially during the summer. Maybe she wanted the shed gone, but she didn't want to burn the cabin down, and she sure as heck didn't want to start a forest fire.

Dawn dialed the fire department, covering the phone's mouthpiece and disguising her voice. Then she ran to the car. About the time she reached it, the gas tank by the woodshed exploded and sent fireworks of flames into the air. She heard sirens and put the car in reverse to get down the driveway, then pushed the gas pedal hard. Speeding down the road, she passed the fire truck on her way out of town. Then tears came in such a gush, she could barely see where she was going.

FIFTY-FOUR

SYL'S PHONE RANG just as she and Roger were catching their breath.

"Sorry to bother you so late," Hendon said. He sounded scared. "Looking for Roger. You know where he might be?"

"I do," Syl said, handing the phone to Roger. "It's Hen."

Syl watched Roger with arms crossed. So much had happened in just a few hours, and she was so damn tired.

Roger uh-huhed and then hung up the receiver.

"Gotta go. Fire at the Winton place." He walked toward the front door.

"Should I come?"

"Nah. You can come by there in the morning though. Unless it's a false alarm. I'll call in that case."

Nothing about Hendon's voice indicated a false alarm.

"We need to talk about what happened here tonight," she shouted as he rushed out the door toward his rig. He waved her away with his hand.

Still so dismissive, even after what they'd just been through.

She watched the truck headlights flash on and then drive away.

SYL WENT TWENTY-FIVE over the limit all the way to the Winton cabin the next morning. She was running on about three hours of sleep even though she'd crashed out right after Roger left.

No way her brain would let her sleep when there was so much to figure out. Gran, the photographs. People around here who knew about it all. The strange thing that happened when Gran showed up and Syl lost all sense of reasoning. People around here couldn't see how the ones that returned weren't *actually* their loved ones, and Syl hadn't been any better. Could she have burned the only remaining photo of Gran if Roger's life hadn't been hanging in the balance?

Syl slammed the door of the Vicky at the end of the Wintons' driveway. There were cars all around, including Roger's rig, perched up high up beside the carport. She walked up the skinny driveway, dodging cars.

Approaching the front doorstep, something looked different. Missing. John's framed portrait was gone. All that remained was a single nail at eye level, where the picture had hung for so many years.

That wasn't good.

Roger's voice boomed from behind the cabin. Syl walked around the outside of it and saw them all standing there, staring at a charred and half-gone structure. She looked at the backside of the cabin. It was slightly burned, but otherwise undamaged.

"How is it possible the cabin didn't burn?" Syl asked.

"Fire crew got here fast. Fastest in history, they said. Just in time to keep it from going up in flames," Roger said.

Syl looked up. "Amazing that it didn't catch the trees at all."

"It's a veritable Christmas-in-July miracle."

"Any idea what happened?"

"No. Except we know gas tanks don't spontaneously explode."

"Sheriff, you need to see this," Hendon shouted from the smoking heap. It looked like they'd been combing through debris for a while, once it had cooled down enough to approach.

Roger unwrapped a piece of Big Red and tossed the foil aside as he took measured steps toward the mess. Syl rolled her eyes and picked up his litter.

Hendon pointed to something in the middle of the ruins. Syl got closer and saw its roundness. A skull.

"Is that a body?" Hendon said.

Roger leaned in, so Syl leaned in, and she saw a pattern below the roundness that confirmed it for her.

"Teeth," she said. "It's definitely remains of some sort."

Roger looked around, then whispered to her, "Maybe John showed up."

It was exactly what she was thinking. Where was his picture though?

"Can I go inside?"

"Back door was unlocked when we got here. That's invitation enough for me." Roger held up his thermos. "Coffee's from home though. You won't find any in there."

It wasn't coffee Syl wanted, but it was nice to know Roger had been home at some point during the night. He must be as exhausted as she was.

One step into the Winton cabin, and Syl groaned. She forgot how insanely cluttered it was. How in the world was she going to find a single framed picture in all this crap?

She came upon Dawn's room first. She knew it was Dawn's because of all the posters of animals with Bible verses on the walls. One poster of the ocean included the "Footprints" poem.

Syl followed the slug path out to the kitchen table, where she found an artist's sketchbook laid open. No drawings though. Just blue and red writing. She thumbed through it, recalling how strange Esma Winton was with every flick of a page. It looked like a conversation between red and blue, but who was she talking to? That's when Syl saw a word that made her skin crawl: Moonstep.

FIFTY-FIVE

SYL OPENED THE sketchbook in front of Roger, who was still sitting on the back steps of the Winton cabin.

"Check this out." She cleared her throat. "Moonstep, Moonstep, misbehave. Moonstep, Moonstep, in the—"

"Stop! God, what's your problem?" Roger went to cover his ears and spilled some coffee on his pants.

What the hell? He acted like she'd thrown a basket of snakes at him.

Roger stood and tried to grab her arm, as if to pull her to the side of the cabin, away from the team working at the site. She whipped her arm out of his grip and stood firm. They still hadn't talked about what happened the night before. What else did Roger know?

"What's *your* problem?" Syl yelled. The team turned around. Roger forced a smile and waved at them.

"Shh," he said and walked to the driveway where the cars were parked, motioning for her to follow. What little patience she was born with was so threadbare it was see-through. He stopped right next to his rig.

"Give me that." Roger put out a hand. He looked it over, half-heartedly. Like he didn't want to fully read through it. "If this is what Esma was up to, then it's probably her in the ashes over there."

"It's just a—"

"Just a little poem, right?" Roger scoffed. "I'm not saying these words on paper resulted in that,"—he pointed at the smoldering remains of the shed—"but it didn't help, either."

"You're still holding out on me. You know more, and you're not telling me. It has to stop!"

He took his hat off and rubbed his head.

"Been meaning to give you this." He reached over and opened the door to his rig. When he turned around, he had a white envelope in his hand. Written on the front were two words in Gran's handwriting: *Sylvia Dixon*. She turned it over and saw that it was already open.

"You read it? Un-fucking-believable!"

"Of course I read it."

"It wasn't yours to read!"

"Look, Syl, you're right. Thing is, I didn't read it right away Didn't read it for a decade. Longer!"

With every word that came out of Roger's mouth, Syl felt weaker. Tired. Like a sleep-deprived mother whose infant wakes every half an hour screaming. She didn't care about Roger's excuses. His justification for something he shouldn't have done. All she wanted was to go home, curl up under Gran's quilt, and read the damn letter. Drink a case of beer, have a good cry.

She walked away from Roger without a word.

"I had to know, Syl," he yelled at her back. "Because…" His voice cracked.

God, was he really going to cry right now? In this moment? Right when she had her hands on something she dreamed about, but never imagined existed. Information he *kept* from her?

Syl sighed. She turned around, glared at him, and tapped her foot so he'd get a glimpse of how little patience she had left. "What?!"

"Because Mary disappeared."

Her mind was slow to comprehend the meaning of his words.

"What?"

"Mary disappeared about two years ago."

Of course she did. Syl didn't want to be a bitch about it, but was he really going to require her to be understanding at this moment? He was in the wrong here. The injustice of all this was hers, and she didn't want to share it with anyone. Especially not him. She had lost her entire family. Grown up without a mom, dad, or even Gran. It was she who had a right to tears right now. It was she who needed a shoulder to cry on, and never had one her whole life. And here he was, asking for her sympathy. And yet… What if he had something important to say? That damn curiosity got the best of her. She didn't soften completely, but she could set aside her anger. Pick it up later and call him to account. There was always a fresh bone to pick with ole Roger Mock.

"And pray tell, how the hell would my grandmother's suicide note help you after Mary left?"

"Read it, and you'll know."

Now she was pissed. Syl rushed over, got into his personal bubble. "I will. And you'll answer my question too. How the fuck did this"—she shook the letter—"help you?"

"I always knew that Lou was into something. The woman was always in the woods, and yet, she always came back. I wanted to know how she did it. Why could she come back? And if she could do it, I thought maybe my Mary could too."

Syl shook her head. The selfishness.

"I'm sorry. I see now it wasn't my place," he said. Then whispered, "Still don't regret it though."

She pretended not to hear and walked to the end of the driveway to get into the Vicky. Roger was not top priority. Reading the letter was.

HOW MUCH TIME had passed? Probably not a full hour, but she was down to the end of the letter, and Gran's handwriting was scattered about the kitchen table. There were only a few pages left to read. So much raced through her mind that she couldn't hold on to one thought long enough to make sense of it. She'd finish the letter and then go back through it. Roger was an asshole for reading it instead of tracking her down and giving it to her, but he wasn't wrong. There was a lot here. It was all connected. To Alex Conder's case. To the portraits. To the Winton fire. Even to the dreams. But her head throbbed when she tried to piece it together. She started reading the last few pages.

PATE, IDAHO

January 1962

FIFTY-SIX

RIGHT AFTER I *threw Rose's photograph into the fire, my head rang hard from the flu. The laughing inside me got louder, the humming went out of control. That bitch in the mine was taunting me. I had to make it stop. That's when I told myself again that it wasn't our Rose I seen. It was something that monster had summoned. I got out of bed and stumbled past Harold. He was saying something, but I couldn't hear what. I pulled up my galoshes, threw on a coat, and went out to the barn for the shotgun. The cold air pinched my face, but the sun was warm, and it made the snow blinding. Grandpa shuffled after me in his slippers.*

"Lou! Get back in bed. What're you doin' now?"

I grabbed a box of shells and put it into my coat pocket. I put on snowshoes. He blocked my way.

"Out of my way, Harold." I went like I was going to push past him, but he wouldn't let me. Everything wavered seasick-like, and I saw double.

"You gone mad? It's thirteen degrees out here."

"Hand me your hat and scarf then."

"Get back in bed, woman! You do what I say." He had tears welling up. But in our whole lives, he'd never told me what for, and it wasn't going to start now. I shoved past him hard, and with my back to him, his tone of voice told me something I never heard before, and didn't hear again after that. He needed me. I always knew he did, but he never let it on.

"Lou, please, old gal. Please stay."

Well, that was when my crying started, but I didn't let him see my tears. I'd already made it along the side of the house and out to the road.

"I'm calling the sheriff! Get back here!" Harold called out.

When there was a break in my sobs, I swallowed hard and walked back to him, leaned in, and kissed his cold lips. Then I turned and walked away again.

Harold went berserk. I'm sure he thought I'd gone mad.

"LouAnn Dixon, what's gotten into you?" he shouted from far behind. I was already in the woods.

I ignored the pressure in my head, the way every hair on my body made my skin ache. That flu wasn't done with me yet, and each step I took sent lightning bolts through me, spun me around and forced me to stop and rest. I leaned against a tree until my vision straightened out. I did this over and over until I had to stop and sit for a while. Couldn't sit too long, though, or I'd freeze. Had to keep moving.

The closer I got to the mine's location, the more out of whack I felt. Like I completely forgot how to be in the woods at all. I got lost, forgot how to work my shotgun. At one point, I couldn't even make a goddamn fire. Just stared at that match like it was a UFO I should know how to fly.

Finally, I got there. The clearing was quiet as death, like it had been before, and I had my wits again. Just a few steps inside that dank mine, I tripped and fell to my knees on the rocky ground.

It was a body.

My foot had caught on the leg of a shriveled-up body! I couldn't tell who it was because the eye sockets were empty, and the mouth was stretched open. At the time I felt numb, like a dead body wasn't the big, fat, hairy deal it should be. I was focused on that damn mine. I pushed past, cocked my shotgun, and started blasting down into the tunnel. I reloaded and fired more shots, careful to send them into the cold darkness, not allowing them to ricochet off the rock walls.

"C'mon you bitch! Afraid of a fight?" I yelled, firing more shots.

My ears rang from the flu and the shots now too. My heart thumped in my head, and every pull of the trigger hurt.

Nothing.

I fired every damn shell in that box. Didn't know what else to do and was sure I'd faint any minute, so I turned to go. A blast of freezing cold air pushed at my back. I gagged because it smelled like death, pup.

Ever so slowly, I turned my head to look back down that dark tunnel.

Eyes. Veins.

Glowing eyes and veins pumping some substance, that same silver that was inside my Rose. Bodies were coming right at me.

That's when I ran. Ran for all get-out. I ran all the way home, tripping, falling, gasping for air. Decided I'd rather die of a fall, or of the flu, than to let one of those bastards get me.

I was almost home before I looked back.

Nothing followed me. Again, I wondered if I was crazy. But no, I'd seen that body in the mine. That was real.

I was lucky to make it back home, but by the time I did, I was real sick. Went back to bed and slept all night and day.

When I woke up, Grandpa was gone. I realized I hadn't seen him when I got home, just went straight under the covers. I stumbled past Rose's room, which was quiet now. Then I called for Harold, but silence was the answer.

Found out later that day that he'd not gone to the mines for his shift. He'd gone to look for me.

I knew he was gone. It broke me. Soon as I could get out of bed, I went to the sheriff.

That damn sheriff was so green, he would have needed help to wipe his own ass. But the old sheriff was in the hospital dying, and so all I had was the young guy. Said Harold called him and was going up the mountain to look for me. He told Harold he doesn't go into those woods, said Harold was on his own. I gave him hell for that.

"You wouldn't go, but you sent my Harold off with a pat on the head?"

The man looked like a kid caught with his hand in the cookie jar. He started rubbing his head so hard I thought his thick hair might all fall out.

"This is on you, Roger," I shouted as I walked out. "Harold's death is on you. I know he isn't coming back. You should have stopped him from going after me if you had a feeling about it."

Back at home, I went through our old boxes and photo albums, and burned every picture I could find of your grandpa. Weren't many. The man hated having his picture taken, but that only made it harder.

FIFTY-SEVEN

THE HUMMING I *felt while I was sick was a regular event now. It grew in pitch, but I pushed on through the years. Nothing ever happened in that spare bedroom again, but I cleared all that shit out and made a right guest bedroom. I accepted my lot—that it was my debt to live with the buzzing of fear and anger. Moonstep Mine wouldn't let me rest, but if that was her only line to me, I could handle it. I wouldn't let that mine demon get me down. I was like some cosmic sponge, absorbing it, welcoming it, until it shrunk into the background of my brain.*

Soon, I longed for Rose all over again. I felt discouraged that maybe I'd never be over her death.

Over the years, though, happier times came. Mason got married, and then you showed up all wrinkled and screaming one day.

Your mother really did die in childbirth, pup. That part's true, although what I told you about your father wasn't true. He didn't die in a trucking accident.

Mason's death is the thing I've been cornering this whole letter.

All these words, and now that I've got it in my scope, I'm tired, and this letter is too damn long. I still don't feel ready to tell you, but since when do feelings get to be the boss?

I babysat you a lot while your father worked as a trucker. Since he was gone for long stretches, I had you for months at a time, and I got to watch you grow.

On your fifth birthday, I was making you a cake. It was a perfect June day, and the sun streaked in through the kitchen windows. Together, with the yellow walls and countertop I had just put in, it shone gold. I loved that shine. It's why I chose yellow for this kitchen. Made me feel like a pirate stumbling upon a treasure chest at high-sun time. Like anything was still possible as long as you hoped for it, and maybe you could be something better than yourself.

You stood on a chair next to me, swiping spilled sugar from the tile counter with your little finger, wetting it in your mouth and then swiping up some more. I swatted at your hands to make you stop, but you only laughed, and that made me laugh too. When I turned to stir the batter, that ache for Rose was gone. You'd done something to patch up my heart, pup. If I tried real hard, I could find that sadness over my lost girl. But you made it seem far away, like something that happened to someone else.

Your father made good money on the road. Gave him an escape after your mom died. For my part, I felt that pushing him to quit the mines was my one and only good deed as a mother.

I've set my pen down a thousand times at this part. Can't find a way to say it that feels right. I figure the best way is to keep it simple. As you know, your dad was home last week. You were at school that day, and Mason asked if I wanted to go out into the woods tracking with him. Like we used to do when he was a boy. I told him no in a lot of ways. Too old, bones get cold faster, can't keep up. But he just laughed and promised to go slow. Your dad could be so convincing, and I was a fool. We packed up, put snowshoes on, and went out for a hike. Once we were in the woods, I realized he wasn't tracking anything. He just wanted to get me out of doors. He knew I loved it. Your father was like that. The sort who could see what people needed and then give it to them.

I started to feel funny, dizzy. The humming grew so loud inside me that I couldn't hear Mason speaking, could only see his mouth moving as he turned and reached for me. It was happening so slow. Then I blacked out.

When I woke up, I was straddling my boy, and all the muscle and fat had been taken out of him. He was shriveled up, like that body I'd stumbled over in the mine years before! His eye sockets were empty, and the only fog of breath I saw was my own.

I screamed and scrambled off him. I had murdered my boy! I didn't mean to, but I did.

I killed your dad, pup. I got no right to live anymore after that. And besides, how could I ever keep you safe? What if that stupor comes over me again, and next time it's you I hurt? That's why after you leave for school this morning, I'm going back out to the spot where I buried Mason in the woods. I'll lay down beside him in the snow and go to sleep. Finally, I'll have peace.

Something happened to me the day I found that lost mine. I don't know what or how, but it's inside me, and I will never be rid of the poison in my blood. The arsenic of violence driven to destroy all that is good, even when I don't want to.

Two days ago, you and me sat at Mason's funeral. It was another sunny winter day, and even though the snow piled up to the bottom of the funeral parlor's window, it shone so brightly against the top of drifts that sparkles came out across the town. You love it when the snow sparkles, pup. You call it Pate pixie dust. I pressed your little navy-blue dress that morning, and you sat next to me, hands in your lap, legs swinging in the chair. The blue was dark enough not to show when your tears dropped on the apron of it. I felt your warmth against my side and tried to be strong for you. Tried not to think about all the pain I caused.

I don't know why I said yes to going out with Mason that day. I should have known better. Nothing had happened for so many years. How many times had I taken you out there without any problems? Why did the mine allow it? I'll never know. But going into the woods on that day was giving it an inch. Mason's smile, asking me to go outdoors, into the place I'd always loved, was too hard to resist. I'd seen the little boy living inside of him in that moment. The little boy I wasn't there for, and I wanted to make it right. Do right by him. I was a goddamn fool.

Life is breakable, pup. Having something dear only guarantees it'll hurt when it's gone. Learn one thing from your old Gran: Enjoy what you have while you have it. Enjoy it because you have it, and because you'll lose it one day. I wish I could give you something more hopeful than that, but I can't.

I'm putting this letter into the hands of that horse's ass, Sheriff Roger Mock. He's young enough that he should be around by the time you turn eighteen. That's when I want him to hand deliver it to you. He knows he owes it to me. He might be a bastard, but he's smart enough to stay out of those woods.

Assuming things work out how I hope they do, you'll be raised by my sister, Shirley, who came up from Boise to live in Spokane this past year. Stranger will go, too, I've decided tonight. Damn Shirley's dislike of dogs.

Pup, my sister's nothing like me. She's sure to be a pushover, and will probably spoil you to high heaven, but she'll love you and keep you away from Pate.

It's morning now, and you're on the couch, sucking that goddamn thumb. You're looking at that old nursery rhyme picture book. Pup, you've got that squeak in your laugh like my Rose had, and it's roaring loud from the den. How I've loved you, Sylvia. How I pray you do better than me.

All My Love,

Gran

PATE, IDAHO

August 1989

FIFTY-EIGHT

SYL WOKE UP with a start. She almost fell off the couch and into a pile of overturned chocolate-covered cherry boxes and empty Doritos bags.

It had been three weeks since she read Gran's letter. Three weeks of avoiding Roger around town. Three weeks of crying. Three weeks of keeping her phone off the hook, again to avoid Roger. Three weeks of watching reruns of *The Andy Griffith Show*, *The Waltons*, or *Little House on the Prairie*. Anything that moved on the boob tube and didn't entail police work. Andy and Barney got a pass.

Syl groaned and sat up, got a whiff of herself on the breeze her lurch forward had made. God, she stank. The yellow robe over baggy gray sweats was a glamorous look, but she needed a shower. Coffee would be a good idea too.

Syl sucked at "processing things," as Carl would say. Processing the letter, for one. She'd always thought simply knowing what had happened to Gran would satisfy her. It hadn't. In fact, knowing only made the deep hole in her heart grow.

The green phone receiver dangled against the wall, stretching its coil cord to the limit, but Syl didn't care. It had to stay off the hook. Surrounding the phone were all of her notes. Connections she made, based on Gran's letter, and based on what Roger had said. She'd compulsively returned to it, despite that she didn't want to think about any of it again.

Disappearances.

Happen in a cycle of sorts.

"High times" lead to reappearances. (Next to this, a separate note asked, "Why?")

Reappearances linked to photographs of the disappeared.

She thought about calling them "the dead," but decided against it. She didn't know if they were dead or not. She didn't know if they were ghosts or aliens or...

She sighed and pulled one of the notes off the wall: *Photos must be destroyed or the disappeared will keep coming back.* She placed it closer to the note about reappearances linked to photographs.

The whole thing was like a popcorn kernel stuck in her gums. She couldn't help but pick at it, try to dislodge something, but nothing came.

At least I still have Lucas.

The thought was so out of left field that it made her angry. It was the last thing she could handle thinking about right now, and too bad if it made her a terrible person.

The doorbell rang.

At first, she tried to hide in the kitchen, but it rang a second time. Whatever, it wasn't like she was a shut-in.

She opened the door to Roger's round face behind a vase of flowers.

Really?

She moved to close the door. He stuck his boot in the way.

"Syl, just hear me out."

She walked into the house and let the door fall open. She didn't have the energy to make him go away. If he was so determined that he thought flowers would help, she might as well get it over with.

"I hate flowers," she yelled from the kitchen. "They always die, stink, and make a mess I have to clean up."

Roger stood in the doorway, flattening his lips, as if waiting for an invitation.

"Well, c'mon! You're letting all the heat in."

He stepped inside and put the flowers down next to the coffee pot.

She poured a cup for herself, careful not to offer him one, and sat down at the table.

"Well?"

He poured himself a cup of coffee.

"We need to talk."

"No shit, Sherlock. Let's start with why you opened my letter."

"I was hoping to start by explaining my theory about why people reappear."

He always did this. Skirted out of important conversations by dangling information she wanted in front of her face. And it always worked.

"Whatever. You've got five minutes."

Roger walked over to the wall with the phone, looked over all her notes. He hung the phone back on the hook. He was sure piddling his five minutes away.

"I know it seems like I'm not busy, but I've actually got a hot date with a shower, so cut to it," she said.

"Mary came back."

"What? When?"

"Just after you showed up in Pate." He sat down across from her at the table.

God, would his secrets ever end?

"You kept Mary's pictures? Even after you knew what could happen?" Syl stated the words slowly, feeling the anger rise behind each one.

Roger rubbed his bald head. At least he didn't bother with the hat at all today. Easy access.

"I know."

"Tell me you've burned them now."

He pressed his lips together again. "Gonna do it. Nothing bad happened. I turned my living room into a visiting room, just like my mom did. It's not like it was with Lou."

How was it that even Roger, who knew how dangerous the reappeared could be, still kept Mary's picture? Then Syl remembered the empty feeling inside when she watched Gran's last photograph burn. People lied to themselves.

They did exactly like Roger, reasoned it away: *It's not like it was with Lou.* Like it'll be different for them. Like they're somehow special.

"Lucky you," she said, "You've got the murderous monster touch, I guess."

He rolled his eyes. "Let me explain."

"Wait. I can't discuss this until you've returned to sanity. You need to burn Mary's picture first."

"It's at home. I'm not that stupid. Listen to what I've got to say, and you'll see why that one little picture of Mary doesn't matter anymore. I'll come clean. Suppose it's time."

"Time? It's so far past 'time.' You should have come clean the day I showed up at Lucky Dog and stooped over Alex's dead body. If not then, how about when Mac and Hendon shouted 'John Winton' and 'Markwells' at us? Or how about the night Gran was on top of you? How about then? Oh, I've got it. How about a good fifteen years ago, when I became an adult? You could have delivered the goddamn letter to me then!" She was shouting by the time it all cascaded out.

"All right, all right. Can you be done giving me the business? I brought you flowers. I'm *trying.* I'm no good at the feely stuff."

"I hate flowers," Syl mumbled again. Then she looked up. "I ask the questions."

"Fine."

"Why the hell did you ask me to help with the Conder case if you already knew it was unsolvable."

"I wanted to keep you close by."

"Why?"

"I thought maybe you were like Lou and were the cause of everything starting up again."

"Huh? What do you mean 'like Lou?'"

"Lou caused the reappearances in the forties, when I came back from the war."

Drip, drip, drip. Here was ole Roger back at it, slow-rolling information.

"Roger, goddamn it! Talk faster. Or say more. Either one works."

"I didn't know for sure until I finally cracked that letter open, but when I did, I put it together. My sister and father reappearing way back in 1946. The strange call I took as a rookie. I told you about it the other day, the Buckley kid seeing his baseball coach. I sleuthed out more instances and none of them happened before about 1941. Lou was in the woods all the time during that period. Looking for her girl, as you know from the letter. Why hadn't Rose reappeared sooner than 1941, considering she went missing in 1933? What took so long? I'll tell you. Lou found Moonstep Mine around 1941. She found it, went in, and then came back out. She just walked right back into her normal life. Except it was anything but normal. She was tormented. You read it. The 'humming' she called it. I think whatever's in that mine got into her and used her against her will."

Syl rubbed her forehead with her fingertips. This was a lot. Too much.

"So, Gran was some sort of evil being, bringing all the disappeared people back to murder their families?"

"No. She was still just Lou Dixon. But the mine used her as a sort of connection. An antenna, I guess. While she lived inside Lou, Moonstep had access. The connection with Lou helped her grow strong and literally reach into homes by returning the missing people. She could harvest more souls without bothering to call them up to the mine."

"So, Gran was possessed?"

"No, because Lou was always Lou. I'm not talking about Satanism or occult stuff."

"Except when she killed my father. She wasn't herself then. Did you forget about that tiny detail?"

Roger grimaced. "Right, except for that. Maybe the person starts out like an antenna and then progresses to a host once Moonstep becomes more powerful. It's still not like possession, though, because Moonstep only takes over for a few moments at a time."

"Feels like you're making shit up, Roger."

But it didn't. It actually made a lot of sense. Syl just hated that it was Gran responsible.

"And why do you keep calling the thing in the mine a 'she'?" Syl added.

"Didn't you read Lou's letter? That bitch is a 'she.' I've been at this since before you were born, Syl. I don't know for sure, but I feel confident that Moonstep needs someone. That she lures people like a Siren, consumes them for years—decades even—in order to get strong enough to find a—"

He fumbled around, looking for the word.

"Just say host. It's easiest."

"All right, a host. Once Moonstep has secured a host, she sends herself out into the town in the form of 'reappeared' people. Think about the silver eyes, veins. Those monsters are powered by silver ore, for lack of a better way to say it. Why not just murder people right away though? I think of my dad. He was really never violent. That part has always had me stumped. How does sending a person back to mess with a loved one's mind benefit Moonstep if the person isn't going to kill their family?"

"Maybe it has something to do with the person, what's already inside them," Syl offered. "What if a person's temperament is what influences how compliant they will be to the mine? She added a question of her own. "How come we don't see a lot more murders during high times? We should be in the middle of a massacre right now."

"I tell people to make a visiting room, like my mom did. Not ideal, but a compromise. Putting photos outside gives them a chance to decide what they want to do if someone they love reappears. What I want to get to is this: There must be an active host right now. I knew it once I saw Alex Conder's body. Just like Lou described Mason's. Like I said, I thought it might be you, but after the Winton fire, I knew it wasn't. Then it was safe to give you the letter."

Syl rolled her eyes. "You should have given me that letter years ago. I've been 'grown up' for a long time. Why do men always think they should make decisions for me?"

Roger put his hands in the air in surrender. "It's not like I knew how to find you! Like I knew where Aunt Shirley lived! I'm not trying to decide shit for you. I can't even decide my own shit."

"Right, and it's not like there's such a thing as a phone book to find people either, right?"

"Didn't know Shirley's last name. She moved away from Pate when I was a kid. What'd you want me to do? Drive up and down every street in Spokane, hollering for you?"

He was impossible.

"What was it about the Winton fire that exonerated me?" Syl asked.

"Mary disappeared again. So, the host must be gone."

"And who do you think the host was?"

FIFTY-NINE

"ESMA? 'A FEW flowers shy of a bouquet' Esma?" Syl asked, then laughed.

"Mary stopped showing up after the night of the fire," Roger said, ignoring Syl's comment. "I think Esma was the antenna that allowed the mine access to the town. Once she was gone, Moonstep lost access."

"I can't see Esma traipsing through the woods."

"There's a sort of trance that happens when people hear that howling. Maybe she heard it outside her cabin and went. It's possible she didn't remember it."

"Great. It's solved then. No more reappearances since the new host is dead. Isn't that consistent with your theory?"

"Yes. Until the mine calls up another host. In the meantime, people keep disappearing. Then it happens again. And again. I became sheriff because I wanted to protect the town. I've failed, but maybe we can still stop it. Nobody is safe while that mine sits up in the mountains unperturbed. Christ knows I won't be around to witness the next high time."

"What do you imagine can be done about it? Gran tried to shoot it up, like some crazy cowboy. That didn't work. You got an idea?"

"Lou was the connection. She *was* Moonstep Mine, in a sense. She couldn't destroy it while she was still alive."

"And let me guess. We can." Syl smirked.

"I don't know if we can or not, but if the host is dead, now is the time to try." He hadn't picked up the note of sarcasm in her voice. He was getting excited, giddy almost. "It makes sense that if the mine is the strongest with an active host in Pate, it's the weakest when the host dies."

He stood up and went over to her notes on the wall. "Maybe she can be destroyed in the time after the host dies, and before she gains strength from calling people into the woods. Before too many people disappear again."

"People never stop disappearing, Roger."

"I know."

"One thing that's never connected up is how the Markwells relate to all of it," Syl said.

"Far as I can speculate, one of them was the first to become Moonstep's host. Everyone around town thinks Lily was to blame for them all disappearing. Her whole family was found murdered in Spokane before she moved to Pate. But I think it was Holver. Makes the most sense if you can follow this…"

Oh goody, more story time.

"Lily was from a high-brow family. Her dad owned a mill in Spokane, they lived in the ritzy part of town. They were high society. The girl probably hadn't gone into the woods a day in her life. Plus—"

"That's a leap. I thought I was a shitty detective, but look at you, clamoring for the title."

"Christ, Syl, just shut your trap and listen for once. How would a being living in the ground, who feeds on human flesh, respond to a huge influx of people—say, the big mining boom at the turn of the century? Moonstep was suddenly overrun with new blood, and most of them spent their days underground. It was a feast. She didn't need to lure anyone during that time because she could pick them off at will. How many unexplained disappearances of miners were there back then?"

Syl shrugged. There was a lot.

"Once mining slowed down a bit, got more organized, safer, Moonstep had to adapt, grow more cunning in order to stay fed at the level she was used to."

"Doesn't explain how one of the Markwells got involved."

"I know. I think based on Lou's letter we can deduce something terrible happened in that shed before the Wintons arrived. My guess? Someone went all Jack the Ripper on the Markwells. Maybe it was Holver. Moonstep doesn't care if the host is bloodthirsty or not. Why does it matter to her how the killing happens? According to Lou's letter, Moonstep draws strength from the death either way. Wouldn't matter though, except for this: one of the Markwells gave Moonstep Mine a taste for luring victims."

"If what you're saying about the reappearances is true, the library should be full of monsters. All those old yearbooks, news articles. Surely for each disappearance, there was an associated article and photograph of the missing person. All stored inside that brick building."

"I burned them all as soon as I became sheriff. Mary's senior picture was the only one that made it."

Syl really needed a shower and a week-long nap.

"How in the…?" she sighed. "Super illegal, but hey, as long as Mary's picture survived, right?"

Sarcasm betrayed her true feelings. She was livid. How dare he burn library property and remove the choice from everyone in Pate, while keeping his own loved one in his pocket.

"I had to make sure it could never get out of hand. Can you imagine a century's worth of disappeared people—maybe more—coming back?"

"Well, all that's left is to go door to door and demand everyone burn their family photo albums. Easy peasy."

"Don't worry about people around here. They know to burn every photo except the ones they choose to hang outside."

"What about people who have someone go missing, but the family keeps the photos and then moves away, say to Spokane?"

"I've never heard of a reappeared showing up in Spokane. I imagine the host's radius is like a signal and has limitations. If someone moves outside of Pate, it might be too far for the mine to reach, but I don't know for sure. That's all beside the point. If I'm right, Moonstep Mine is weak right now. We have to act *now*."

"*You* have to act now. I got what I came here for, thanks to Gran's letter. All I need to do now is pack up this house and put it up for sale. Then I'm out of here."

Roger could stomp his foot and throw man fits until the cows came home. Syl wasn't getting further involved in this. She'd rather return to Spokane and beg her old boss Cummings for another shot at detective. Hell, a lifetime of patrol would be better than playing demon hunter with Roger Mock.

"I'm not going into those woods," he said.

"Are you kidding me? Your play was to convince me to do it *by myself*?"

"You know the land."

"So did John Fucking Winton!"

She was close to punching the guy in the face. "Thanks for the flowers. Leave." Syl turned Roger's wide body around, and pushed it until he was outside. She shut the door without another word.

SPOKANE, WASHINGTON

September 1989

SIXTY

LIGHT FOUND DAWN'S face through the part of the motel curtains that didn't fully close. She rolled over in bed. The alarm clock said 11:40 a.m., the day half gone. She didn't care. The only thing she had to do today was get herself back home to Pate. The cost of this motel room, along with pizza delivery for most meals, had used up her savings; it was time. She'd see about a funeral for her mother, pick up the pieces of her life, no matter what became of her. It was time to talk about what actually happened to Dad all those years ago. She'd put it off for weeks, but it was pointless to think there was an end other than telling the sheriff the details. They had started coming into focus after Mom's death.

Dad had given Dawn a bad feeling in the days leading up to the Apocalypse Survival Week. He was even more strange than usual. He thought she was turning into an unbeliever, trying to steal his stash, planning to abandon him when the End of Days came. It was stupid, really. How would an eight-year-old manage an apocalypse without parents? Logic didn't factor in. It never did with Dad. His paranoia wouldn't allow it. Only made the spankings more frequent.

Dawn had to escape. She made a plan to do it at the first chance and run back home to Mom. Tell Mom everything before Dad could return. Surely Mom would believe her, and they'd move away together.

But telling Mom everything would be the hard part because she'd have to tell about the cleansings.

But the closer Dawn and Dad got to setting up camp for the night, the surer she was that Mom would not believe her. The few times Dawn had told Mom about minor things Dad said or did, Mom sided with Dad. How could Dawn be sure she wouldn't just wait until Dad returned, and then there'd be hell to pay for Dawn? She couldn't trust Mom, no matter how much she wanted to.

She was on her own.

In the past, whenever they had camped in the woods—it didn't matter where—Dad would set up a chopping block, made out of an old stump. He always wedged the axe into it when he was done splitting wood. Dawn could never pry it out. But that first night, when he was done chopping wood for the morning's fire, he had set the axe down next to the stump, handle facing up. Dawn had thought that was weird.

Then something really bad had happened in the tent at bedtime. Dawn couldn't recall that part in a lot of detail. She didn't want to. She had cried and cried afterward, and Dad spanked her for crying. He fell asleep after her spankings.

Dawn laid awake in the dark tent for a while, listening to the owls call out. The wind tickled pine trees. If she focused real hard, she could hear the river far below. It was wide and deep at this part of the woods, rushing hard. Not like the little stream at the base of the cabin. She pictured floating in it. Floating away, out to the ocean. Then she had to pee.

Slipping her little feet into white canvas shoes, now a weird shade of gray from overuse, she tried to be invisible while unzipping the old canvas tent. If she was quiet as a church mouse, he wouldn't wake up. Head first, she came out, then one leg, the other leg. The sky's stars went on forever that night, without a cloud at all. She cried looking at them, no warning, the tears just came. Seemed like the stars always had each other. It was so rare to see one alone in the sky before another popped out of blackness. When one wasn't visible, it was usually because none were. Why couldn't she be one of them? Never be alone.

After she'd done her business, Dawn poked her head back into the tent, and even though it was dark, she saw him lying there.

His long, dark mop covering a usually scowling forehead. He snored as if he didn't have a care in the world. As if life was easy, and he had nothing to fear. Dawn pulled her head out and looked at the stars again. Where fear usually lived inside her small bones, anger grew. She went back out and sat at the edge of the cliff that led down to the river, not ready to be back inside the tent. Would she ever be ready again?

It was still dark when she heard the soft crunch of pine cones underfoot. She was lying on the earth, in a nest of tall weeds, asleep. Dad stumbled along the edge of the cliff, body heavy from slumber. He hadn't seen her. Probably taking a pee, same as what she'd done. She should get back into the tent before he returned. What would happen if he came back more awake than when he left, and saw her missing? He'd spank her again. And then... The thought of another cleansing was unbearable.

She stood, and something she didn't recognize took over, moved her feet quietly to the chopping block. That thick wooden axe handle was just sitting there, so Dawn wrapped tiny fingers around it and waited beside the tent. Listening, breathing, staring at the stars, never before feeling so strong, so sure. Dad's steps crunched pine cones all the way back to the tent's opening.

He pushed his head into the tent, with his rump sticking out. "Dawn?" he whispered. "Dawny? Where you at?"

Dawn swung hard, sending the sharp point of the axe into the thick flesh of his ass. That was what came to her mind in the moment too. The bad words, "his ass."

The blade lodged deep into muscle like it did when you wedge an axe into the chopping block. As he yelled and fell forward into the tent, she held on tightly so the axe came free. It almost didn't, and then where would she be? Thankfully, there it was in her hands.

Now what? she'd thought, calming her breath. He was in pain, hollering and carrying on, but he was also moving around, trying to get to his feet, and he was angrier now than ever before. She had to do it again. Even if she didn't want to, and Dawn didn't remember if she wanted to or not. Didn't think about it. It was like shooting a bear in the hind leg. You had to take another quick shot, or it came at you. It was you or him.

It was him.

She hit the tent with the axe, and it fell down on top of him easily. This bought her a few more minutes as he struggled to get free of the canvas. She could make out his shape in the moonlight, and down came the axe again. Hard. Again. And again. She didn't know which parts of him she was hitting, but every time she swung that axe, he cried out, so she must have landed most of the blows.

He finally got the tent off. She looked at him, and he looked at her. He struggled to get up but he couldn't. Gouges littered his body and blood poured from where the axe had made contact. His face and head were unharmed, but of course, he'd been protecting his head. He was covered in crimson, but even so, he reached out an arm, asking for the axe. She pulled it back. He tried to stand again, but couldn't. That first hit alone would make standing impossible. He cried. She had never once seen him cry.

"Dawn, what are you doing? How could you hurt your father like this?"

She wound the axe up high, higher than she had before, and holding it there for a beat, she said, "You can't make yourself clean, so I have to do it."

Then she brought the metal blade down on his head. It landed in an explosion of blood and stuck right into his forehead. He stopped moving, but she wasn't sure he was dead, so she waited. She couldn't get the axe out as easily now, so she gave up. She let go of the handle and took a step back, dizzy from the strain.

There in the moonlight, the wet metal blade glinted as it intersected Dad's skull. She cocked her head to the side and felt nothing. Nothing at all. That's when the painting, hanging in their living room miles away, came to mind. Jesus on the cross. His red-soaked body, crown of thorns, hands and feet pierced through with nails.

Blood and metal and pain and suffering was God's love.

Dawn fell asleep.

SIXTY-ONE

IN THE MORNING, Dawn cried.

Her dad's body had fallen over, but his eyes were open, crimson drips running from the point of the axe down his face, like tears. What if he didn't stay dead? This was back when she still thought that old black and white portrait of Holver was him, thought he had everlasting life on earth, that he always had been and always would be. Yet, there he was, grotesque on the outside, just like she always knew he was on the inside. Still, Dawn needed to make sure he was dead.

What she'd done to him hovered over her like a heavy brick, waiting to drop, to crush her. But then a Bible verse came to her and made her feel better.

If anyone comes to Me and doesn't hate his father, he cannot be my disciple.

Maybe God wasn't mad at her for hating Dad, killing him even. She didn't know if she wanted to be God's disciple anymore, if she wanted to serve a god who would kill his own son and tell others to hate their family. A god who had turned her dad into a violent, disgusting man. But what mattered was Dad could never hurt her again. She had to make sure nobody could find him, nobody could know what she'd done. She'd make him disappear. So many people disappeared in these woods. Why not him?

Once a few crackers had taken the edge off her hunger, she got to work.

Dawn pulled the axe from Dad's head after a few times of trying. Her muscles were sore from swinging it the night before. It really was like she'd wedged it into the chopping block. It came loose with a squelch and bits of his insides. Maybe his brains. She gagged and gagged until finally she produced some vomit.

Dawn whacked at his neck until his head lolled off, attached only by what looked like a rope. It was just like chopping through rope too. It took her a few times, but eventually the head came loose. and she took it by the long, greasy hair. At the edge of the cliff overlooking the river, she hurled it as hard as she could, but even that wasn't hard enough. It hit the side of the cliff and bounced down until it splashed into the water. Next, his legs, arms, body, cut into smaller sections. She tossed his right arm off the cliff, but buried his left using the small spade Dad always attached to the back of his pack. Then she rolled what was left of him into the tent fabric, like the way Mom would make Pigs in a Blanket, and dragged the mess deeper into the woods. On the way, she heard something, and it made her stop. Could it be a person? Nobody was out this far.

There it was again.

It sounded like a howl. A cry from some sad animal.

She ignored it and kept walking because there was very little daylight left, and she wanted to be rid of all of Dad by the time the sun went down.

Crows cawed, and she took pieces of Dad to them, set out his left leg for their supper. Hiding behind a big pine tree, she watched them swoop down and get started with great delight.

On she went like this until dark, burying some of him, and feeding some of him to the scavenging animals, until all she had left was the blood-stained tent.

Just as the sun was dipping below the mountain and bringing the light-blue haze of dusk, she heard that howl again.

Should she go after it and see what it was? Maybe it needed help. Her hands were stained red. Her clothes, her little shoes, now a deep rust brown. Maybe a different day. Tonight she needed sleep, and then home. She wrapped the bloody tent around her small frame and fell into sleep immediately.

In the morning, Dawn buried the tent deep so nobody could find it. She tossed the spade aside and ran down the hill to the river.

The river was cold, and as she stepped in, she didn't even care if it took her away, if she drowned. But she didn't. She stood on smooth river rocks, the icy current tugging at her from underneath. She laughed, but then felt bad. It wasn't funny. Nothing about this was funny, yet she couldn't stop laughing. Her body shook, and her legs were numb, and then laughter gave way to sobbing.

Removing her clothes, she scrubbed and scrubbed them. At least she wore the dark striped tee shirt and navy-blue shorts. You couldn't really tell even if they were stained a bit. She dug at her fingernails to remove all traces of blood, thought about how Dad was feeding the earth, and other creatures would go on because he died. Even that was more than he deserved. When she was clean, she tossed her stained shoes down the current. There wasn't much left of their sparse camp, but she buried or tossed all of it.

She couldn't wait to get home to Mom. It would be just them now. But when she arrived, the only thing Mom seemed to care about was Dad. Where was he? Was he coming home? Why did Dawn leave him out there? The police asked her a few questions, but it was easy for Dawn to say she didn't see what happened, she didn't know, and then as the days went on, she really didn't know. The whole thing became a big, black hole in Dawn's memory. The police wouldn't go into the woods to look for him. They never did. Mom's hysteria over losing Dad reinforced Dawn's earlier thought. Nobody could ever know what had happened to him. Or what he'd done to her. Not in the woods, not in the shed.

PATE, IDAHO

September 1989

SIXTY-TWO

SYL DROVE THE Vicky slowly up the Wintons' driveway. It felt wrong to be there, like an intrusion. But maybe Roger was right. Maybe they could stop whatever was happening before more people got hurt. Syl could be a stubborn jackass, but she wasn't selfish or stupid.

Still, there was no way in hell she was going into those woods now that she knew everything.

Coming back here seemed logical, but what exactly was she looking for? Proof that Esma was actually the host? What would that even look like? She didn't know, but something compelled her to return and check the place out.

The front door was locked, and nobody answered, so she walked around to the back and let herself in.

Dawn was at the kitchen table.

They stared at each other, and neither said anything at first.

Then Syl started, "Dawn, I'm sorry, I didn't know you were home…"

Dawn sighed in defeat. "I can't run away my whole life."

"Run from…" Syl looked behind her, indicating the ash heap that used to be the Winton shed.

"No! I didn't kill my mom. I loved her." Tears welled up in Dawn's eyes. "But even though I didn't kill her, it doesn't mean I'm blameless."

Dawn weaved her way along the slug trails to the couch and sat down. Syl did too.

"I killed my dad."

Syl's mouth dropped open, but she quickly caught it and returned her jaw to the closed position.

"Hard to believe, I know. A little girl. He abused me daily, and after one bad night, I decided I'd had enough. I don't think I meant to kill him—I don't know though—I don't remember thinking it through. But once I'd hurt him, I saw in his face he was going to kill me, so I had to finish it. I'm going to tell the sheriff about it today. It's why I came back." She wiped her eye with a single finger swoop.

"You were only eight," Syl said. When she couldn't find words to comfort the girl, Syl stood and wound herself around the clutter to get a roll of toilet paper from the bathroom. When she came back into the living room, a clatter rang out from behind.

"Is someone else here?"

Dawn shook her head slowly.

Footsteps on the wood floors of Dawn's bedroom.

"Someone's definitely here," Syl whispered, reaching for her gun, realizing she'd left it in the Vicky.

Dawn reached behind the couch and gripped a wooden baseball bat. The one Syl had noticed on her first visit.

Syl started toward the sound, but Dawn pushed her little body behind and mouthed, "I have the bat."

Embarrassing to need the eighteen-year-old to protect you.

Coming up to Dawn's bedroom, bed springs sang out. Was the person sleeping in her bed? Bouncing on it?

Dawn pushed the door open and there sat some guy with silver eyes.

"Monte?" Dawn said.

"You know him?"

Dawn nodded, fresh tears running down her face. "He's my boyfriend."

"Not anymore. This isn't Monte. It's something else. You must have a photo of him. Where?"

"I don't know. I let him take one of us weeks ago, but I thought I threw it away. I kept our relationship a secret. I was afraid of my mom finding out. Which seems so...stupid now."

"The picture. We have to find it."

Dawn set down the bat and opened dresser drawers, threw clothes on the floor. Monte seemed out of it, but Syl knew that wouldn't last long. What sort of monster would he be? Maybe he was like Roger's dad. Maybe not.

"I have no idea where it could be," Dawn said.

Then Monte was right beside her.

"Ashamed...of...me," he said.

"No! No, Monte," Dawn cried. "I liked you. I'm so sorry I couldn't protect you. I tried. You wouldn't listen!"

Syl tiptoed behind Dawn in the tiny room. She needed to get that bat.

Monte struck Dawn across the face. So much for hopes of non-violence.

"Being...bad...girl..."

Dawn scampered between the bed and the wall, trying to get away.

Syl grabbed the bat. "We have to find that picture. It's the only way."

Dawn looked under the bed. "It's there! I see it under the nightstand."

Syl was too far away, and Dawn had the bed blocking her reach.

Monte was on the mattress, looking down at Dawn. "Bad... girl..."

Syl cracked him over the back with the baseball bat. He turned his silver eyes on her, and then his whole body lit up with silver. *That must happen when they get really mad*, Syl thought even though it was not the time to analyze it.

She hit him again and Dawn slid under the bed, landing fingers on the Polaroid. She tore it up.

"No! We have to burn it," Syl said.

"Matches are by the fireplace. Here, I'll distract him." Dawn's hand jutted out from under the bed, and Syl took the shreds of film from her, gave her the bat in return.

Then she ran out on the slug paths and saw the box of matches on the hearth.

She fumbled with sliding the box open.

Dawn screamed.

Syl finally had a single match in hand and struck it against the side of the box. She watched the pieces of the Polaroid fizzle away.

Silence.

Dawn walked out of the bedroom, her straight hair frizzed out on one side, jaw slack.

Syl sat on the couch. "Any chance you've got a smoke?"

Avoiding cigarettes, the one thing Syl was determined to succeed at, was now the one thing she craved.

"Sorry."

Syl waved it off, and they sat there in silence for what felt like ten minutes.

"So, how religious are you?" Syl asked.

Dawn sighed. "I try. The whole reason I went back to religion was because I thought it'd help me deal with the guilt for killing my dad. But I suck at being good. Why?"

"I think there's a bit more to life—life after death—than we thought."

"I had a run-in with one of them already," Dawn said. "The one who took my mom. It was Holver Markwell. I didn't know about the photo thing at the time, but it makes sense because his portrait was in the shed. My parents put all the important Markwell stuff in there when they moved in. Dad didn't want to get rid of it, seeing as it was his only connection with his family."

"You were there when the fire started?"

"I started it."

"But you said you didn't kill her."

"I didn't. She was already gone."

"How did your mom…go?"

"Same way as Alex Conder."

Syl was shocked for the umpteenth time today. "We never released Alex's cause of death, or any details about the condition of his body. How do you know how he died?"

Dawn smoothed out the knot in her hair. "Because I was there."

SIXTY-THREE

ROGER PULLED HIS rig into the driveway of the small rambler he and Mary had lived in since the time of the dinosaurs.

Slow day at work wasn't a bad thing, but it made the days inch by. He crossed the threshold he'd carried Mary over the day they got married. The door slammed behind him.

He startled and turned. When he came about again, Mary was in his face, red lipstick and bobbed hair. Silver eyes. God, she was beautiful.

"Mare! You're back!"

"Come…for…you."

He reached out as if to hold her, and she allowed him the embrace. Her arm snaked around his waist and he smelled the scent of her hair, felt young again, holding her like this. It was like he could hear her laugh, the ring of it. How much fun they had all those years together. Life was shitty with Mary gone. He'd gotten used to it, found a certain pattern in his days, but it had crushed him when she disappeared into the woods. What, after all those years of vigilance keeping himself, her, their kids, away. What were the chances she'd go missing after just one time? But that was the thing about the White Pine mountains. It was a risk. You never knew if the mine would lure you after one visit or five hundred, or at all.

On the day it happened, Roger had come home to a note from Mary. "Went hiking with Sue and Nola. I know you'll be mad, but I couldn't say no this time. Be back for supper."

His hand had trembled as he crumpled the note up. He hadn't allowed the thought that she'd disappeared come to mind in that moment. It was too soon. And yet, he looked at his wristwatch. It was 6:15 in the evening. A six o'clock supper time was the closest thing Mary had to religion. She wouldn't be late.

Roger called Sue's house. Her son was in town, answered the phone and said they were just sitting down to supper. Sue included. He called Nola. She said Mary had been with them the whole time, but then she had to go. They assumed she needed to get home earlier than they did. Mary had turned around and left them there on the trail. Nola had been frantic on the phone. "Roger, she was walking back toward the cars. How could she have gone further into the woods?" Roger slammed the receiver down without saying goodbye. If he went into the woods to look for her, he could end up just like his dad looking for Winny. Like Harold going after Lou. Roger might get lost, disappear, and then what good would he be? But how could he just leave Mary out there?

He drove his rig right up to the edge. Up to the river that bordered the vast mountain of trees. He got out of the rig and hollered for her for hours. Walked up and down the border of the woods. It was dark, well into nighttime, when he got back into the rig. All he could do was cry. Maybe he was a pussy, after all. The love of his life was in danger, and he couldn't even budge a foot over that river.

There was no point. He knew it. How many times had he taken calls just like this? So-and-so loved one was supposed to return at such-and-such time. Those people never turned up. He bought a bottle of Johnnie Walker on the way home and drank the whole thing.

When Mary returned, he'd scrambled to get everything out of the living room. Every knife, every mirror, anything with glass, any statue or object that could be used as a blunt instrument. He'd created his own version of his mom's "visiting room." Except it was worse in his case because he knew it wasn't Mary. Still, he'd lived all these years without her and wasn't going to lose her again.

Sure, Mary had said crazy shit during those few days after she reappeared. But she was back. Then she left for a few weeks. Where had she gone after Esma died? No matter, she was back again. He would enjoy the time they had together.

As he held her now, a thought formed in the back tunnels of his brain. It took a while to travel to the forefront. Then it arrived.

If Mary's here, Esma must not be dead.

Then who did they find dead in the Winton's wood shed? Dawn? How could Mary return again if Esma was dead? Roger looked into Mary's silver eyes and then focused on those plump red lips instead. Her eyes creeped him out. She pushed up against him tighter, and he went to unbutton her blouse. This new Mary was really something else. Not modest like the old Mary. Not at all.

Maybe Esma wasn't the host.

The thought pulled him out of whatever reverie he was in, and when he looked down, his own gun was pointed right at his big gut. Mary had grabbed it off its holster when he thought she was getting fresh with him.

"Mary, no."

He stepped sideways to the fireplace mantle, where her black and white picture sat, now without Mary in it at all.

She pulled the trigger.

Roger staggered a step back. He felt the wall behind him and slid to the floor.

The last thing he thought about was his own stupidity. That he should have burned that damn picture.

SIXTY-FOUR

"EXCUSE ME?" SYL thought she heard wrong. "It sounded like you said, 'I was there.'"

"I lied to you, I'm sorry. I was afraid of getting in trouble," Dawn said.

"No shit, Sherlock."

"Monte asked me to go with him to Lucky Dog Mine that night. Alex was his dealer, and he needed to buy more weed."

"Why the hell would you do a drug deal in an abandoned mine?"

Roger's voice in Syl's head rang out, *Let them tell it their way!*

Syl took a deep breath and sat back down on the couch.

"When you inspected the crime scene, did you have any idea Alex was there for a drug deal?"

Syl didn't answer.

"How do you think Alex was able to parade around town as a family man? Abandoned mines."

Fair point.

"I didn't want to go," Dawn continued. "I was trying really hard to be a good Christian, get my life right. But I really liked Monte. He wasn't a bad guy, he was just a little reckless, that's all."

"Whatever. Fast forward the defense of Monte Shrake. Get to the part where Alex Conder got sucked dry."

Dawn held back a little laugh.

"What?"

"Monte made a blowjob joke like that when we left the mine that night. It made me mad, so crass. But it was funny still."

"Sounds like a real winner. Blowjob jokes after a guy dies. I can't understand why you didn't introduce him to your mom."

"Sorry." She grimaced. "I still don't know exactly how it happened, or why. I've thought about it constantly. Alex said his price. It was higher than what he'd told Monte on the phone. Monte got mad, said no way, he wouldn't pay that. Said he could drive into Spokane and get it cheaper. Then Alex came at him. Monte hit Alex across the face. Monte was a big guy, but more like a teddy bear than a fighter..."

Syl didn't get any teddy-bear vibes a few minutes ago in the bedroom.

"Well, Alex grabbed a rock and hit Monte over the head. Monte fell very near to the edge. That's when I sort of passed out, I guess. The next thing I knew, I was on top of Alex, and he looked like a shriveled mummy. I got off him just as Monte was coming back to his senses."

"You," Syl said. Her heart picked up like a gun had just signaled the start of a sprint. "It's you."

"It's me, what?"

Syl stood slowly, took steps backward toward the door.

"You're it. You're the host."

"What? The host of what?"

"When did you find Moonstep Mine? How long ago?

"I don't know. Months ago, I guess. I just found myself there. Was the weirdest thing. Heard that howl when I was younger, but it never meant anything to me until recently, when I was out in the woods, and I followed it. I couldn't resist it. It was like I had to know what was making that sound."

Syl was almost to the door.

"Why? What does it mean?"

"Get in your car and meet me at the diner," Syl said. "I'll explain—hell, I'll even *show* you—but I'd rather be in public."

SIXTY-FIVE

DAWN KNEW WHAT it meant. She had asked the detective for clarification, but deep down, somehow, she knew.

This was all her fault.

I killed my mom.

The thought kept looping in Dawn's mind after the detective left. She lifted the loose wood slat under the kitchen table and retrieved the torn wedding picture of Mom.

Barely able to see through the wall of tears welling in her eyes, Dawn finally blinked, and a drop landed directly on the picture. Mom's face, that huge smile, long hair, parted down the middle like a proper hippie. A crown of white flowers. She wiped the picture dry.

First, Dawn took Dad away from Mom. That had ruined her mom's life, even as it saved Dawn's. And then Dawn took Mom's life too.

I killed my mom.

Sure, Mom was already gone by the time she found her, but Dawn was the one who opened the door for all of this. She was *the host,* as the detective said.

It made sense.

Of course Dawn was to blame for this. Just like Dawn was to blame for Alex Conder. For Monte. For Dad. Even if Dad deserved whatever he got, Dawn was the one who murdered him.

Who else would Dawn hurt in her lifetime? As long as she was breathing, nobody was safe.

Dawn stood, folded the picture of Mom in half, and put it into her jeans pocket.

She should go into the woods. Just be done. What was there to live for now that Mom was gone? Especially now that she saw so clearly how much pain she caused. And yeah, she'd had a hard life, but how much of that was a result of her own poor decisions? Her own *wickedness* that she could never make right. Then, a Bible verse came to mind. One that Dad had made sure Dawn knew by heart. *The heart is deceitful above all things and desperately wicked. Who can know it?*

She would never be good. Even if she imagined that she was, her heart was deceitful. She couldn't trust it.

Dawn looked around the cabin.

The sense of Mom was everywhere. Down to all the crazy clutter that she refused to organize.

Tears streaked Dawn's cheeks as she thought about Mom's last moments. How scared she must have been.

I killed my mom.

Walking out the back door, Dawn made sure not to let it slap. Mom hated that. Dawn stared mindlessly at the big, charred pile where the shed used to be. She got stuck there, just staring, and by the time she realized she'd been standing there for a while, her face was wet with tears.

Maybe her heart was deceitful, but she could admit she'd done some good by ending that monster in the shed. *Both* monsters.

But it wasn't enough. There was still one more monster left.

Dawn got into her car and sat there.

What should she do now? There was nowhere to go. Nothing left for her.

She could find that camping spot she and Dad had occupied so many years ago and fling herself over the edge of the cliff. Just let the water's current take her out to the Columbia River and then into the Pacific Ocean. Sheer oblivion.

But another part of her said to drive to the diner, just to see what the detective had to say. If it was worthless, then she could find that camping spot and do as she planned.

What did she have to lose at this point?

SIXTY-SIX

EVEN THOUGH SYL stopped at Gran's first, she still beat Dawn to the diner. She used the phone there to call Roger at the station. Hendon said he'd already gone home.

She tried his home number, which she now had memorized. Of all the useless things to carry around in your head.

No answer.

She sat down and ordered coffee while she waited for Dawn to show up. What if Dawn bolted again?

Shit. She had to do it this way though. What good was she if Dawn "sucked her dry" right there in the cabin? Although, was it safe here? She didn't know. Gran had tried that trick on Roger in her kitchen. She knew very little about the rules of this game.

Her coffee arrived, and Dawn came shortly after. She looked tired, like a child kept up too many late nights in a row. Her ponytail had fly-aways galore, and her shoulders slumped like she thought she was in trouble. She was. That was the cold, hard truth. The girl was in huge trouble.

Syl needed Roger here. She tried him again on the diner's phone.

"Sheriff been in today?" she asked Josephine.

"No. And I been working a double. Did breakfast, and now I'm doing supper. I'd have seen him if he come in."

Syl slid back into the green vinyl seat opposite the blonde mine monster. No, she shouldn't think of Dawn like that. Gran wasn't a monster. Was Holver? Why did it matter now? Focus.

"What do you remember from your first visit to Moonstep Mine?"

Dawn played with her napkin and said, "Not much. Went in, saw this massive silver vein along the rock wall. It shined like crazy, practically hypnotized me. Then…"

Syl waited.

"Then what?"

"It sounds insane, that's why I didn't tell anyone. I have weird dreams, and I thought afterward, maybe it was just a dream. Maybe I didn't see what I thought I saw."

"You did. Tell me what happened next."

Dawn rolled her eyes the way people do when they're embarrassed. "There was this lady. She was blonde like me, but with this old-style braid. Her hair was longer than mine too. She wasn't pretty, but she wasn't ugly either. Just normal looking, I guess. Whatever that means. Told me she could give me whatever I wanted. Just one thing, but I had to say yes to her. I didn't know what I was saying yes to! I was stupid to do it, but it felt right, and I was desperate, more desperate than I can explain. I told her what I wanted, and then she turned into… Well, I don't know what, but it wasn't human. I don't know how much time passed, but when I came back to myself, I ran home."

"What did you ask for?"

"For my mom to really see me, to notice me. For us to be together."

"Did it happen?"

"No." Dawn looked down at her hands.

"Most people don't leave the mine. You have to know that." She nodded.

"Just a second." Syl put up a finger and slid out to call Roger again.

Still no answer. Not even an answering machine. Was he stuck in the sixties?

When Syl came back, she caught Dawn up on Roger's theory.

Disappearances, Moonstep gets stronger, calls a host, portraits, reappearances.

"I'm the host," Dawn whispered, as if she already knew.

Syl pushed Gran's letter across the table. "Read it. I'll be right back."

Syl tried Roger again. No answer. Did he have a heart attack in his rig? She called Hendon and asked him to go check Roger's house. Yes, it was an emergency. The heart thing, remember? Hendon agreed.

Syl drank three cups of coffee while Dawn read. At least the girl was taking it seriously. She watched Dawn's face and caught flecks of recognition. A few winces, some tears.

The diner phone rang.

"Sylvia, it's for you," Josephine called out.

Syl got up from the booth and headed over to Josephine, took the phone from her waiting hand.

"It's Hendon," said the voice on the other end. He was breathing hard, hesitating, "Roger is... He's dead, Syl. Someone shot him with his own piece."

Fuck. Mary!

"You're not safe in his house," Syl said. There's a picture of Mary somewhere. He said it's in his living room. Find it and burn it."

"Burn it? What the hell?"

"Listen to me, Hen. Do it."

"You got some crazy ideas on you, you know that, right? I thought when we first met—

—The hell was that?" Hendon interrupted himself.

"Hendon. Forget the picture. Get out of there!"

"Well, I got the picture, but I thought I heard something in the hall. Should I go look?"

"No! Do you have your lighter?"

"Course."

"Torch the picture *now*."

The strike of his Zippo once, twice.

"Shit, need to get this lighter—Whoa! There's some girl here! She's a babe. Looks like some pinup model from—"

"Burn the picture!"

"There's nobody in the picture."

"For fuck's sake, Hen, burn it!" Syl shouted so loud the whole diner looked at her.

The line went silent.

"Hen? You there?"

"Yeah, I'm here. Just realizing the crazy stories my uncle used to tell me might be real. That hot chick disappeared when I burned the picture."

Syl sighed in relief, but immediately thought of Roger and felt tears pinching at her nose. "It's real, Hen. It's all real."

SIXTY-SEVEN

"**IT HAS TO** be me. I've got to do it," Dawn said after a few hours had passed.

Josephine had let them stay past closing, with a comment about how she had three days off after this and didn't mind serving them coffee as long as they wanted. If Roger were there, he'd demand chicken fried steak. But Roger wasn't there.

Syl had been on the verge of tears all day. It still didn't feel like time to cry though. Dawn had read the letter, and they'd spent a long time brainstorming ideas.

"I can't let you do it," Syl said.

"It has to be me because I'm the host. If you go in there, you'll die, and she'll live on."

"Gran tried to destroy the mine when she was the host. It didn't work."

Dawn rubbed her eyes. God, she was just at the beginning of her life, barely an adult.

"Gran tried to shoot at it like some last stand. But I think the host has to die first, before the mine can be harmed. That's when it's the weakest. Isn't that what Roger said?"

Dawn had taken to calling her "Gran," instead of "Lou," like everyone else. Syl liked it. She liked Dawn. She wished they'd bonded at some town social instead of while wrestling a mine monster that had killed almost everyone they both loved.

"Yes, but Roger didn't know jack shit about a lot of things. Nobody really knows. Feels like a big chance to take when we aren't even sure it'll work."

Dawn took a sip of her coffee. She drank so little of it that it was probably cold.

"It'll work. I know where to find a few sticks of dynamite."

"How?—"

"Don't ask. And you can't come with me to the mine, either. You can't be anywhere near. In fact, I want you sitting here at this booth when it happens."

"I have to come up there with you."

"Absolutely not. You're in danger just sitting here with me. Imagine how much more dangerous I'll be inside the mine."

"Doesn't mean I can't go. I have nothing keeping me here. I've failed at everything I've tried. I'm ready to go, if need be. You shouldn't have to be alone."

"I've always been alone." Dawn smiled through tears. "I can do it."

Syl cleared her throat. No tears. Not time yet.

"It'll be two explosions," Dawn began, as if the discussion of her suicide would lighten the mood, stop them both from crying. "The second one will be delayed, set to explode after the first one goes off. As long as I'm dead by the time the second explosion happens, it'll work. I just know it."

God, she was talking so much sense, and Syl hated all of it.

"This feels right to me. It feels more right than anything else in my life. Except maybe taking care of my mom. But she doesn't need me anymore."

Syl sighed, so Dawn continued. "This checks a few boxes for me. First, I get to make up for what happened to Monte. I knew the woods were dangerous. Maybe I didn't know everything, but I knew people went missing, and I still took him out there. Second, that thing in the mine killed my mom. I thought I did, and in a way, I am responsible, but still, I get payback. Third, the only other thing I care about are the kids around here. I get to stop the murders. Forever."

"None of this is your fault," Syl whispered.

"That doesn't matter now. I'm doing this. You can support me or not, but I'm doing it."

IT WAS INTO the early morning hours when Dawn reached the silent clearing up in the mountains. The place she'd buried the dynamite was so close to there, it caught her by surprise. Another surprise was that she was even able to find the spot. That she'd opted to bury the dynamite instead of tossing it into the river. Being there, where she'd killed Dad, steeled her resolve even more, and now she had a small backpack with two sticks of dynamite, and matches from the diner. She left one wick long, and trimmed the other nice and low. No need for the time it'd take to escape that one. Dawn wasn't going to escape.

There she sat on the ridge where the hill evened out and became the mine's clearing.

This was right. It was exactly what she had sensed needed to happen, and here she was, being given a second chance of sorts. An opportunity to finally do some good.

Dawn watched as the first light of morning rose over the mountains to swallow up diamond stars.

"Soon. I'll be there soon," she told the stars under her breath. Closing her eyes, the still, autumn air chilled her cheeks. Tears ran freely.

Dawn stood up and brushed off the back of her jeans.

Show time.

But just as she took a step toward the mine, the ground wobbled, like a small earthquake that didn't stop, like the mine knew she was coming, was trying to ward her off. She lost her balance and fell to her knees.

Until Dawn was inside with a lit stick of dynamite, she did not have any advantages against whatever this was. She could feel its strength.

She made her way across the meadow, falling every few steps, then crossed the little stream, and trudged through the grass and weeds that led the way to the mine.

Slow obey is no obey!

She ignored Dad's voice in her head.

Where's your father? How could you come home without him?

Mom's voice. That was a new one. The mine hadn't tormented her with it yet. She kept going.

I can't make myself clean.

She winced, pushed on.

Images flooded her mind. Her dad, the shed, her mom as a shriveled corpse. Dawn let herself cry. She wailed, but she kept going.

Now, sharp pain in her body, like metal spikes in her head, her hands, her feet.

God's love for you, Dawn.

She looked at her hands, nothing. It was all in her mind.

Just inches from the mine's entrance, the ground stopped shaking. She peeked inside.

Silver eyes everywhere in the distance, the cavern, where the source vein was located.

A cold blast of air.

She reached into the backpack and took out both sticks of dynamite.

Silver streaks came at her, like all the people the mine had collected since who knew when. She couldn't fight them, had to keep going instead. Had to get to the cavern, hit the mine where its source of power came from.

They were almost on top of her now, so she closed her eyes, willed her legs to move forward instead of running away.

"Dawn?"

Mom's voice.

Dawn opened her eyes.

All the corpses with silver eyes were gone. It was just Mom now, standing in her crinkle skirt, bandanna in place. She smiled.

"Honey, go back home. You'll die if you stay."

Dawn hadn't expected it to be this hard, for the mine to defend itself like this.

"You're not my mom!" she screamed.

"Yes, I am." Mom reached out a hand.

It couldn't be Mom. Dawn had seen her dead body, had lit it on fire afterward.

"Look at the picture," Mom said.

Dawn pulled out the torn half that only had her mom.

Mom was in the picture still. If this was one of the mine's projections, Mom wouldn't be visible in the picture, right?

"Why are you here?" Dawn asked.

A blast of heat came through the tunnel, so hot Dawn screamed again. Her skin burned like she'd been in the sun all day. She was giving the mine more time to defend itself, but here was Mom. The very thing Moonstep promised to her and hadn't delivered.

"I didn't want you to be alone."

The mine quaked, and Dawn almost lost her footing again.

"But I saw you. You were shriveled up like Alex."

Mom smiled. "I have special gifts, remember?"

Dawn narrowed her eyes. "What do you mean?"

"You always said you thought the Lord would use me." Mom reached for Dawn's hand.

"Mom, I have to tell you something. Something bad I did—"

"I wasn't there for you," Mom interrupted. She was now crying too. "I should have protected you from him, and I failed. That's the only thing that needs to be said. Please forgive me."

Dawn cried hard.

"I'm here now, sweetie. You're not alone. But we have to go."

Dawn looked at her and nodded. They held hands and ran down the mine's tunnel. Dawn tripped and fell, got up.

The walls rumbled, and dirt clods fell on her, but she kept running. Another blast of heat, hotter this time. Her skin peeled a little, and she cried out in agony. But she was almost there.

The tunnel opened up to a wide cavern, and there, the silver vein glowed.

An electric current shot out from the vein like lightning and ripped through Dawn's body. A charge, like the humming she'd felt inside her body all these weeks, but amped up a thousand percent. She was dizzy, like she might collapse. Mom held her.

Mom helped her wedge the first stick of dynamite into a crack in the mine's wall. She lit the long fuse. It sputtered and sparked at first, but soon the fire was snaking up the wick.

They ran to the edge, and Dawn held the second stick of dynamite close to her heart.

Mom wrapped her arms around Dawn as they stood, facing each other, inches away from the pit.

Dawn looked down into darkness.

"Don't look down. Look at me."

Dawn smiled and took a deep breath.

She struck the match and lit the tiny stub on the second stick of dynamite just before they stepped off into the black hole.

THE FIRST EXPLOSION woke Syl up. She'd fallen asleep, head down on the table inside the diner. It was 3:57 a.m. Goddamn witching hour.

Then she remembered where she was, what she was doing.

The second explosion came just a few seconds later, and it rocked the town even harder than the first. A cloud of smoke curled up from the mountains. Syl tasted saltwater and looked to Dawn's half-full, now cold cup of coffee.

"You did it, kiddo."

AUTHOR'S NOTE

DEAR READER,

If you're still here, I want to thank you so much for picking up *The Vein*. I wrote it for you, which is why I'm putting this note to you before the Acknowledgments. If you liked this story, I hope you'll consider leaving a positive review so other readers can find it and decide if it's for them or not.

Small press and indie authors rely heavily on word-of-mouth recommendations in order to get visibility in a world filled with absolutely incredible books. Trust me, your two-sentence review matters.

Again, thank you for reading. xo

FREE PREQUEL STORY

THE LAST CLAIM JUMPER

By Steph Nelson

After two prospectors are skunked by the California Gold Rush, a rumor of untouched silver in the mountains of Idaho Territory seems too good to be true. Upon arrival, they must resist their own lust of silver, or risk their lives trying to mine it. *Includes small spoilers for The Vein.* Scan the QR code to download.

ACKNOWLEDGMENTS

I ALWAYS SAID I'd write a novel. It'd be when I was old. When I could hole up in my house, not have to wear pants, and learn to survive on Fruity Pebbles alone. Maybe I'd even pick up smoking cigarettes and sleep at all the wrong times, a slave to the muse like some off-brand Patricia Highsmith.

Then the pandemic happened, and the joke became a reality of sorts when I, like so many others, had time enough on my hands to tinker around at a computer with a story idea (pants gloriously optional). Soon, I had a story, then a real book, and now the thing is out there in the world with my name on it. Pinch me.

It has taken an absolute army of beloved humans to help me shape this hot mess into an actual book.

First, I want to thank my husband, Chris. He's a voracious reader, and had a lot to say to help me find a first draft I felt good about. You've done so much in order for me to spend early mornings and weekends with the door shut, communing with the weirdos I created in my head. Not many women can say their husband shoulders a bulk of the household and child-rearing duties while also working a full-time job, and I'm lucky to say that mine does. And because of it, I finished a thing. You're a keeper. And you're a way better cook than I ever was.

My children, Cameron and Jonathan, have been absolute gems, as I've been grumpy about their interruptions. I'm proud of the people you're both becoming. Thanks for your patience with me. Love you both two lots. And to my angel, Evelyn, thank you for continuing to shape who I am even though I only had you for two weeks.

Thanks to my mom, Denette Dresback, whose love and support has been constant from my earliest memory. Thanks for being a listening ear, a sounding board, and a cheerleader. At times in my life, when I felt like I had nobody, I always, always knew I had you. Also for helping me comb through your family history to learn more about silver mining in the Coeur d'Alene district. It's a pretty cool legacy.

Thanks to my dad, Jim Dresback, for the hours upon hours spent answering my questions about police work and investigating homicides. Thank you also for your words of wisdom at crucial times in my life. (PSA: Any shoddy police work in this story is my own.) Thanks to my stepmom, Diane Dresback, for your enthusiasm about my writing, and for putting up with my dad.

Thank you to my extended family: siblings, grandparents, aunts, uncles, cousins, the saintly people who married them all, and on down the line. I can't name all of you because you are legion, but I want to call out a few. My Aunt Sue Walker, a bottomless pit of information, excitement, and dedication to our family's silver mining history. And two who are no longer with us: My grandma, Norma Stutzke, who provided a lot of the inspiration for Lou Dixon; and my uncle, Mark Dresback, who we lost unexpectedly during the time I was working on this novel. A freshly painful reminder that life is breakable.

Thank you to Noelle Ihli, Anna Gamel, and Rachelle Nelson, all talented writers who are a newbie author's dream friends. You all encouraged me and pushed me to publish this story.

Thank you to my amazing beta readers! Noelle Ihli, Rebekah Dresback, Kelsey Zedwick, Destiny Irons, Evelyn Woodhead, Ashley Hildebrand, and Jacque Fries all read this book and gave valuable feedback that I was able to use. Thanks to Patti Geesey, who had a first stab at editing and helped me shape it into something I could try and get published.

Thanks to early readers and reviewers. You're doing the Lord's work in horror and thriller books, tirelessly trying to help match new titles up with the right readers. Thank you for picking up *The Vein* and sharing it on social media and blogs.

Thank you to Sadie Hartmann and Ashley Saywers, who lifted me out of a massive slush pile and published my first ever horror story in *Dark Matter Presents: Human Monsters*. You are the ultimate advocates and badasses. I wouldn't be publishing with Dark Matter INK if not for you. Literally. Sadie, thanks also for all your support and help promoting this book. For sending out ARCs and all the things you do behind the scenes to help horror thrive and find readers.

Huge thank you to Rob Carroll with INK. I'm seriously so lucky to work with you. From my first email interaction with you regarding my *Human Monsters* acceptance to present day, you've been nothing but supremely encouraging and positive. It's not just me either; your other authors say the same thing. It's like you don't see a world where any of us could fail. Such a rare find in our industry.

Lastly, thank YOU. I am a reader, too, and I know what it's like to have a TBR pile that's both exhilarating and, at times, overwhelming. I'm honored that this book made it to the top of yours.

—Steph Nelson

ABOUT THE AUTHOR

A LIFELONG PNW girl, Steph currently lives in Boise, Idaho, with her husband and their two teens. Her short fiction appears in *Dark Matter Presents: Human Monsters* and *Mother: Tales of Love and Terror*. Both are Bram Stoker-nominated anthologies. Her novella, *Sawtooth*, is forthcoming through Cemetery Gates Media, and her next horror novel, *The Threshing Floor*, is forthcoming through Dark Matter INK in November 2024. When she's not working on her next story, she's devouring horror, thriller, and even romance books. Find her on Twitter @stephdresnelson, and on Instagram/Threads @stephnelsonauthor.

Monster Lairs: A Dark Fantasy Horror Anthology
Edited by Anna Madden
ISBN 978-1-958598-08-5

The Bleed by Stephen S. Schreffler
ISBN 978-1-958598-11-5

Chopping Spree by Angela Sylvaine
ISBN 978-1-958598-31-3

Free Burn by Drew Huff
ISBN 978-1-958598-26-9

The House at the End of Lacelean Street
by Catherine McCarthy
ISBN 978-1-958598-23-8

The Off-Season: An Anthology of Coastal New Weird
Edited by Marissa van Uden
ISBN 978-1-958598-24-5

The Dead Spot: Stories of Lost Girls
by Angela Sylvaine
ISBN 978-1-958598-27-6

When the Gods Are Away by Robert E. Harpold
ISBN 978-1-958598-47-4

Grim Root by Bonnie Jo Stufflebeam
ISBN 978-1-958598-36-8

Voracious by Belicia Rhea
ISBN 978-1-958598-25-2

Abducted by Patrick Barb
ISBN 978-1-958598-37-5

Darkly Through the Glass Place by Kirk Bueckert
ISBN 978-1-958598-48-1

The Threshing Floor by Steph Nelson
ISBN 978-1-958598-49-8

Available or Coming Soon from Dark Hart Books

Rootwork by Tracy Cross
ISBN 978-1-958598-01-6

Mosaic by Catherine McCarthy
ISBN 978-1-958598-06-1

Apparitions by Adam Pottle
ISBN 978-1-958598-18-4

I Can See Your Lies by Izzy Lee
ISBN 978-1-958598-28-3

A Gathering of Weapons by Tracy Cross
ISBN 978-1-958598-38-2